Every Dark Place

CRAIG SMITH

MYRMIDON

Myrmidon Books Ltd
Rotterdam House
116 Quayside
Newcastle upon Tyne
NE1 3DY

www.myrmidonbooks.com

Published by Myrmidon 2012

A catalogue record for this book is available
from the British Library.

ISBN: 978-1-905802-53-1

Typeset in Sabon by Ellipsis Digital Limited, Glasgow

Printed and bound by CPI Group (UK)
Ltd, Croydon, CR0 4YY

1 3 5 7 9 10 8 6 4 2

In loving Memory of my father, Stanley Smith, and my nephew, David Smith. Too soon gone.

Prologue

Night.

MISSY WORTH WEPT AS SHE STOOD in the trough of earth that was to be her grave. She wore only the rags that had once been her underwear. She was a tall, willowy girl of seventeen, never beautiful like her sister Mary but pretty and fun. Not made for something like this.

She could not remember the last time she had slept or think back to a time when her bones did not ache. They were standing in a field... somewhere. Trees stood between them and the river. It was raining and dark and cold. She had not seen sunlight from the start.

Will stood outside the grave and watched her dig. His face in shadow, he was dressed in jeans and an army fatigue jacket. His hands were plunged deep in his jacket pockets. A baseball bat lay at his feet. It was filthy with the blood of the others.

'That's good enough,' he said. His voice was hardly more than a whisper. 'Now put the shovel here.' He pointed his toe to a place next to the bat.

'Don't do this to me, Will!' Missy Worth's cry echoed back from the trees.

'I want you to lie down, Missy.'

Missy's body shuddered. She wrapped her arms around her chest, twisting nervously. 'Will, you *promised*!'

'Missy, lie down in your grave.' When she still hesitated he touched the bat with his toe purposefully. 'You heard me.'

Missy tumbled back into the mud unable to keep from bawling. 'Not the bat! Please, Will, not that!'

'Lie down like you're going to sleep, and I won't use it on you.' His voice was soft, insistent.

Missy's teeth chattered. Her throat and mouth made sounds she no longer controlled. Will picked up the shovel. Starting at her feet he began dropping the heavy earth on her. Missy pleaded softly as he covered her feet and legs. Her body trembled as she struggled for control. A heavy shovelful of mud dropped on her belly, and Missy could not help herself. She began to cry loudly. It was a sound of another's voice. It was another's death she watched. Will placed several scoops almost delicately over Missy's chest. He continued heaping it up until clods began to run over her neck. The whole dark mountain of it began shaking as she convulsed in terror.

She was certain he meant to cover her face, but he stopped at this point. When he knelt down, leaning his face toward her own, Missy stopped her prayers and pleadings. She listened with the attentiveness of an errant lover hoping to be forgiven.

'If I could only trust you, Missy...'

A breath of hope stirred. 'You can, Will! I swear to God you can!'

'You say that now, but they'll ask you... and they'll keep on asking you. Finally, you're going to think you have to tell them *something*.'

'No!' Missy rocked her head back and forth. Tears ran wildly across her cheeks. The weight of the earth made it hard to breathe, but she nearly shouted the words. 'I won't! I won't say anything, Will!'

'You'll think I can't hurt you anymore. That's what they'll tell you, too. They'll promise to protect you...'

'I know you can hurt me.'

'I'll come back for you if you're lying, Missy. I'll come back from the dead, if I have to.'

'I won't talk, Will. I swear to God I won't!'

After a moment of consideration Will said, 'What are you going to tell them when they ask?'

Missy felt a spasm of joy tearing through her. She did not want to die. Not tonight. Not like this. 'I'll say it was always dark. I never saw your face!'

'Is that a promise? Are you going to keep your word, if I trust you?'

3

'YES!'

Will Booker stood up. 'You know, I think I believe you, Missy. Just so you believe me.' The gunshot came as a surprise. Missy heard the echo crackling back from the trees as she was gasping at the incredible pain in her chest. She tasted earth, her scream strangling in her throat. The next bullet jolted her, hitting below the ribs. She heard the second echo from the trees. She saw the smoke rising oddly from Will's jacket pocket. She searched the shadow of his face. Missy wanted to speak, but if she could say something, she was not sure what it would be. Perhaps only, 'This is exactly what I deserve.'

The last bullet came without echo, punching into the bone at the centre of her chest.

Part I

Legends

Let a bear robbed of her whelps meet a man,
rather than a fool in his folly.

Proverbs 17: 12

Chapter 1

'TRUEBLOOD,' I SAID into my cell phone.

'Rick?'

I had known Pat Garrat's secretary nearly four years. Even on the phone I knew she had bad news. I could even guess how bad it was. 'Yeah, Sandy,' I answered, my left hand on the steering wheel of my big county-issue sedan, the right up by my ear.

'Garrat wants to see you as soon as possible.'

'I'll be there in half-an-hour.' I put my phone back in my pocket and pulled into a farmer's driveway so I could turn around. I had been firming up a list of witnesses about a burglary spree the sheriff's department had interrupted a few weeks earlier. We needed live bodies in the witness stand so a jury could understand the nature and extent of the damage these kids had done. Naturally folks were reluctant to help. About half of them wanted their stuff back without bothering to take a day or two off to see justice done. The others worried about retribution.

And why not? The thieves were juveniles; no matter what we did they were going to get another chance and sometimes second chances take the form of revenge. I was too old to marvel at such legal niceties, but for the past couple of days I had been telling people that when the prosecutor finished with these thieves, they weren't going to remember who testified. All they would be thinking about was getting out of Shiloh County! It was a method that worked with a lot of people. Pat Garrat was new to office but as tough as tempered steel. Remind them who was running things, and they would smile and tell me I was probably right.

Of course there were some of the older ones who told me Pat Garrat was not half the politician her daddy had been. I never disagreed with such sentiment, and I had been hearing it since Garrat had started campaigning for the prosecutor's office over a year ago. I would answer instead that I had had the honour of working for Governor Pat Garrat and that in my opinion no one was ever going to be the equal of *that* Pat Garrat, but if anyone was going to get close to his sort of integrity his little girl had the best chance. More often than not people got a private smile on their faces and a look of hope that comes when something grand is stirring to life.

I took State Road 159 north into metropolitan Hegira, blinked, and hit the raw open countryside again. I passed through yellow fields in fallow, vast acreage of farmland ploughed and disked to a wet black and waiting seed, a smattering of woods, and small clumps of working class houses trying to be a suburb. The countryside was breaking out of wintertime, but a cold mist took away the pleasure of it.

I GOT BACK TO the office close to forty-five minutes after Sandy's call and left the parking lot whistling contentedly. At the north door I passed through the security checkpoint, then ambled on until I came to the county prosecutor's suite of offices. Garrat had seven prosecutors, a couple of them looking to be very decent lawyer-types if you could forgive them their green, but they were all young. In a particularly morose period of my life – as I recall it was a week or so after Will Booker's appeal case broke over us like a canker sore – I had tried to decide if all the lawyers together, including Pat Garrat, had as much work experience as I did. When I finished the tally, I still had room for the three paralegals and Sandy Willis, who was huffing her way toward a reluctant early middle age. After that only my bartender could console me. She said if I was counting *real* work, there wasn't a soul in Shiloh Springs with less experience than I had.

There was a smoked glass window from floor to

ceiling next to the entrance of Garrat's outer office. I usually checked myself in its pale reflection just to make sure I was not going to be mistaken for a lawyer. This morning there was no chance. With more than a bit of the barn about me, I actually looked like a conservation officer. Country folks have an unusual hierarchy, with conservation officers standing several rungs above investigators for the prosecutor's office. A little straw stuck in your pants cuff will get you through a farmhouse door a lot faster than a badge, so I had purposely dressed the part.

I smiled at my reflection like an old friend, pretty much the only one I had – at least the only one I could trust. I stand an inch over six feet and weigh a few pounds beyond the two hundred ten mark. My chest is broader than my waist by a whisker, and I am as bald as a friar. Handsome as a sunrise, too, even if I do say so myself. Fifty-eight years can kill a lot of moral failings in a man but not his vanity. Vanity needs the grave to stop it cold.

I RAISED MY EYEBROWS when I opened the door. 'How is she doing?' I asked in a whisper.

Sandy was on the phone, but her saucer-sized eyes and wagging chin let me know things were not good. I went down a long hall to the last door on the left, my cubbyhole. There I dropped off my winter coat and slipped on a wrinkled wool sports jacket. It was a good cut of cloth but older than most of our lawyers. I got a tiny notebook that fit into my frayed jacket pocket, bummed a Bic pen from Sandy's desk on the way back in exchange for a confidential wink, and then got some coffee.

I went through Garrat's door without knocking. Garrat, Steve Massey and Linda Sutherlin, the paralegal, were at Garrat's conference table just to the left of the entryway. Massey was in a trial lawyer's uniform, a three-piece wool blend in midnight blue with a scarlet tie hanging under his square chin. He had dark brown hair that had a few nice waves and a rambunctious curl or two to finish the effect. He wore old horn rim glasses for reading, and loved nothing better in the courtroom than to take them off with a flourish, imagining, I suppose, a startling transformation. In my opinion it was wasted effort. With or without them, Massey had an expression that looked like wildlife caught in the headlights.

Linda Sutherlin sat between Massey and the chair I usually grabbed. Sutherlin wore a black slip and, as far as I could tell, nothing else but shoes. She was rail-thin and kept a spike through her nose and another at the bottom of her lower lip. It was my studied opinion that Sutherlin used the extra weight to keep from blowing away. She had a few miscellaneous rings on her fingers, a studded band about her neck, and one tattoo that I could see: the word MOM written in a shaky scrawl high up on her thigh.

11

'You're late, Rick,' Garrat announced.

It wasn't a tone I especially took to, even from Pat Garrat, but I didn't answer it in kind. 'Traffic,' I lied. Knowing I had been down in Hegira, which doesn't even make most maps, Garrat gave me a long, smouldering glare, and I braced myself for a weird ride.

Chapter 2

Wednesday 10:30 a.m., March 17.

AS FAR AS BOSSES WENT, Pat Garrat was usually the stuff of dreams. She was honest, full of wit, and had more than her fair share of empathy for what other people were up against. But sometimes, backed into a corner and her political career in jeopardy, she could get as cranky as the best of them. My guess was cranky flew right by about an hour ago. Garrat was working on a full blown tear.

All the same, she was a beautiful woman. She was thirty-one and possessed an athlete's body. It was compact, muscular and so full of grace the photographers could not take a bad picture. Her hair was a simple wash and wear, a dirty stone-blonde that fit the image of a serious woman. In the wind, she looked positively philosophical. She had a square, forthright face and a quick, lively smile that did not look put on even when it was. Never hurried and never slowing down for distractions, Pat Garrat had always seemed a child of destiny.

I had known her when she was still called Patty. After her father's assassination, which I had watched in horror, we both left the Governor's mansion and went our separate ways. She was in law school when I met up with her again. The occasion was not a happy one for either of us and nothing had come of that reunion but a lot of talk and another funeral.

When Garrat had finished law school the following year, I saw in the local paper that she was joining an elite firm of attorneys over in the capital but that she had moved back to the family farm, just east of Shiloh Springs. I thought then she was setting roots even while she was off building bridges, and I was right. Just under three years later, the boys of the club offered her a partnership but Garrat resigned on friendly terms to open her shop 'back home.' It was a manoeuvre worthy of her daddy and undoubtedly a part of the grand scheme, though she had never admitted to anyone that she had ambition for political office.

Garrat called me the moment she began contemplating the opening of her new office and asked me if I would be her full-time private investigator. It was pretty much what I had been doing for about six different law offices on a piecemeal basis anyway. But neither the ease of the job transition nor the relative security she was offering me meant very much. I joined up with Pat Garrat because I knew where she was going, and I wanted to be with her when she arrived.

'Will Booker just got his conviction overturned,' Garrat told me, though I had already guessed that much. I tried to act surprised, but the effort was wasted. Garrat was looking right through me. 'That's the bad news,' she announced. 'The really bad news is Judge Lynch has given us sixty days to bring him to trial or he walks.'

I pulled my notebook out and checked my watch for the date and time. I had been getting cases ready for lawyers long enough to know sixty days was tight. Most real law is practiced before the *voir dire*, so too all the legal research and the motions that mean very much. According to my quick calculations, sixty days meant I should have finished my investigation a couple of months ago. Normally such a situation would constitute a serious interruption in my drinking schedule, but I knew about Will Booker and his crimes. As far as I was concerned we could be ready for trial in twenty minutes. What evidence we had ten years ago was all manufactured by Sheriff Nathan Hall or it was so tainted it would never get into court a second time. As for witnesses, I could round up friends and relatives of the victims with a single phone call. The only critical witness, the only evidence at all against William Booker, was a gal named Missy Worth. Missy I could find anytime I wanted in a little drinking palace she managed called the Dog Daze End.

As for her testimony, ten years ago it had been just what the prosecutor ordered. It was anyone's guess what she would pull out of her bonnet these days.

'What are you going to do about it?' I asked. I kept my head tipped in the direction of my little notepad. I was scribbling nothing furiously.

'Appeal.' I looked up from my notepad and studied her face. She meant stall. 'Same as we're appealing his release,' she added.

'He's out?' I asked incredulously. It is standard procedure in the American judicial system for mass murderers, serial killers, and homicidal maniacs to stay locked up while their lawyers make mischief. It took an incredibly lazy, stupid, or angry federal judge to turn one of them loose on the issue of habeas corpus. Federal Circuit Judge Buford Lynch was neither lazy nor stupid.

'As of noon tomorrow,' Massey grunted.

'What are the chances for an appeal on the release?' I pressed. I could not believe Will Booker was going to be walking around Shiloh Springs as a free man.

Garrat shook her head. 'I doubt an appellate judge will even listen to an argument, but I intend to go over to the capital tomorrow and get some help from the attorney general.'

'Sixty days is not a lot of time to get ready for a murder trial,' I offered blandly.

'The problem isn't time,' Garrat answered. 'The problem is we now have no evidence.'

16

'You still have an eyewitness,' I told her.

'With public opinion about her where it is,' Massey interjected, 'I'll be laughed out of court if Missy Worth is all I can produce.'

I gave Garrat a quick look, but she was not answering looks at the moment. She had assigned Steve Massey to the case because there was no hope of winning it. I knew it as well as the lawyers did, but I could not condone the idea of surrender – not to a man who had murdered five kids and left the sixth for dead. 'The story Missy Worth will tell,' I said, 'is nothing to laugh at, Steve.'

Massey slapped his pen down. '*Lynn Griswold* is his lawyer, Rick!'

'Missy Worth spent thirteen days locked up in Will Booker's hell.'

'When Griswold is done with his cross-examination of Missy Worth, the jury won't believe she could ID her own mother!'

'Her mother didn't do it,' Garrat answered. 'Will Booker did.'

'Give Will Booker the benefit of the doubt for a minute,' Massey said with relative calmness.

'I prefer not to,' she answered.

'Say Missy Worth was indoctrinated with misinformation.'

'She wasn't,' Garrat answered flatly. I gave Garrat a quick, admiring look. She had been sitting quietly on her opinion about the innocence or guilt of Will Booker for over a year – trusting the legal procedures that were in place to take care of such matters. It was an approach that had allowed her to crush her opponent six months ago in a county election, but now she had to pick a side. In my opinion she had chosen the right one.

'You mean she didn't see Booker in the hallway in handcuffs before the line up?' Massey asked. This was a standard tactic for some police agencies. It tended to get solid, irrefutable IDs. It was also one of the better ways for appellate attorneys to afford their summer homes.

'That's substantiated,' Garrat admitted.

'And the photo spread?'

Garrat smiled bitterly. Sheriff Hall had possessed the knack for getting the right picture picked out of a photo spread. 'Bernie Samples was right about that much,' she said. Samples had been the newspaper writer whose articles had first generated public interest in Will Booker's appeal. 'But we are not talking about a quick look at the man and a shaky identification.'

'So why did Missy Worth tell Nat Hall when they first talked that she never got a good look at the guy?' Massey asked.

Garrat looked at me with a suddenness that took my breath away. 'That's what Rick is going to find out for us.'

Chapter 3

Wednesday 2:00 p.m., March 17.

IT HAD BEEN A PRETTY GOOD meeting up to the point that the entire case got shoved down my throat. The rest of it involved Pat Garrat fighting off the look of having to put a favourite old pet to sleep. I could not help feeling set-up.

I should not have been surprised by it really. It's how things work. Rising political stars are only as good as their glimmer. It never pays to look too closely or worry about the substance behind the light. Will Booker's case threatened Pat Garrat's political future. There was no easy way out from under it, so Garrat was sending her lone investigator out to find a lead on a trail ten years cold. And when he came up empty, which was only to be expected, she would have her scapegoat. I gave Linda Sutherlin a quick, calculating glance, wondering if I could get her to take some of the blame, but it was useless. Nothing at all sticks to twenty-four. I was the heir apparent for this one.

Every politician knows how to play the game. I had seen Garrat's daddy do it a few times, though not with me. It is the nature of politics. No one ever seems to worry about the staff members who come and go as long as they are loyal and quiet on the way out. What I minded was Pat Garrat with that coy I-know-you-can-do-it-big-guy look as the meeting broke apart.

I went to my office hoping Garrat would call me back or slip down to see me once she had pampered Massey's fragile ego. I wanted her to tell me straight out this might turn nasty, maybe cost both of us our jobs. Something kind and wise: an intimate little shrug and that pretty smile of hers. If nothing else, some sweet nothing to let me forget I was about to take that long and certain road to nowhere. When she didn't show up, I flipped a coin a couple of times, best out of five, actually, to see if I should drink or work, and finally getting it right went off to get started on an early, long, and very wet lunch.

AROUND TWO O'CLOCK, FACING the prospect of never going back to the office or making some gesture at finding out the truth about William Booker, I called Max Dunn's cell phone.

Max answered with a voice as raw as wet hay. 'Sheriff.'

'Rick Trueblood, Max. I've got a favour to ask.'

'What do I get out of it?'

I had my answer ready, 'Not a damn thing.' Max had always appreciated me for my honesty with him, but he told me I could go to hell with an offer like that. 'How about I don't tell your wife everything I know?'

After a thoughtful pause Max said, 'Do you think she'd leave me any money, Rick?'

'Not a penny.'

'So what do you need, buddy?'

An hour later, pushing it to make the appointment since I'd downed a couple-three more beers before taking off, I pulled into the Stuckey's parking lot on South 641 and found an army brown sedan with black wall tires waiting for me. Max Dunn sat in the front seat with the patience of a man who's been on too many stakeouts over the years. He lifted his chin, which is country for hello and pretty much the way we tell folks to go to hell too. 'Rain ever going to stop?' he asked. Settling into his cruiser, I told Max the rain helped the crops grow. It was like cranking the handle on an old toy. 'Who gives a damn?' Max snapped. 'That's what I want to know! They got corporations growing things now, Rick. There's not a man on a tractor anymore that owns the land he's working!'

Max Dunn was a big man, about six-three and a good fifteen pounds heavier than I was. His chest was long and square, and when he got in a huff, like he always did when he got on the subject of corporate

21

farms devouring the small farmer, you would swear he was wearing an armoured vest. He had black hair with a bit of grey to soften the effect, flinty eyes that were quick and mean. Like a lot of men with a physical presence it was second nature for Max to turn his opinions into pronouncements. And not always with a lot of concern for the facts. For a politician on the stump such habits win votes. In the electronic age it was a style that could get you in trouble. The painful truth was the subtleties of political double talk escaped him. Max Dunn said what he thought and paid for it. He had managed to succeed his corrupt boss Nathan Hall as sheriff only because he had been second-in-command when Nat ate his own bullet. Even as an incumbent the election last fall had almost gone the other way. What saved Max was the fact that he was in the same party as Pat Garrat, who had swept into power on a wave of sentiment that pulled a lot of lesser political talents into office with her.

We pushed past the remnants of a farm that was turning into another makeshift suburb and Max shook his head like a man who has seen paradise, then drops by the local dump for a comparison. 'Another farm gone to hell, Rick. You can't make a living farming!' It was a canned speech, but I still loved it. Part of my innate appreciation for a criminal's ability to justify himself. About twenty-five years ago Max had climbed off his family tractor and answered a sheriff's advertisement for deputies. Unlike a lot of farmers going out of business, Max held onto his land though it cost him the luxuries the rest of us think we can't do without. A few years later, using the acres to leverage a healthy loan with a friendly banker, Max joined in with Sheriff Nathan Hall and his cronies to form a company that bought up options on choice spots of real estate just ahead of public announcements of land use. It was as illegal as bank robbery but all the watchdogs were in on it, including Herm Hammer, the former county prosecutor, and a couple of local judges. These days the Dunn family farm was fenced in with white board, and Max raised some of the finest quarter horses in the country.

Max took us into a countryside spotted with tiny ponds and rough low gravel mounds held together with scrub pines. It was a land that had been raped and pretty much lay useless these days, too raw and rough even for another housing development in the middle of nowhere. 'Here,' Max announced, pulling his cruiser to a halt on the rutted gravel road.

I had been expecting something a bit more than a wide spot in the road, but that's all North Shore Point was. Not even a rusty sign to announce you had arrived. The weeds and brush were close by; even in a light mist dust hung in the air out of habit. Off to the side of the road the land plunged down so that we were looking at the tops of a thick grove of trees. Max led me to a narrow path, then down the hill until we came out at the side of a fairly nice-sized pond. It was hardly the lake I had imagined from the lone photograph I had seen in the newspaper about a year ago when it was reporting the injustices committed against William Booker.

'This is it,' Max told me.

Chapter 4

Wednesday 3:25 p.m., March 17.

'YOU INVESTIGATED IT?' I ASKED. As I figured it would, this got a nervous jerk of the head. I had wanted Max to show me the place not because I couldn't find it, as I had told him, but so I could get a feel for the thinking that had taken place during the original investigation.

'I looked at it like everyone else. Not much to see.'

Max did not look comfortable. Whether it was the actual guilt of helping to frame Will Booker or simply the danger of appearing to be part of it, I couldn't tell. I didn't really care. The Reverend Connie Merriweather, who had spearheaded the drive to free Will Booker, had done enough damage to the local political scene. I couldn't see how ruining another career for the sake of Will Booker was going to help anyone. 'So how is the fishing?' I asked genially, just to soften the air between us.

Max flashed his big horse teeth. 'Like as catch a mermaid as an old mud cat, Rick. Least ways, last summer we caught us some. Three girls and one lucky boy naked as the day they were born. Frolicking.' He thought about it for a time, then explained, 'They were college.' *College* covered a number of lunacies, including frolicking, and Max Dunn left it at that.

I kicked around the small shoreline. There was very little space between the water and the heavy under-growth of bushes and weeds, no shore at all around the rest of the pond. The water itself reached out about thirty yards or so before coming up against a dense grove of pines on the opposite shore. The pond was three times as wide but came into a muddy swamp at either end. 'I thought the place would be bigger,' I said.

'Well, it's plenty deep,' Max answered. 'We lost a kid out here three, four years back. He came up on his own eventually, but we sure couldn't find him.'

'Got a question for you,' I said. Max's gaze stayed on the water and the spittle of rain that dashed against its surface. 'How did Will Booker know who was down here?'

'What are you talking about?' Max got a flinty look of curiosity about him, but he wouldn't look at me. I don't think he especially trusted me at the moment.

'The way I understand it, Will Booker arrives at the top of the hill, and first one boy then the other goes to see who's up there.'

'That's right. He shot the first and clubbed the second one to death.'

'Then he comes down the hill here for the girls.' I pointed at the path we had used. Max nodded. 'My question,' I said, 'is how does he know what's waiting for him? As far as I can see, it could have been you and me with those boys. And somehow I don't think Will Booker would have cared for that.'

The sheriff frowned with a bit of uncertainty. 'What's your point, Rick?'

I looked over the pond and lifted my arm to indicate the far shore. 'What's beyond that hill?'

'Another filled-up gravel pit. They're all over the place. This is lake country, or what passes for it.'

'Down there?' I pointed at the far end of the lake.

'Hell, I don't know, and I don't want to go find out. As far as I can see, it's just brush and thorns and mud!'

'So the theory goes, Booker, or whoever killed those kids –'

'Don't tell me you've joined Connie Merriweather's church!'

'I'm just saying he drove up without seeing who was here and took what he found, a couple of boys and four teenage girls, but it could have been my handsome mug or a deputy sheriff named Max-by-God-Dunn packing his big .45?'

'Yeah, I guess.'

'And nobody had a problem with that?'

'I did some background on Booker down south, Rick. I wasn't part of this mess, thank God.'

'Nobody's trying to draw you into it, Max. I'm just asking you if you remember them talking about it?'

Max gave me a suspicious look. It was too late for any kind of indictment, but if he ended up closer to the case than folks now believed, Max was likely to go the way of Herman Hammer: politically dead-ended. Pat Garrat needed blood if she was going to survive. Maybe she wasn't too picky whose she got. 'Nat and a couple of the others handled the whole thing, Rick. If they talked, I didn't hear it.'

He was lying. He's a good liar, too, at least practiced, but I didn't doubt my judgement on this point. I also didn't call him on it. In the absence of true friendship, any friendship at all suffices, and Max Dunn was about as close as it came for me. Instead, I asked about the background on William Booker. He didn't want to answer that either. 'It's been too many years to remember. You can find it in the files, buddy. That's why I wrote my report!'

I had tried an old trick, testing a liar's memory against his last account of the facts, then picking at the discrepancies, but Max had been in this game too long for it to work. He wasn't talking short of a serious game of Russian roulette.

At the top of the hill, though, Max stopped and looked around thoughtfully. There was no way to see down to the shore to know who or what waited below. Finally, he nodded. 'I see what you mean about him not knowing what he was going to find down there, but maybe the cars gave it away. Bumper stickers with school logos, tubes of lipstick on the dash. Teenage girl things, you know?'

I gave an agreeable shrug, 'Maybe.'

Chapter 5

Wednesday 4:08 p.m., March 17.

SOUTH OF BETHEL FALLS, WHICH is nothing but a kink in the road with a church and a broken down tavern, the river bends west and the highway goes south. The land between is low and flat, river bottoms turned to farm country, laced together by a network of dirt roads. An occasional house stands empty along the way. Sometimes whole settlements of crumbling shacks line up against the levee.

'I bet they get a good crop out of this soil,' I told Max. He had gotten quiet since we had left North Shore Point, but at the mention of farming he waxed lyrical.

'Rule was five years of good crops, one year washed out with floods. He pointed at a solitary house with the sky for a roof. 'When you got a couple flood years in a row, you lost it all. Course, not anymore! At this point the corporations own all this land...'

He went on like this as we ran parallel to the river about a quarter of a mile out from it. When a grove of trees forced the road toward the river, we had a choice of following a grass lane back into a field or driving right into the water. 'Ferry still work?' I asked. There was a little place across the river where I could see a big flatbed raft that looked like it could carry a couple of cars. There was nothing on our side but a steel brace and a low slung cable stretching out over the river to the other side. A faded sign next to a rusted bell said to ring the bell to call the ferry.

'When the old boy feels like coming across to get you it works,' Max told me. 'Why?'

'How about ten years ago?'

'Same as now. Nothing on this side but crops and a road to nowhere. Old boy over there, Josh Lawson, he was ten years younger, just as ornery. You don't live out in a place like this if you *like* people.'

'Anyone interview Josh Lawson about what he saw and heard?'

'He's the one who pulled Missy Worth out of her grave, Rick. Said he heard gunshots in the middle of the night and came across the river early the next morning to have a look around. She was down in that field – not far from those trees.'

Max turned into the field on a hard-packed lane and we continued due south, the river maybe a hundred yards away at this point. There was a nice cover of trees and weeds tall enough to swallow us up, and we found the abandoned farm we were looking for a couple of minutes later. There were four buildings still standing. A muddy field ran up close against the structures. The house was made of clapboard, probably built about eighty years ago, when farmers were still people. It was a one storey, poor man's paradise with high ceilings and an enclosed porch. The ceilings were mostly fallen in now, the windows all broken. All that remained of the roof was a skeleton. The front steps had been stolen like some of the clapboard. The weeds and trees coming up from the foundations were taking the thing back to nature by degrees. The barn was worse. People had taken about everything they could carry off. Half of it was collapsed in on itself. The garage had fallen down completely, a rubble of rotting boards. Only the milk shed had survived relatively intact. It was made of stone blocks and had a concrete floor. The roof was rotten but still mostly together. A stainless steel lock secured the door.

'He pried off a hasp and staple to get in,' Max announced, pointing at an old scar in the doorframe. 'Then he put his own lock on here.' Max showed me a second scar. 'Sheriff's department replaced it with one of ours.'

'Did you bring the key for it?' I asked. I had told him I wanted to look at the place when I called him.

'We couldn't find it, but I don't think it matters.'

Max reared back and kicked the door. The sheriff's good lock held, but the wood anchoring it exploded and the door whipped open. He grinned at me and winked. 'There you go.' I stepped in and looked around. The place was close and damp. There were no windows. I saw only a dead light switch on the wall by the door and an empty light socket overhead. There was a big sink just inside, but when I turned the faucet, nothing happened. 'There's a pump outside that worked ten years ago, but he didn't turn it on,' Max said. 'Whatever water he gave them, he brought in from the outside.'

'From the river?'

'No way of knowing, but I'll tell you something. If he gave them water from *that* river, I'm surprised they lasted as long as they did.'

There were only two other items in the room, a big work table that had been painted white and turned black of its own accord and a walk-in refrigerator, which was nothing more than a concrete room with a thick oak door. I went to the walk-in. Max told me that the heavy brass lever that would have originally locked the door had been taken away to avoid someone accidentally getting trapped inside but that Booker had put one on of his own making. It was gone like the first lock. The interior was three feet deep, not quite six feet wide and just over five feet high. 'He kept *four* girls in here?' I asked incredulously.

'The first one was dead after two or three days, Rick.'

'I want to go in,' I said, after a moment of consideration.

'You're too fat.'

'The hell I am,' I growled and slipped in easily, all two hundred-ten-plus joyful pounds. 'Push that table against the door and give me fifteen minutes in here.

'You're crazy.'

'Humour me.'

Max Dunn actually grinned as he started to shut the door. 'Tell me again how you voted in the sheriff's race, Rick.'

'For the other guy!' The door closed. A moment later I heard Max pushing the table against the door.

Chapter 6

Darkness.

I KNEW THE MOMENT THE DARKNESS had swallowed me that I had made a mistake. 'Can you hear me?' I called, but Max made no answer. I called out more loudly. 'CAN YOU HEAR ME NOW?' I was certain he would answer. I got silence for my troubles. Fifteen minutes of it, I thought grimly.

Twenty or twenty-five minutes, knowing Max. With my head tucked against my chest in order to fit inside my temporary prison cell, I reached up and searched the ceiling. There were no soft spots that I could claw at. I turned and tested the outer wall, then stepped away from the door and tried again. I caught a draft of musty air. I felt around for the crack and found it with my fingers. I played at the edges for a while, but nothing was coming loose. I called out to Max again, but he still didn't respond. I turned and lowered myself to the floor. I could sit without hitting a wall, but when I stretched out on my back, I had to bend my legs slightly in order to fit. A second person would have been virtually impossible to endure for any length of time. Four living, miserable girls in here must have been like something out of Dante.

I wasn't sure but it seemed to me I caught the old scent of piss and fear aged on river air. It was probably only my imagination, but my pulse kicked up some after that. My chest burned with a bit of pressure that scared me. I stared straight ahead, listening for Max, and I felt a surge of irrational fear. I tried not to think. That wasn't possible. This was too close to Sarah's end. The fear my daughter had faced before her own murder washed over me. It was a feeling I knew well. One of my more developed talents, as a matter of fact.

I had spent too long searching for her killer. In doing so I had relived her final hours in my imagination so many times that I could fall into dour moods without even realising what was happening. There had been a time when I could dream of nothing else. The feelings would still resurrect in my weaker moments. They enveloped me now. I was powerless to stop the surge of emotion – the utter emptiness that comes of such a loss.

I felt myself looping back to a time that began eight years ago when I had given up everything in my life for a revenge I never delivered. There was a divorce in the middle of my search, a drunk that had carried on past all reason at the end of it. Then Pat Garrat had made a phone call and asked if I'd like to go to work for her. Things got better slowly after that, but there were still times when I slipped. Sometimes there were whole nights when I imagined Sarah's cries for help. Too often I struggled vainly to change what history had already written. When that happened there was no way back until sunrise.

Suddenly, I could almost believe I was in the middle of it again. I knew I ought to be able to control things this time, this was just a case, but it didn't feel that way sitting in Will Booker's homemade hell.

A footstep scratched against the floor. I had lost my sense of time, and for a moment I could not have said if I had been locked up fifteen minutes or eight long years. I remembered my folly with a surge of embarrassment, and I shouted as loudly as I could, 'GET ME OUT OF HERE!'

'You had enough?' Max's voice was muted by the thick walls.

'OPEN THE DOOR!'

I heard the table move, and then the door opened. Standing in a square of pale light, Max Dunn looked down at me. 'You want to try it a full night? I can come back and get you tomorrow.'

I swore at him roughly and reached up to take his hand. I rolled out as awkwardly as any fifty-eight-year-old. 'Where were you?' I asked, my voice barely holding its manufactured calm.

'I drove down to the river, trying to find just where Missy Worth was buried, but it's all overgrown now.'

'I didn't hear you leave.'

'I could hear you shouting when I stood right here, so I went outside to see if I could still hear you.'

'Did you?'

'Not a thing.'

I shook my head and walked out of the milk house and into the rain. The air felt good in my lungs. 'I thought I could smell them,' I told Max. I kept my back to him so he couldn't read my face.

'When we first looked in here, there was a pretty good stench to it.' I felt dread crawling up my throat, as if I would have to go back inside. I knew what it meant: I wanted Will Booker back on Death Row, but I wasn't going to get him. He was going to get away with his crime, the way Sarah's killer had done, and it was going to be on my head.

'What's wrong with you?'

'Nothing,' I said sharply. Then remembering I was talking to Max, I said, 'I got to thinking about Sarah while I was in there. How it must have been for her.'

Max thought about it for a minute, then nodded as if he understood, though I doubt anyone can understand that sort of madness. 'It wasn't a whole lot different, was it? The way she went and the way these kids got it?'

There were differences, too terrible to consider, but Max was right. The basic outline was the same. Sarah had been abducted and held for nearly a week. Then she had been murdered. 'Sarah has been gone over eight years, Max, and I still think about her a few times every day.' Max said nothing to interrupt the hard silence of memories. Finally, I looked at him with a bitterness I let few people see – at least when I could stay sober enough to hold a mask up. 'I can't imagine what it would be like if they had caught the bastard and put him on Death Row, then a decade later decided his rights had been violated.'

Max looked ready to tell me something, but seemed to change his mind. Confession is maybe good for the soul, but it rarely assists one's career in law enforcement. 'You get what you came for?'

Chapter 7

Wednesday 5:30 p.m., March 17.

AT STUCKEY'S I GOT OUT of the sheriff's cruiser and thanked Max for running me through things. Max laughed with the humour of watching someone walk on ice. 'Worth absolutely nothing, wasn't it?'

I gave him what he expected, a lonesome shrug, then got in my car and drove back to town. I dropped my county car off at my house and wandered over to Simple Simon's for last call on happy hour. It was just over a city block from my house, crawling distance in case things got serious. I didn't see a soul over forty in the place, and it was packed. I felt my gut tighten and started to leave. That was when Darrel Liffick took my arm. I had worked piecemeal for the firm where Liffick was a partner. Better than most, Liffick had put up with my nonsense, usually by looking the other way when I was too drunk or hung over to function. Seeing him, I felt like I had run into an old friend, but only because I had forgotten there is no such beast in the world of lawyers.

'Is Garrat going through with it,' Liffick asked, 'or just barking like the bitch she is?'

My affection for the man washed, though I answered him all the same. 'What do I know? I'm just the office grunt.'

'Let me buy you a drink, big guy.'

I never turned down a drink from a lawyer. They knew the kind of money I made, so never expected me to buy them one in return. Of course, what Liffick and the rest of his kind wanted for the canary piss they bought me was information. Sometimes I gave it to them, if only to keep the lines of communication open. In the business of law it is a commonplace that today's opponent may well become tomorrow's ally. So I took a seat where Liffick indicated and found myself next to Kathy James, one of the field reporters for WSLO. Liffick sat to the other side of me, effectively holding me in place for the interrogation. He called to the waitress and signalled for her to bring me a glass of beer. Kathy James was the one who spoke. 'I heard Garrat's going to be cutting her losses once the storm passes, Rick.' This was purely a fishing trip, and I knew it. She had heard it from Darrel Liffick, who was merely speculating. Pat Garrat confided in no one. It was how she had climbed to the top of the political dung heap by the age of thirty-one. That and a serious family fortune.

'You think she's going to have losses?' I asked innocently.

James leaned in closer, as intimate as a dagger, 'There's no way in hell Garrat's going to convict this guy. All she wants out of this mess is a scapegoat. The way I hear it, you and Massey are the leading candidates. Everyone I know is betting on the bald guy.'

I was working on a comeback to this when a man put his face in front of us. Kathy James smiled like an innocent and I was forgotten. My beer came. There was some nonsense to bat around with Liffick and a few more people I knew who weren't all that keen on local politics. Before I left, though, Liffick got me aside and put a friendly arm over my shoulder. 'She's not like her old man, Rick,' he told me in a whisper that barely missed turning into a kiss. 'Don't think she is or she will break your heart, pal.'

I MIXED BOURBON AND water the colour of strong tea when I got home, then another while I watched the news, which was mostly about Will Booker and his influential friend, the Reverend Connie Merriweather. Somewhere along the line I thought about dinner but the refrigerator was empty. I wasn't legal to drive anymore, and I was too drunk to walk four blocks to my neighbourhood restaurant, so I just poured another drink. Like the old days. Around midnight I found some stale bread the mice had refused and washed it down with the last of the booze.

Chapter 8

Thursday 8:00 a.m., March 18.

THE NEXT MORNING I STOPPED at St. Jude's, an old Gothic Revival filled with plaster saints and guarded by cheerful gargoyles. I spent a few minutes on my knees at one of the side altars and ran out some rusty prayers from my protestant upbringing. Then I just stayed there waiting for God to answer. He had been quiet a long time, so I wasn't expecting the skies to open this morning. I just wanted to give him the chance to point me toward a piece of evidence no one knew existed – something to send Will Booker to a well-deserved execution. I usually went to St. Jude's two or three times a month, never when they were actually having services. I wanted the quiet of the place and to believe for a few minutes that what we do matters.

Before I left I looked at old Jude himself. His emblem is the club. It is how he was martyred. The thing I always noticed about the old paintings, these folks took their pain with more ease and forgiveness than I ever did. It had never made sense to me not to fight back, but then no one ever mistook me for a saint. They say Saint Jude had no cult for centuries since he bore the name of the arch-betrayer Judas, but some wag a few centuries back came up with the catchall of 'lost causes.' Now there's not a saint with a larger following.

I got to the office around nine and had pretty much decided to go in and face Garrat with the scapegoat theory. What did she really want from me? Was I supposed to take the blame if nothing turned up? Well, fine, but just tell me up front. Don't insult my intelligence with lies of omission! I was ready for a knock-down-drag-out if it came to that, and I've had a few with different folks over the years so I'm practiced at it, but Sandy told me Garrat wasn't coming to the office. 'She's meeting with the attorney general's people,' Sandy explained. 'Didn't she tell you?'

I nodded. She had. Wrapped up in my own worries and paranoia, I had forgotten.

'If she calls again, I'll let her know you want to talk.'

'That's all right,' I drawled, my anger and arguments failing me suddenly, 'I'll talk with her tomorrow.' There was a chance, after all, Garrat could do something about this case at the federal appellate court level; still a chance, too, *I* could pull something off. I looked at my watch. Solve the mystery before happy hour, find the truth, save the day.

Blame it on my prayers to Jude and the good bourbon I had found in my cupboards, but I actually thought it was possible. Not likely but possible. I had the whole case on paper, the lies all documented, and one rather nasty suspicion about the initial attack. All it really took was the right question, the appropriate perspective, one explanation nobody had thought to offer. And maybe a small miracle from a quiet God. My optimism lasted about fifteen seconds, until, in fact, I ran into Steve Massey. 'You got anything for me yet, hotshot?'

I smiled innocently. 'Maybe. Do you want a meeting?' I asked him.

Massey's face lost its colour. Nobody needs another meeting. He was back-pedalling by the time his words hit the air, 'That depends on what you've got. Have you got something or not?'

I pushed on in a mood to tear my door down rather than unlock it. I got my computer started, went for coffee, and then started making some calls on a couple of unrelated matters. Folks down in Hegira still had to be coddled and cooed. After about an hour I was feeling ready for murder and plunged into Booker's case with both fists knotted. As most of the evidence in the case was now officially worthless and had been entered into the appellate case Booker had just won, I concentrated on the background reports. Several of these were signed by a sheriff's detective named Max Dunn. These I read fondly. Max Dunn, though not an especially competent investigator, could spell better than the average Shiloh Springs law enforcement officer. Shortly before noon, I set the case files aside, checked on an address, and headed out for lunch. After a couple of beers and a roast beef sandwich I couldn't finish, I found myself driving by old working class houses that had been partitioned into apartments for the college kids. A bit closer to campus, the properties were mostly shacks with front porches attached.

I found Missy Worth's address close to Seventh and Elm. The yard was a pad of dirt. The front porch was cracked and collapsing. The curtains looked to be made of worn-out sheets. I knocked at the front door, then walked around back. The house was not more than fifteen paces from the railroad tracks. A service road of cinders and weeds lay between the tracks and the cinder block that served as Missy Worth's back porch. I considered briefly going out to find Missy at the bar she managed but let it go. There was still work to do at the office.

I ASKED ABOUT GARRAT'S PROGRESS with the appeal, but Sandy hadn't heard from her. I saw Heidi Cameron, our domestic crimes prosecutor. She was at her desk, holding an ink pen and contemplating a quarrelsome comma. Nobody did it better. Settling into my government-issue chair, I poured a little Jack Daniel's straight into my drinking glass, and continued with the history of William Booker.

In Manassas, his hometown, Booker had been arrested

once for trespassing, age ten. That was the extent of his criminal record, though Max Dunn had turned up a lot of suspicion that he had dealt grass. He was extremely bright, according to some of his teachers, but his schooling was spotty. He had made a habit of missing school as often as he attended it, and his grades reflected it. Having grown up from the age of eleven under the guardian-ship of his maternal grandfather, a retired Army sergeant who had spent three years as a POW, Will was a reclu-sive and generally disengaged student, with no social life. He had no close friendships, no romantic attachments. 'Invisible,' was the way one of his teachers described him to Deputy Max Dunn. 'Whether he was there or not, it didn't matter. No one paid any attention to him.'

At twenty, Will's grandfather committed suicide. Will inherited a little over ten thousand dollars from the old man. It was not long after this event that Will moved north to Shiloh Springs. He picked up and dropped a couple of different jobs after the move but eventually spent most of his time hanging out at the University's Student Union building, where he claimed to be a full-time student on an academic scholarship and sometimes sold an ounce or two of grass.

A lot of people at the university claimed to have seen Will in the months leading up to the mass abduction, but few admitted to his acquaintance. No one inter-viewed had any idea where he lived. No one had noticed any person Will might have considered a friend.

Chapter 9

Thursday 4:15 p.m., March 18.

NOT HAVING LEARNED MUCH from the files on William Booker I closed them up for good and headed out to find Missy Worth at her place of employment.

The Dog Daze End was a little bar I had carefully avoided even in my wildest years of alcoholic excess. It sat off at the side of a county highway about the length of a pickup truck, which was something of a waste of space since only motorcycles were parked in front of the tavern. Sixteen if you bothered to count them, every single one a Harley. I parked at the corner of the building and studied the place warily. The building was painted white with big paint-peeled scabs of cinder block showing through. I saw four dirty windows in the long low wall, each covered with a set of bars. Dead centre there was a jailhouse security door that had been swung open and tied against the wall with a weathered string. The main door was made up of patched plywood decorated with bullet holes. I looked back at the road, then toward the field and woods beyond. I had come across the river and into the wilds.

The smoke of the place billowed out and the stink of spilt beer hit me hard the minute I opened the door. The place was crowded with only twenty or so people inside. I counted three women with a quick glance but with the long hair and standard-issue costumes of denim and black leather, I might have missed one or two.

I did not miss the one standing behind the bar. Mid-twenties but looking ten years older, Missy Worth was a plain, overweight woman with powerful sloping shoulders and dark, dull, mean eyes. Her hair was a shabby washed-out brown that hung limply to her shoulders. Almost anything could have improved her looks but nothing was ever going to make her pretty. She wore baggy jeans, a dark, torn t-shirt and a faded denim jacket with praises and salutations for one of the more famous West Coast gangs. Coming out of the top of her t-shirt was a tattoo of a spider sitting in an enormous blue web: jailhouse code for a killer. It covered one side of her neck and anyone's guess how far down her chest the web went. I knew her parents were society sorts. Dad was somebody's vice president at the university; Mom was a professor of psychology. They lived in the suburbs, drove nice cars, polished their shoes. That sort of thing. I was pretty sure they didn't talk much with their friends about their daughter Missy.

'We're closed!' Missy Worth shouted when she saw me. It was 4:45 in the afternoon.

Another voice shouted, 'Let him in, Missy. I need the money.'

'You still blowing folks for quarters, Curly?' she shouted. Several of the men laughed. Curly, whoever he was, had no answer, and I stood there feeling like Missy Worth's straight man. 'So tell me, sweet cheeks,' Missy Worth said as she sauntered down the bar toward me, 'are you lost or just stupid?'

'You're Missy Worth?' I asked, as I held up my identification. Missy Worth's face twitched. The eyes did a quick take on the ID. Then she tried to stare me down. I felt like road kill.

'Stupid,' she said finally and walked away. Grabbing an empty glass from a customer, she poured him a fresh beer at no charge that I could see and set it before him. Then she joined a big man at the end of the bar and lit a cigarette from his pack. She ignored me passionately.

'If you're Missy Worth,' I said, walking down the bar and knowing exactly who she was, 'I want to talk to you.' I had run a quick check on the woman's record of accomplishments. All in all, Missy Worth was one nasty female. Nothing had crossed over to a felony conviction but not because she hadn't tried. There was plenty to show she had a hair-trigger temper and a history of assaulting men. Seven arrests for it, actually. There were quite a few intoxication charges of one kind or another in addition and half-a-dozen traffic violations. Even one solicitation of prostitution that was nothing more than a misunderstanding, according to her lawyer. Such was the record and being neither a neophyte nor uninformed, I had been expecting anything but a quiet drink and a friendly discussion about the county prosecutor's plans for her. Still, I was not prepared for the woman's physical toughness and sheer raw power: the scarred hands, the snarling mouth, the murderous eyes. These are the sorts of things photographs and even TV cameras just can't quite capture.

'And just what are we going to talk about, sweet cheeks?'

'I want to talk about William Booker.'

Missy Worth let a nasty grin smear over her face, as she shook her head. 'I got it, Doo. Patty Garrat's *boy* here just needs the facts of life explained to him, that's all.' I looked back and saw a wall of big-bellied flesh between me and the door. The man named Doo nodded solemnly and lifted his chin. It was a signal to the two monsters to either side of him, and they walked back to their table. I had my exit again if I needed it.

Missy pulled a bottle of Budweiser out of a chest and popped the cap, taking a long drink of it. Absently, she studied the crowd, and seeing something I couldn't she went to pour another pitcher. I followed her down the bar as she did this, pushing myself between two men to get in her face. 'The prosecutor has ordered another investigation,' I said.

A cool smile, distant eyes, 'Look, I told the reporters, I'm telling you, I'll tell Max Dunn, and I'll even tell that prissy little boss of yours, if she ever has the guts to get face-to-face with me, I've got nothing more to say about it. I said what I had to say in court ten years ago, and that's the end of it. If people don't like it, I don't care. I ain't going into no courtroom and saying that stuff all over again.'

'Actually,' I told her, 'Garrat is hoping this time you might try telling the truth.'

The head on the pitcher rolled over the plastic edge, and the beer kept flowing. Missy Worth didn't seem to notice. 'You've got a mouth on you, don't you?'

Another customer came to the bar. He wanted three bottles. He looked at me like he was trying to decide how many bones he'd like to break. 'You Curly?' I asked and blew him a kiss. His answer wasn't even polite. Missy Worth gave him his beers, then dumped half the pitcher she had screwed up and refilled it. She went out into the room to deliver it. When she came back, she rang up the sale before she finally looked at me again. She tried to pretend she couldn't believe I was still there.

'So what's it going to be?' I asked. 'Are you going to talk to me here or down at the county jail?'

'Look, I told the truth at that trial. The cops screwed it up. It pisses me off, but I'm damned if I'm going to go out of my way to help them straighten up their mess. So don't try to threaten me. It won't work.'

'You're scared, aren't you?' Missy Worth's face went white, but as much as she appeared to want to, she couldn't quite find the words to answer. 'You think now that he's out he'll come after you if you agree to testify.'

'What'd you say your name was?' Amused, superior, but under the surface wanting to let loose.

'I'm right, aren't I? You're so damn scared of that guy you'll let him walk before you try to put him back where he belongs.'

Missy Worth's emotions seemed to shut down suddenly, and her voice went cold, 'Why don't you leave while you can still walk, pal?'

'Is your boyfriend going to hurt me if I don't?' I tipped my head out toward Doo, who was watching everything through tight slits. Once you discounted his twenty friends, Doo was all guts and beer.

'*I'm* going to hurt you,' she answered.

'I think you're all *talk*, Missy.' I said it loud enough for everyone in the room to hear me. Missy Worth grinned at her audience, but she was not happy. I saw in the mirror over the bar every face in the room staring at us. Nobody looked worried for the bartender.

'Did you put the wrong guy on Death Row, Missy? Is that why you're not talking?'

Missy Worth reached under the bar and came up with a policeman's nightstick. 'I asked nice. Just remember that when you're in the hospital.' She held the thing in her right hand as she put both hands down on the bar. She looked ready to come over the top if I didn't back off. It didn't look like a bluff either.

'The guy killed your sister, and you want to let him walk? Only way that works in my book is you either made a mistake or you're just plain scared.' The whole place got deathly quiet suddenly, and for a terrible second even Missy Worth was frozen. I nodded with the pretence of satisfaction. 'So which is it? Are you scared or stupid?'

Her face flooded with colour as she came over the bar with a roaring curse. Her hip hitting the wood surface she swung her feet over fast. As she dropped, her right hand came off the bar, cocking the nightstick behind her waist. Her eyes were hot, and I could see she meant to finish things with the first swing. I stepped forward before she got to the floor.

That was not something Missy was expecting. I reached under her wrist and took her forearm into her shoulder blades. I heard her scream. I heard the nightstick hit the floor. I looked around and saw everyone in the bar standing up. I put my mouth close to Missy's ear and hissed, 'Not scared, huh? Well you must have picked out the wrong man from the line up.' No answer. Doo and two friends were coming toward us fast, so I let her go with a hard push. 'Just leaving,' I told them.

I kicked the nightstick out of the way and looked at the three men to see if they meant to try to stop me. My size was not going to mean much in that crowd, but the thought of arrest seemed to slow them down half-a-step, and I sauntered to the door before anyone thought to cut off my retreat.

'I'll tell Pat Garrat you got the wrong man, Missy.' I said this loud enough for everyone to hear. 'It'll save us all a lot of trouble.'

'I DIDN'T GET THE WRONG MAN!'

The voice was different. Her savagery was suddenly stained with a strange sort of girlish panic. The eyes were changed too. In her face was a look of uncertainty and fear and powerlessness and dumb rage. I knew the expression well. I had carried it around for a few years after Sarah. Sometimes I could still see it in the mirror.

'Sure you did,' I told her. 'You thought you ought to know who did it, so you let Nat Hall convince you it was William Booker.'

'I know who it was! You think I could forget something like that? *Thirteen days of hell?*'

One of Doo's friends stepped toward me, reaching his hand out like a peacemaker, 'Why don't you leave her alone, man?' It was a polite question, but there was nothing polite about the man's face. After a moment, I nodded. Outside, my new friend escorted me part of the way to my car. He stood and watched as I got my keys out. The tavern door opened again and the fellow

named Doo came out. He was staring at me with undis-
guised curiosity and I hesitated. Doo sent his friend
inside and came toward me. He was wearing only a
dark t-shirt and jeans. He didn't seem to notice the cold
or rain.

'You tell Pat Garrat this thing's over,' he said. 'Will
Booker did it. He served his time. That's all there is to
it.'

'Are you a friend?' I asked.

'You're damn right I am, and I don't want to see
Missy messed up by this thing!'

I reached into my rumpled, sports jacket for one of
my business cards and handed it to him. 'Tell her to
call me if she feels like talking about it. Maybe I can
help.'

The guy took the card and studied it thoughtfully,
then stuck it in his jeans with a big showy shrug of his
enormous shoulders. 'No point. She ain't going to call.'

'Give it to her anyway,' I said.

I found a friendly bar after that. Maybe it was a
couple. Somewhere past midnight I stumbled home and
mixed myself one last drink. William Booker was out,
and looking to stay out. The only thing I was not sure
about was how much mischief he was planning.

Part II

Whispers

...Behold how great a matter a little fire kindleth!

James 3: 5.

Chapter 10

Thursday 8:30 p.m., March 18.

TAMARA MERRIWEATHER COMES to Will's bedroom door. 'Mom said to give you a towel and washcloth.'

Will steps toward her. Her eyes meet his tentatively. A big girl, he thinks. Tall with broad shoulders and big haunches. Soft. Pudgy. Eighteen, still the child. Tabit is in the hall pretending to walk by. Tabit watches enviously as her sister stands one desperate step inside Will's bedroom. Sixteen. Thin. Tall. So tall these girls of Pastor. Buds for breasts, the both. Hair long and golden on Tamara. Tabit's black like the sin she dreams. Tabit with that look. And there is a question in it that Will cannot untangle.

'It's just down the hall,' Tamara tells him.

The shower, she means. 'Thanks,' he answers.

Tamara wants to ask him something. With her big

59

grey-blue-grey eyes like a cloudy day. The pink lips of her mouth so tiny. So clean the skin. Pie-fed-plump. A virgin because no one has tried. Her dark-haired sister Tabit is the pretty one. Baby sister is the pretty; with baby sister boys have *tried*. And big sister hates it. Poor, sad Tamara Merriweather. Curious. Lonesome. Ready for miracles.

'I better go study.' Tamara drops her eyes miserably.

'Pastor says you prayed for me, Tammy.'

She smiles. How pretty she is when she smiles and blushes at the same time. Her plump, milky flesh burning suddenly. And what did you pray for, Tamara? It is the question Will does not need to ask. 'We have a youth group?' Uncertain, frightened, eager. 'This past year,' she tells him bashfully, 'we prayed twice a month in the group, then in private, too.' Her private prayers have turned the world upside down. Will is here before her in the flesh.

'Is your boyfriend in the group?' Will asks.

'I don't have...' Silence for an ending. Blushing the colour of her lips. Blushing hot.

WILL SLIPS TO THE BATHROOM like a shadow and takes a long hot shower. Finished, skin puffy with a clean he has not known for ten years, he leaves his hair a bit damp for the girls to see and steals the scents that lay forgotten on the white porcelain. Lavender for love.

Tamara in her room listens to headphones as he passes.

She looks up. Smiles. At dinner Mamma Rachel asked about homework. A lot, Tamara said in answer. So solemn and determined. Then to Will, she had better go study. But here she is looking at her quiet desk, listening to some dreamy song. Will goes on without pausing and sees Tabit peeling her sweater over her head just as Will comes past her half-opened door. Looks up now that she has done it. A wrinkled blouse that is pulled out of her jeans. He catches a glimpse of her flat belly, but that is all she shows him. That and the pretence of surprise. She heard you coming! This is for you. Black hair tousled. Black eyes testing. White flesh teasing. A Preacher-man's daughter is the devil's own!

For Tabit, Pastor weeps in the night. Dark and thin and so hungry for... something. Does she even know? Of course she knows. Those eyes know from the beginning of the world. Tamara dreams; this one is different. Thin red lips with a snake of a tongue; little hatchet blade of a nose, like Pastor's. Flat small butt, quick, lean thighs. What won't you do when your day comes, Tabit? Will glides quietly into his room, closing the door behind him. He stares a moment through his lone window into the cold wet night. Pastor lives in the suburbs, but the city is not far away.

He studies the night only a little while, the divinity of darkness, then pulls his curtain. He slips the bathrobe off his shoulders. It falls in a wrinkled heap at his feet. An obscenity of disorder in a room that he has already straightened twice this evening. He walks around the piled cloth with wicked glee, then picks it off the floor guiltily and hangs it neatly. He wipes it carefully so there are no wrinkles. Now he walks in a prison-cell-circle. He watches his own nakedness in two mirrors. One shows most of his body. He is weed-thin, a tiny man who should have been a girl. His blond hair is long. His face is thin. His eyes are his glory: hypnotically blue, dazzling blue. Bluer than the sky.

Will falls to bed with a sigh that he does not utter. His first sleep as a free man. He tries to think about pretty Tabit Merriweather, but her image fades. He dreams again of other times. The dark and the rain. Missy in the hole she thinks will be her grave. *Missy*. Beside the likes of Missy, Tabit and Tamara are lilies of the field. So pretty and soft, so soon to pass away.

Chapter 11

Friday 8:00 a.m., March 19

I STOPPED FOR BREAKFAST ON the way to the office. I had had enough mornings like this to know the routine. Heavy on the grease, a few extra cups of coffee. I had wanted to hit the ground running, but it took a while. I was sore and sick and tired. Just looking at folks turned my stomach sour. I kept feeling I was on the hunt for Sarah's killer again. I kept waking up from my foggy thoughts with a cold shiver. By the time I got to work, I was feeling physically ready to take on the problems of the day, but I had somehow worked myself into a low boil of a rage, as though all of this were very personal. I caught Garrat just as she was walking out the door. On impulse I asked her if we could talk. She saw at once the ragged edges of a sincere hangover. 'Ten minutes,' she told me, and led me back into her office. 'I talked to Missy Worth,' I told her.

Garrat looked faintly curious, nothing more. I expect she smelled the booze melting out of my pores. 'Will Booker is the man,' I told her.

'I never doubted it.'

I walked to the window and stared at the empty grey sky. 'I talked to some people. Lawyers. There's a rumour going around that you're planning on cutting your losses when this thing blows up. And we both know –'

'What the hell are you talking about?' I turned and saw an honest face: the kid I'd known years ago who thought nothing of walking in on the governor's meetings. Only the kid had died in Pat Garrat the night her father fell, and *this* kid was a lie. As good as they come, but a lie no less.

'If you need for me to fall on my sword, I will, but don't play games.'

Garrat swore. 'Don't turn paranoid on me, Rick. I need you.'

'If you want Will Booker, you're going to have to take him on yourself. Sending Massey after him is just smoke and mirrors. People who know this business see right through it, Pat. That's all I'm saying.' She looked at her desk, and I knew I was right. She knew exactly how she meant to play this thing. A bit of catastrophe, a bit of housecleaning afterwards. Maybe Massey because he was worthless but definitely the old drunk.

'Look, Rick, nobody knows how this thing is going play out.'

'Save it for the kids! You've got a problem on your hands and you're dealing with it. Fine. Do what you have to do. Just be up front with me. I had a job when I came onboard. I'll get another one when you bounce me out of here. Just don't throw the friendship away.'

'Sit down.' I took a seat and worked hard to meet her gaze. We were like a couple of teenagers who had just found out that the world was not going to coop-erate with our fantasies. 'If there's a way to try this case, I'm going after it,' she said staunchly.

'*You're* going after it? I thought Steve Massey was prosecuting this.' She hesitated. I had caught her in another lie, and she was doing a fast shift-and-sort on the best way out of it. Truth being the last option. 'I don't expect you want to hear it,' I said, 'but when your daddy was the prosecutor in Shiloh County –'

'You're right,' she snapped, cooling the air between us. 'I don't want to hear it.'

I looked away as I murmured my bit of truth, 'He took the big cases, Pat. He didn't run and hide when the likes of Len Griswold was coming to town.'

'The world's changed, Rick.'

'Nothing changes, Pat!' I caught her up in my eyes. 'Nothing ever changes!'

Lazily, a woman suffering her fool's jests, 'So how would my old man handle it?' There was a twitch some-where in the smile she offered, the way a cat will move its tail when its patience is gone.

'With eloquence! Evidence be damned, he would talk that maniac back to Death Row!'

'First rule of politics, Rick, in case you're interested. You don't have to win them all, just make sure you don't lose the big one.'

I swore angrily. 'You sound like Steve Massey!' She did not blink, and she did not back down either. I was five seconds from the unemployment line. So I took a shortcut. 'Get another investigator, lady. I'm done.'

She showed genuine surprise. Whether or not she was relieved, I could not say. 'You want to think about that, Rick?'

'It's all I've been thinking about. You're making a mistake, Pat. I won't stand by and watch it.' I stood up and put my back to her. At the door, I thought about one more shot, but instead I just kept on going.

I got a couple of boxes together and had my desk cleared in about five minutes. Mostly dead ink pens, bent paper clips, and empty whiskey bottles.

Chapter 12

Friday noon, March 19.

THE FIRST THING I DID WAS head for the Dug Out to bolster my resolution. Around noon, I remember, I swaggered into the Shamrock with a good buzz going and pushed toward the bar like a man on a mission.

So began the long drunk that is never finished. At least that was my goal. I had spent too many days like this not to know how to do it up right. It's more than alcohol. It is a state of mind. It is the art of thinking about the poor suckers who work for a living while you smack your lips on a cold bitter brew. It is the righteousness of never being forced into a compromise.

Drunkenness as an act of holiness. A mostly desolate tavern on your first day of unemployment. Leaning on a pool stick and playing hard for quarters against other loafers as the afternoon fades. Tapping a fender as you drive away at four and not giving a damn either.

Dodging the amateurs at happy hour, and going where only the serious drinkers bend an elbow. Catching a ride somewhere and stealing a few crackers so the last dollars of the day can be used for what God meant them to be used on: more beer, by God!

Chapter 13

Friday 6:30 p.m., March 19.

A KNOCK AT WILL'S bedroom door. He comes out of his holiness and into the dirty light of day. 'Will?' the voice calls. Tamara. Sweet, soft, cherubic Tamara. Will sets his Bible on the bedside table and stands up. He straightens the covers. He opens the door. Tamara steps inside. Tamara stands close. Too close for it to be an accident. 'My dad wants to see you in his study.' She steals a glance around his room. Her eyes fix on his bed. 'Something about the lawyer calling,' she murmurs.

Will does not answer for a moment. He stares into her grey-blue-grey eyes until she looks at him. He studies her plump cherubic cheeks as they flush under his hot gaze. Pink goes to red. Her breath catches. Her weight shifts awkwardly. 'Close the door,' he whispers to her. *Why?* She asks with a tilt of her head but not a word spoken. 'Close it.' She studies his naked feet. 'Are you afraid of me, Tammy?' A whisper, a dare. She shakes her head, but her eyes cannot lift to his. 'Close it,' he tells her again.

She turns and steps out of the room, then closes the door until only her face peeks back at him from the dark hallway. A timid smile. She is playing with him. Closing the door as he asked her to do. 'I'll tell him you're coming down,' she says. There is no sound beyond his door after the latch clicks shut. She is listening. He listens, too. Finally, she moves away, but he knows she has almost come back to him.

'I GOT A CALL FROM Len Griswold just now, Will,' Pastor announces when Will comes to his study. It's a big room with hundreds of books. Will scans the titles and thinks about Pastor's good life. Pastor has never wanted, never suffered, never sorrowed. The Lord loves him as purely as he loves the Lord. Like Job, Will thinks. Blessed Job, whose soul, the Devil wanted. 'It's good news, son. The appellate court has refused to hear the state's appeal! Len says he expects Pat Garrat will drop the case in a week or two. No way now they can win!'

Will nods simply. 'Praise God.'

'Dinner, you two.' Mamma Rachel, with the trim figure and pretty smile. Will turns and meets her gaze. Her faith is like Pastor's, but Will wants to know where her God is in the dark of night. When the Lord withdraws his protection, will she curse His indifference or pray all the harder? She leans into the stairwell and calls up to the girls. Pastor and Rachel and Will wait together for the two girls to come down the stairs. Tabit arrives first. She meets Will's gaze when her mother is not looking. She lets him know with a glance that if he's after Tamara he's wasting better opportunities. Tamara follows. Tamara's step falters when she sees Will's quick smile answer her sister's look.

That is good. She won't deny him the next time he asks her to do something.

Chapter 14

Midnight.

I WROTE A CHECK AT the pool hall Saturday morning. I wandered back and put a couple hundred balls away in a kind of dreamy world. I spun the stick. I kept my feet dancing. I sent the balls sliding across the felt and wondered that such a broad expanse could remain perfectly level. So different from the world. I went for a big lunch at a place called Jeff's Grill. Jeff burns his hamburgers on the outside and somehow keeps the meat juicy within. How the saints will fix them at the eternal cookout. I fended off a print reporter who was mostly just curious about what Garrat intended to do since she had lost her appeal. That she had lost her appeal was news to me. When I asked him for the details, he wandered away in search of greener pastures.

After that I sauntered out to my car and drove to the Pastime on Poplar. At about six o'clock I ran into some

professors at Charley's. We spent three hours talking baseball, books, and the meaning of life. When it had finally
settled on the one eternal, I sent them off to the Shady
Lady, one of our local strip saloons. Myself, I passed on
the chance to fall into a seat stage-side for a bleary eyeful
of the feminist counter-culture. Not virtue, mind you. I
just didn't have the cash for anything but beer.

I lose a few hours now. I do not quite know where
I went, only that it was midnight, give or take a decade,
and the prettiest gal in town and I were dancing in the
street, just outside Simple Simon's. We were oblivious
the rain and traffic. Laughing at it, in fact, because folly
is an aphrodisiac. Then there was a light, as from heaven.
I recall looking around and seeing a friendly face in a
blue uniform peeking out from a city patrol car. Maybe
I wanted to move it inside, he said. He passed me a
grin and a wink with the advice.

I know all the old cops and most of the new ones.
I was a city cop myself before I went over to the State
Troopers, but that was a lifetime ago, so I walked toward
this patrolman with a friendly smile.

My next coherent memory is sitting with eight other
men in the city jail drunk tank. I had a cut lip, bloody
knuckles, a hotness at one eye, and some real heaviness in my back and leg muscles where I had enjoyed
an apparently much needed 'attitude adjustment.' I'll
say only this of my night in jail: the tough boys let me
be. And why not? I was the nightmare their mammas
had warned them about.

Chapter 15

Sunday 2:00 a.m., March 21.

RAIN. A WEEK OF IT AND no letting up. Missy Worth stood in the parking lot by her low slung Buick Skylark. Because the new Harley don't come out in the rain. Probably a pretty nice car twenty years ago. Now even the chrome was rusting. She looked up angrily at the sky. Was it ever going to stop?

Behind her a motorcycle blasted to life. Missy climbed into the Skylark and turned the key. It groaned before it turned over. She played the engine out for a while, as touch-and-go as a virgin. And she'd had one or two, so she knew all about virgins. She pressed the pedal with several light taps, then heard the rumbling take hold. She brought it on fast until the backfires started up. She looked over at Doo, who shook his head, laughing quietly at the old Skylark. She had to get a new car, but with the Harley payments who could afford it?

Missy waved at her friend with her middle finger and pulled out from behind the building, rocking through what looked like a footpath to the front where everyone parked except her and Doo, then to the pavement. She was beat down from five hard days of two-to-two. Not that she didn't like the work! It was the greatest! Best job ever. It was only that... well, a month off would be great. Month off and roll!

She had the trip planned if she could get the time off, or she got her ass fired. Start through the hill country further south, roll down beside the river and slip over to the Ozarks. Quick stop in Stillwater to see an old friend and then head southwest again. Destination: Santa Fe. On roads out there you could hit a hundred and the cops would just wave at you as you blew by. She grimaced suddenly. The river. She always felt something crossing it. Something in the air. Something old and mouldy in her memory. When she was a kid it was different. Loved the river. Loved the woods. Loved night. Stars in the sky: that was the best. The last ten years things had been different. She thought about her sister. How if Mary could come back, what she would see. Besides Will Booker walking the streets a free man.

Missy shook her head with a familiar rush of rage and a sewer-full of guilt. If Mary came back, she would not recognise anything including her own sister. Eighty pounds heavier. Missy swore and reached into her purse for her cigarettes. She needed to go on a diet. She finished her smoke as she pulled up in front of her house on Elm Street. She tried to remember the drive. Like a blackout from the river onwards. She had them sometimes. Just go through the motions and then wake up and wonder what had happened. Sometimes it lasted for the length of a cigarette. Sometimes longer.

Missy studied her house as she sat in her junkyard special. The house had all the appeal of a dose of clap, but the rent was right. For a whole house, right as rain. It had three rooms and a kitchen. The bathroom was smaller than most closets but what could you do? The porch was broken down. You could open the front door with a credit card – or a good kick if the banks didn't want to give you any credit. The back door was worse. Security was nothing more than a hook on a u-shaped nail. A burglar's dream, assuming the guy wasn't dreaming big.

Probably the worst thing about the place was the railroad tracks forty-seven feet off the back step. Once you got used to the trains coming through your bedroom at all hours of the night, even that wasn't so bad. Better than some sex she had had, actually. At least the ones she could remember. Missy checked her watch. She had sixty hours off. Lugging a case of Bud she had stolen out of the back of the Dog Daze, Missy kicked the storm door open, braced the box between her ample belly and the door frame and unlocked the front door. Stepping in, she snapped the light on. The place was a mess, as usual. The front room had a tattered couch and a couple of cat-frayed easy chairs she had stolen from a Goodwill drop-off. In the next room was her pride: a Harley where a dining room table ought to be. It was as black as a moonless night, its chrome like stars. And fast as a back-seat promise. She shuffled through her front room admiring the big bike in the mirrors she had hung around it, hardly noticing the newspapers covering her floor or the tumble weed dust balls in the corners of the room. Maybe once before she died she would clean house. Maybe. She kicked a pizza box out of her way and dug into a drawer by the TV for her dope. 'Come to Mamma,' she whispered as she brought out a big bag of grass and hit the CD, setting it out of habit for the second band of Terri Clark's best. 'Poor, Poor Pitiful Me' was what passed for the national anthem in Missy's world.

Sitting on the ratty couch and carefully throwing a pair of men's underwear to the floor, Missy pulled an oily clump of grass out of the bag. She tossed it on her rolling pan and broke it apart. She sucked up the sweetish scent of it. She scraped the seeds out by letting them roll down the tray while she dragged the leaves up into a neat pile. She pinched three loads into an EZ wider and rolled a fat joint with quick sure fingers. She licked it with the delicacy of a fellatrix and dried it with a lit match. Now she set the tip on fire and blew the smoke out after a long, lazy drag. Best grass she had had in months. One minute she was Missy Worthless. Next she was pulling down dreams out of the sky.

Chapter 16

Darkness.

MISSY WALKED AROUND THE ROOM with the joint smouldering in her fingers. She hit the auto repeat on the Terri Clark song because she wanted to listen to it all night, full blast. Neighbours might not like it, but they knew better than to complain.

She sang along raucously, '*Poor, poor, pitiful...*'

She took a hit. The song went on without her. She blew the smoke out through her nose, hit another and held it until she went dizzy. The stuff leaked out her ears and trickled through her toenails. Good stuff! 'Caesar! Here, kitty!' Give the cat a shotgun. Old yellow bastard comes-a-running, nose in the air.

Nothing when I get home, can't be bothered to get off the bed, thank you, but the minute you offer him the good stuff. Here I am! Here I am. Here am I.

'You like to get high, Caesar? Sure you do. We all

78

do, hon.' She took the joint into the curve of her tongue, the fire at the back of her throat. A thick line of white smoke shot out of her mouth and hit the cat. Caesar flinched and recoiled and shook his head, then swooned to the floor and staggered away, one leg crossing the other, front and back.

Missy was still watching the cat when she heard a rattle at her back door. She felt her gut go hollow, and set the joint down. She caught her baseball bat, which she liked to keep in the kitchen, and looked out the cracked glass of the back door. Nothing. But it had sounded like someone checking her door. She popped the hook and pushed the door open. Down the way maybe thirty yards there was a streetlight where the tracks crossed the road. There was a security light at the back end of the college where the fence shut out trespassers. She came off her step and stood listening. Nothing but her imagination.

Back inside, she walked through the house until she came to the front room. She moved a curtain aside and looked out into the blackness just to be sure. Nothing, but then as she pulled away she was sure something had moved. She swore hotly, and looked again. Only the night.

She went to the front door fast. She was sure she was going to catch someone sneaking around the house. As suddenly as she began, Missy stopped herself. She knew who it was. All those years waiting to get out.

And now he had come to make good on his promise. Because she had broken hers. Because she had sworn on her very soul...

Tears broke over her cheeks, and without thinking, Missy turned and ran for her bedroom. She dropped her bat as she went. Like a child running from ghosts. Only no ghost had ever scared her like this.

She tasted copper on the back of her tongue. She opened her closet door quietly and then rolled down to her knees and crawled in among her shoes and dirty clothes. She reached back nervously to close the door and listened.

A creaking noise at the back door now. A footstep in the kitchen. The song again: *Poor, poor, pitiful me...*

Shivering, Missy pulled back deeper into her tiny space. She tried to draw breath, but at the thought of Will standing on the other side of her door, she found herself making odd, spasmodic sounds. Did he hear it? Not a movement, not a sound. He was there, just waiting for her to open the door. '*Missy... Missy!*'

The years gone like the snap of her fingers, they start it all over again. Missy feels herself shaking as she lets go her piss. She smothers her sobs with dirty laundry stuffed into her mouth. Even as she does, another sob ratchets out of her.

She is seventeen. She is naked and cold and scared. Beyond the darkness, Will is whispering to her again. '*Time to come out and play, Missy.*'

Chapter 17

Sunday 7:30 a.m., March 21.

PASTOR'S CHURCH SITS ATOP A BIG bald hill cut out of a forest. A huge white box crowned with a cross you can see for miles. It has a few acres of parking for the faithful. It is fourteen years old. Pastor built it with the Holy Word of God and other people's money. God still smiles on them all, but only for a few more days.

'The sanctuary will hold eight hundred sinners, give or take,' Pastor announces proudly. 'Saints,' he tells Will with a wink, 'have to go on down the street.' Almost blushing at the fuss folks have made over him lately, Pastor shows Will the video booth, the three big screens which multiply Pastor's image. He shows a few seconds of a video in the control booth so that Will can get an idea of how the place will look filled up. Will can feel Pastor's pride, which extends to more than his pretty sanctuary. Pastor is a movie star who stands in an artificial garden before an adoring crowd.

Will sees all the school rooms, the gymnasium, the vast library. Pastor walks through the building, *his* building, flipping lights on and off, talking to Will as he goes. Will likes the basement's dark intimacy. Pastor shows him a beautiful study. Couches, chairs, rug, lamps, a wall of books. There are two steel doors at either end of the room with keyed deadbolts. No windows. A lovely room for the work of God. 'The youth group meets here,' Pastor tells him. Will feels a shiver of desire. The lights go off; they prepare to go on.

Pastor says he needs to spend some time in his office. He needs time alone before the first service begins. His speech breaks off suddenly. A man and a teenage boy are coming toward them down the long basement corridor. Something cold stirs in Will's chest. The boy looks to be about sixteen or seventeen. He is tall, lean and dark. He is his father's image, except that the father has lost most of his hair. They walk like each other, a shambling gait with a joyous little bump to finish every step. The father blinks in the same manner as the son. The man is Pastor's age but in better condition. Broad shoulders, flat belly. He has a long bumpy nose, a fat bulb at the end. Brown eyes set tight. An athlete's cockiness.

'You must be Will Booker!' the man announces with a Midwestern bawl of good cheer. He has a quick smile, broad flat lips. In his eyes he is deciding Will's guilt or innocence. He believes he is a practical man, a man of the world. A businessman almost certainly, Will decides. Yet he dreams of peeking into another man's soul to know him. Will dislikes him for that. The feeling is passionate and immediate. Pastor is speaking. Pastor's voice purrs solicitously. Will does not know this tone. He has never known Pastor to purr to anyone. Pastor talks to God man-to-man. What *mortal* could possibly inspire him to ingratiate himself? '...Ben Lyons,' he says with gravity, 'and his son Benny.'

Old Ben shakes Will's hand. It is so good to see justice finally win out! Will glances at Ben Lyons's boy. Boy Ben has his father's shoulders and vanity. Not yet the hypocrisy.

Chapter 18

PASTOR IS BORN FOR THE pulpit. He loves his small stage for the power it gives him and for the vanity of his holiness. He prays mightily. He sings of joys and sorrows in the Lord with a voice fit for mountaintops. As he prays, he glows. This is the man Will has known for the better part of the last decade. Pastor tells his flock about doubt. *'The feeling that we are in a room praying... to one big Nobody! A natural response to the life of faith. Natural... but not right! Because he IS there! The proof is sitting right here!'* He points to Will. *'...an innocent man who prayed in the solitude of a Death Row cell that justice would finally win out...'*

Will is inspired by the fact that he is the supreme example of faith. Holiness buzzes in him like a maddening fly. Tamara is beside him. Too tender for taking blood. Like Tabit, who has not enough rage for

84

what he wants. Will is bored with them both. He watches Ben Lyons instead. Proud Ben Lyons. And Boy Ben, who is handsome and seems to watch a certain blonde, who watches him back with careful glances. Will studies their game curiously, but soon finds something far more interesting. She sits between Mother Lyons and Boy Ben. She is a large, lanky girl, trim and muscular like papa. Like Benny, not yet the hypocrite. Bitter as the dawn. Miserable. Angry. He can feel it from here. This is a spirit that wants only... *expression*! God's own, this one. God's own!

'Does Benny Lyons play sports?' Will asks Tamara quietly. These are his first words since the service has started. Will never talks during worship, but he *needs* this. He can't wait.

Tamara stirs; she studies the Lyons family critically. Her breath smells of oatmeal and chocolate. She says she thinks he plays baseball. Tamara obviously does not care. 'He's stuck-up,' she explains. Will smiles to himself. Benny likes the pretty blonde across the way, has never once given Tamara Merriweather his adoring brown eyes.

'Is that his sister next to him?' Will whispers.

Tamara warms to Will's attention. 'Penny is Benny's twin. Penny is okay,' she tells him. 'She used to swim, but she quit.'

Penny. He likes the name. He likes the girl. There is murder in this one's heart!

85

Part III

Judgement

And Ehud said, I have a message from God unto thee.

Judges 3: 19.

Chapter 19

Sunday 2:00 p.m., March 21.

I KNEW A DOZEN GOOD lawyers, but I did not call any of them. I took my breakfast, then my lunch, ready to sit it out until my court appearance Monday, at which I would proudly defend myself and probably get a year in lockup for the crime self-lawyering. A radical alternative to AA, I'll admit, but I was in the mood for getting sober without making confessions.

I watched an old priest come through. It was Sunday. He talked to some of the boys, blessed a couple, had a prayer book that he gave one occupant. I just stared at the old man as he passed me by. He had the good sense to keep going. Most of my new acquaintances were out by two o'clock. Parents, friends, bail bondsmen, lawyers: somebody loved them. I hung on like mould, having no one to call. My luck ran out when a jailer took me up to a conference room.

Max Dunn was there, missing only his .45. 'Are you out of your ever-loving-mind?' he asked me. The first words he spoke.

'Who told you I was here?' I answered.

Max looked away, shaking his head, his voice echoing my words, 'Who told me you were here? Let's see. What *was* her name?'

'I'm staying until I talk to a judge.'

'Get off your Cross, Rick. They're cutting you loose.'

'They can't do that.'

'They already have, and if you raise hell with *me*, I'll put you in Crazy Cate's, where you belong!'

Jails didn't bother me. Doctors, with their opiates and needles, did. I felt the air running out of me like a blown tire. 'I don't appreciate you butting in, Max. It's none of your business what happens to me.'

Max looked away, seriously irritated. 'She'll take you back, Rick. To tell you the truth, I don't think anyone knows you even quit!'

'She can go to hell.' I said this evenly, sincerely. Pat Garrat had broken my heart.

Max gave me a speculative look. 'I'll do you a favour, buddy, and not tell her you said that.'

'If I walk out of here, I'm just going to get drunk again.'

'It's Sunday, Rick. The only joints open are respectable.' I swore and looked down at the scars of the table we sat at. Hell is a friend who knows your haunts. 'What's under your skin, buddy?'

I looked up in anger. 'She's going to let this guy walk without a fight, Max.'

'Is that what this is about?'

'Part of it.'

'Let me ask you something. Why do you even care? It's one less headache as far as you're concerned.' I had no answer. 'Rick, you've got to be tougher than one fight.'

'Her old man would bury this kid!'

'HER OLD MAN IS DEAD!' Max brought his voice back to room temperature. 'It's been seventeen years, Rick; when are you going to get that through your thick skull?'

'I'm tired, Max. I'm tired of wanting things right and finding everything wrong.'

'What you're tired of is this binge you're on. Now why don't I take you home? You need to get some real food down you and some sleep. Tomorrow you can go into the office and get back to work like nothing at all is the matter.'

'Just like that?' I asked, almost laughing at the ease of it.

He gave me his patented gap-toothed grin, 'Your sins are forgiven, my son.'

Chapter 20

Sunday 2:15 p.m., March 21.

DOO PARKED HIS HARLEY behind Missy Worth's broken down Buick on Elm Street. Missy had scored some really good grass. She had told him he ought to come by first thing Sunday. Two-fifteen. Doo gave the grey skies a friendly grin. Two-fifteen was as early as it ever got on a Sunday.

He hit the front door with a hard, quick tap and waited. He heard music inside. Maybe she hadn't heard him. He hit the door again, a long, loud rattling. He wandered down to the window. The curtain was drawn aside just a bit. The lights were on. Missy's bag of grass was on the floor out in the open, the stuff all spilled out. There was more sitting on her rolling tray. A dead joint sat on the ashtray. Doo dropped off the end of the porch and went around to the back. She wasn't in the yard, but the back door was unhooked. The cat appeared, circled nervously, and skittered back out of sight. Doo felt his gut tighten as he went forward tensely, calling Missy's name. The CD started playing the same song again.

In the dining room Doo slipped around Missy's Harley and picked up the baseball bat that lay on the floor. He went back to the kitchen, setting it up next to the doorway. He checked the bathroom to make sure she had not passed out in there. Something was wrong.

He called Missy's name several times. He watched the cat come out of the bedroom and return. Doo followed it. He checked under the bed. He opened the closet. It was a mechanical motion, simply checking all the possibilities, so he wasn't ready to see Missy sitting under a pile of dirty clothes. She stared up at him with dark wet eyes. The closet stank of her piss. He started to swear. Then he tried to laugh. What the hell? Then it hit him. She didn't recognise him.

'Don't hurt me,' she whimpered.

Chapter 21

Sunday 3:00 p.m., March 21.

AT THREE PASTOR ASKS WILL if there is anything special he would like to do. The public library, Will answers. Lots of books here you're welcome to look at, Pastor tells him. Will knows that, he says; then he smiles bashfully, but it isn't the public library.

A phone call. Yes, the library is open until nine every evening but Saturday. Pastor asks Tamara to drive Will into town. Pastor tells her he will pick Will up later, when he calls.

It is not raining, but the sky is still grey. For a couple of minutes neither Will nor Tamara talks. Then Will tells her to turn right. Tamara protests but she turns where he indicates. They leave the asphalt at once for a gravel road. Soon they are in open farmland. Five, then eight miles out from town. Will remembers the road. Almost nothing has changed along the way. Then he sees it ahead, what he is seeking. An abandoned property. Still there, still desolate. A quarter of a mile distant six new homes stand where there were once only fields, but here there is still the quiet of decay. A fence tangled in briars. An old lawn turned to high weeds and heavy brush. A broken concrete lane leading to a bald patch of dirt.

'In here,' Will tells her.

Tamara looks at him strangely, but she obeys. They are hidden from the road the moment she turns into the lane. The weeds and trees press close, scratch the girl's banged up Chrysler. A few feet more and they have a view of the pad of dirt where the house stood. Behind it is a broken down shed. Beyond that was an abandoned barn, where he had once found a bat and shovel. The new houses down the field might as well be miles away. Here they are absolutely alone, perfectly invisible. 'Come here, Tammy,' he tells her. Tamara does not wait this time when he asks. She comes quickly. Her lips find his. Her breath pours over his face as they kiss. He tastes the Sunday staleness of her. The green beans they have eaten, mashed potatoes, beef and gravy. Cherry pie. He holds her neck reverently. 'Do you like that?'

'Oh, Will!'

He looks away sadly. 'I know it's wrong,' he tells her, 'but I can't help myself. The moment I saw you…'

'It's not wrong, Will!' After a long, quiet kiss, she

finishes, 'If two people care for each other it's *never* wrong.'

He studies the girl's face. 'For me, knowing how you prayed to get me out, the moment I saw you, I knew this was what I wanted.'

'I wanted it too!'

'Your parents aren't going to understand.'

'I don't care!'

'We can't tell them.'

'I could keep driving,' she tells him. He stirs from his thoughts and focuses on the girl. He is not sure what she means. 'No one would ever find us, Will.'

She is serious. Eighteen always is. 'They'll put me back in prison if I run, Tammy.'

She throws herself at him. She weeps and kisses his face. It's not right what they've done to him. It is not fair. He should be free! *They* should be free! Will holds the girl tightly while she laments. He thinks of things past; he summons pain, hunger, cold. 'We have to wait,' he tells her with quiet decisiveness. 'Once I'm free, it will be different. Then it won't matter what your parents say. It won't matter what anyone says.'

He kisses her mouth to seal the promise. 'How long do we have to wait?'

Will shakes his head. 'That's up to the law.'

'My dad says there won't be a trial!'

'If he's right about that, we won't have to wait more than sixty days.' While she considers the changes in her life that might come in the next sixty days, he tells her, 'We'd better go, Tammy. I need to... I mean I should spend some time in the library, since I said that's where I'm going.'

She starts the Chrysler and backs out to the road. A car comes toward them, forcing Tamara to wait. It sweeps past them, a rock kicking into Tamara's rear bumper. Tamara swears brightly, and Will thinks she is worried about the damage the rock has caused. 'I knew that woman!' she tells him, 'It was Mrs Breen. She goes to our church!'

Will closes his eyes. A mistake. A bad one if the woman really saw them. 'Pull back inside,' he whispers.

Tamara does as he tells her. 'What's the matter?' she asks.

Will thinks he should kill Tamara here and now. It is not what he wants, but if Pastor finds out about them before it is time for him to know the truth...

'Tell me about Mrs Breen.'

'She's an old busybody.'

'Is she your mother's friend?'

'They don't get along. My mother hates her.'

'You can't say anything about us,' Will whispers. 'If your father finds out...'

'He won't.'

'What about your mother?'

Her gaze drops away. 'I won't tell her,' she answers quietly.

'She'll know, especially if Mrs Breen calls her.'

'Mrs Breen won't call her.'

Will stares at a patch of weeds in the distance. Then he looks across the overgrown property to the barn. He is not ready. He needs time, a day or two more. For Penny.

'Are you going to tell Tabit about us?'

'It's none of Tabit's business what we do!' Tamara is bitter. She hates her sister's slender dark beauty.

'We won't have to hide from anyone once I am free,' he tells her.

'Oh, Will!'

'We better go.' She hesitates, wanting his promise to be true. 'Go on,' he tells her. He is smiling like a lover. 'Take me into town like you said you would.'

Chapter 22

Sunday 9:43 p.m., March 21.

A KNOCKING AT THIS BEDROOM door stirs Will. It is late; he is back from his studies at the public library. He is reading his Bible, the story of Job, who kept faith. When he opens the door, Will sees Pastor's face is stricken. Will is certain Pastor has found out about Tamara.

'The sheriff is downstairs, Will. He wants to talk to you.'

'The sheriff?' Pastor does not answer him. Will has no choice but to follow.

Will recalls the other sheriff vividly when he gets to Pastor's study. The gun in his mouth. The dirty words he spoke. This one is a big man too. 'I thought I better come see you personally,' he announces at once, 'because I don't want any confusion between you and me on what I have to say. Do you follow me, William?'

Breath of booze, eyes red, mean. 'I'm not sure I do, Sheriff.' Will feels his guts boiling. 'We had a complaint about you!'

Pastor moves in by one big step. Mug-to-mug, Pastor's head tipping down into Sheriff's face, 'What kind of complaint, Max?'

Sheriff looks uneasily at Pastor. Pastor scares him. All the same, Sheriff stands square. Gets mean when he is scared. Like prison guards and dogs. 'I'll ask the questions, Connie.'

'Then maybe we'd better call Will's lawyer.'

'Call a baker's dozen! All I want to know is where William was this morning.'

Pastor grins. He does not like Sheriff Max Dunn. 'Will was with me from six-thirty until close to three this afternoon; is that good enough for you?'

'I asked *him*.'

Will blinks in confusion, then answers. 'I went with Pastor to the church this morning. At three I went to the public library.'

'And you were up at six-thirty this morning?'

'Yes, sir.'

'Sunday is a work day around here!' Pastor chuckles.

Sheriff ignores him passionately. His frown tightens down on Will. 'William,' he drawls, 'have you seen Missy Worth since you have been out?'

'No, sir. Not to my knowledge. Maybe she was at church this morning. If she was, I didn't recognise her.'

'She wasn't at *church*!' Pastor answers with a laugh. 'Not Missy Worth! Is that your complaint, Max? You think Will here was making eyes at Missy Worth in church?'

Sheriff angers, 'They've got Missy Worth up at the hospital, Connie.'

'The *hospital*?'

'Catherine Howard. They've got her in for observation until noon next Sunday.'

Pastor gets a strange, questioning look, his head leaning out like a leering mask. 'She's had another breakdown!'

'They don't know what it is.'

Pastor looks at Will. 'Catherine Howard is a psychiatric ward, Will.'

'Her parents are beside themselves with worry. They think your friend here came to see her and made some kind of threat.'

'This morning? Well that proves she's a liar, doesn't it? Or just plain crazy! Now let me tell you something, Max. They're grabbing at straws so they can send Will back, but they made a mistake this time. Will has an alibi! You hear me? That's proof positive, isn't it? Your eyewitness can't be trusted!' Sheriff has no answer. He cannot quite figure this out. 'I asked you a question, Max.'

Sheriff's face flushes, 'Don't you take that tone with me, Connie Merriweather! I came out here –'

'I'll take any tone I like! You come into my home and treat Will like he's done something wrong because you've got a poor woman locked up in a psychiatric ward. Well, she's a drug addict, as I have pointed out many times. Is now and was ten years ago! It's a tragic situation, I'll grant you that, but so is her accusation against Will! Especially as it cost him ten years of his freedom!'

'You're a damn fool, Connie Merriweather!' Sheriff shifts his glare suddenly to Will, murder in his eyes. 'Talk your Jesus to this fool all you want, boy! But I know the devil when I smell the sulphur!'

'You get out of my house, Max Dunn! Your welcome has worn out!'

'And let me tell you this, *my Sweet William*, if you get the *urge* again, you had better go do it in someone else's county! If I find dead kids in my jurisdiction I'll load all six before you and *I* play the game!'

'That's a threat! I'm a witness to that, Max! You're talking about Russian roulette. Don't think I don't know exactly what you're saying!'

'Go back to your pulpit, Connie. You don't have a hog's breath of an idea what's going on here.' One last look for only Will, his big finger pointing. 'Mind what I say, boy, or I'll *get* you! You hear me? I will!'

Pastor's voice cools. 'Max, I want you out of this house, now.' Sheriff only has eyes for Will as he leaves. Like a dog driven off, barking all the way. A bad man, he is. As evil as the last. And godless, too.

102

Pastor opens the door for him as he leaves. 'You have not heard the end of this, Max Dunn!' They have words again, but Will cannot hear them all. The word *fool* is clear. He hears the name of Rachel, then mention of Pastor's two little girls. Does he want them all to die? Whatever Pastor answers, Will cannot hear it. When he comes back into his study, Pastor is shaking his head, pretending a calm he does not possess. His face is red. Will thinks Sheriff has scared Pastor with his warnings, but it isn't so. Pastor is thinking about Will. About the trial. Will focuses on Pastor's face, nods and answers as he must. He cannot follow everything. He knows only Pastor believes Sheriff has made a mistake. Pastor wants to call Mr Griswold about it. Will is not so confident. He fears this sheriff as much as he did the last, as he feared the guards and the convicts at Graysville Prison. Against such men even God is quiet.

Chapter 23

Monday 11:15 a.m., March 22.

I DID NOT GO BACK TO WORK Monday morning. I did not call to say I would not be in, either. Max Dunn meant well. Pat Garrat, even. But I was finished with it. Finished with politics and the dreams that take you places where you don't belong. I walked down to St. Jude's and spent a hard hour on my knees. I told the Lord to take me where he would because I was finished with Pat Garrat. The Lord had absolutely nothing to say to any of this.

Afterwards, I found my car in the lot of one of my favourite taverns and drove to a cafe, where I bought a couple of big newspapers and settled down to a life of leisure. I'm pretty good at loafing, and I did it up right that morning. I got back to the house a little before eleven and made a couple of calls to the newspaper. Rooms for rent at my house. PI for hire. I cleaned up the place some and then decided to go see Sarah's grave. In the back of my mind I had couple of options after that, a tavern or a gun shop, and I was not real sure which I would take. Dead or dead drunk, I mean. At that point it did not seem to make much difference. I don't know now, even, what I would have done, because I got a phone call as I was heading out. And that changed everything. The voice was heavy, somehow familiar, but the name meant nothing. 'This is Clint Doolittle.'

'What is this about?' I asked, running the name through my memory and wondering why I knew the voice.

'You said you might be able to help Missy.'

Doolittle. Doo. Missy Worth's boyfriend. I started to explain that I was not with the county prosecutor's office anymore, but I was a little slow getting started. It's hard sometimes to say a truth we hate.

'Well, she's in trouble, and she wants to talk to you.'

'What kind of trouble?'

'That freak came by her house Saturday night. They got Missy up in Catherine Howard for a week and he's still walking the streets.'

I went through things with Clint Doolittle for another few minutes, but I was still pretty much in the dark. So I called Garrat.

'Rick? Are you coming in?' Garrat sounded like nothing at all had happened last Friday. It was no concern of hers if I spent Saturday night in the drunk tank. I was already on the road, not more than six blocks from the office. 'I was thinking about it,' I answered, 'assuming you haven't changed the locks.'

'No reason to do that, but we've had some developments in the Booker case, if you're interested.'

'The attack on Missy Worth?'

'You didn't get that on the news, did you?'

'Clint Doolittle called me, Pat. The boyfriend. He said Will Booker broke into Missy's house and terrified her all Saturday night and early Sunday morning.'

'Mr Doolittle has a perspective that does not necessarily accord with the facts.'

I put my signal on and caught the light. 'What are you talking about?' I asked her.

'Why don't you get in here, and I'll tell you what I know?'

I slipped my car into one of the prosecutor's parking slots. 'I'll be there in a minute.' Getting out of the car, I dropped my phone into my sports coat, slammed the door shut, and trotted toward the north entrance. They waved me through security and inside of a minute I came through Garrat's door. The joys of technology. She barely blinked, but I could tell I had surprised her. 'Max called me last night,' she said without preamble. 'Said Booker appears to have an ironclad alibi for the whole of Sunday morning. There is no way he was at Missy Worth's house, unless it was well before six in the morning.'

I stopped dead in my tracks. 'I thought he was holding her at gunpoint, threatening her. Now you're telling me... what?'

'Twelve hundred witnesses, give or take, put Mr Booker in church Sunday morning. He attended *both* services and got back home about the time Clint Doolittle found Missy Worth.' I grunted at this. 'But there are still a couple of hours Saturday night unaccounted for; so maybe he was there. And maybe he wasn't. At this point I'm getting a lot of different stories. They've got her levelled out some now with the meds, so I sent Massey over to sort things out. I wanted to see if there is any chance Booker actually showed up sometime before dawn Sunday. Missy said she would only talk to the old bald guy.'

'So why didn't you give me a call?'

Garrat smiled wryly. 'I asked Clint Doolittle to do it for me.'

I shook my head at the con she had run, mad at myself for not seeing through it. 'Did you tell him to say Booker was at her house with a gun?'

'Doo's been hanging around with Missy Worth for a few years, Rick. In all that time he never saw her back down from anything but a smart decision. He found her yesterday afternoon hiding under some dirty laundry like a frightened kid. Whatever he told you is what he believes.'

'But you're not convinced Booker was there?'

'Talk to her, Rick. Find out what happened. See if it makes sense. At this point, all I need is for the thing to sound reasonable. Right now, we have got her home at say two-thirty, three o'clock Sunday morning. Booker was up with Connie Merriweather at six-thirty. It's a tight window of opportunity, but it's still possible – unless Missy is claiming that Booker was talking to her after the sun was up. Right now, I've got statements suggesting that, but they were made while she was still upset.'

'If Missy Worth gives us a credible story, are you going to charge Booker with witness intimidation?'

'If I believe it, I might.'

'You don't have any doubt about Will Booker, do you, Pat?'

'I'll tell you what scares me, Rick. It's that Connie Merriweather doesn't. Did you know the guy has two teenage daughters, and he has put Booker in a room across the hall from them?'

'Is that preacher out of his mind?'

'He's invested over eight years in his cause, Rick. That's way too much for him to admit he could be wrong.'

Chapter 24

Monday 11:45 a.m., March 22.

MISSY WORTH WAS IN BED sleeping when my escort knocked on her open door. 'You feel up to another visitor, Missy?'

Missy's eyes fluttered briefly, then seeing me, she smiled a lazy, drugged grin. 'You come to give me another chance at your sorry ass, sweet cheeks?' The attendant beside me got a little edgy, but I thanked him. I said I would take it from here.

'How are you doing?' I asked. I had come into the room but was standing just beyond arm's reach, the way folks do at the tiger's cage.

Missy had a slack jaw and dull, listless eyes. She looked like a woman who had been asleep for days. 'Feeling better than *you* look. What happened to your face?'

Touching my black eye, I answered, 'I ran into more beers than I could handle.'

'Hey, the docs all have top-of-the-line drugs, but I could sure use a beer. You want to go get drunk with me?'

'Maybe later,' I said, taking a chair. From where I sat, I had a better view of the spider web. The spider's body on her neck was about the size of ping pong ball, the legs of it taking it out that much farther. The web was executed with some real skill, and I knew she had paid good money to mutilate herself.

'I like the work,' I told her.

She pulled her gown free and dropped it completely down so I could see… everything. 'Cool, huh?'

I tried not to stare, but Missy had a lot to try to avoid looking at. 'Local work?' I asked.

She shook her head in disgust. 'New Orleans. I went down there just for this one guy. Years ago! If you're going to do something permanent, do it right. You know what I mean?' She covered herself finally and I quit looking at the floor like some dried up old priest.

'You got any?' A tattoo, she meant.

I shook my head. 'A woman in our office has one,' I told her. 'It says MOM, right here,' I pointed to my thigh about two inches from my crotch and sketched the design.

Missy smiled lewdly, 'Turn her upside down, it says WOW. You ever think about that?'

'I probably won't be able to stop thinking about it now that you've brought it up.'

She seemed to laugh at this, then to think about things. Finally, she told me, 'Hey, you're pretty quick for an old man. I thought I was going put you down the other day!'

'Yeah, well, before I became a rich and successful businessman I was a city cop for a couple years, then a state trooper for almost a dozen.'

She gave me the once-over. 'What happened to rich and successful?'

I grinned at this and gave her something like the truth. 'My ex-wife got the security business I started. I went back to working for a living.'

'You call busting people work?'

'I let other people make the busts. I do follow-up investigations, help the lawyers prepare their evidence and witnesses – that kind of thing.'

'You any good?'

I laughed and shook my head. 'I'm pretty old. In this game that counts for something.'

'You're not *that* old. I'd do you if I was drunk enough.'

I won't say I didn't react, but I sure hurried to change the subject. 'Missy, what the hell happened the other night?'

Missy's eyes closed, and she tipped her face toward the ceiling. I thought for a minute she had gone to sleep. 'Nothing,' she said. Her voice seemed to crawl out of her throat. 'Not a damn thing happened.'

'Doo said Will Booker showed up at your house.

111

Made threats. Put you in the closet. Said Will told you he'd kill you if you came out.'

'Look, you're all right, man. I mean you have got some guts. I like that. Let's just forget about it, huh?'

'Was he there or not?'

'What difference does it make?' I didn't answer her. After a moment she dropped her gaze. 'I can't prove it was him. I can't even say for sure someone was there.'

'You didn't talk to him?' She shook her head. 'You didn't see him?'

'Look, forget it. The guy was there, but there is no way I can prove it. Will is untouchable. I'm the one in the nut house.'

'They tell me you're in until noon next Sunday. That's a pretty good chunk of time just to give up.'

'Observation.' Missy's head rocked like a drunk's. 'If I screw up in here it could be a lot longer.'

'I assume you have salary insurance? A good medical plan?'

She laughed at me. 'What planet are you from, sweet cheeks?'

I didn't even smile. 'Will Booker hit you pretty hard for not even touching you, don't you think?'

After a long silence that threatened to fade into sleep again, Missy answered me. The voice was still raw, but there was an element of confiding that had nothing to do with the playful flirtation she'd been manufacturing just to get me off stride. 'He was whispering my name for a while; at least I think so, I'm not real sure; it could have been me just remembering how he talked, but I'm telling you, I *felt* him. I don't know how else to put it. Ten years, I never felt the guy; last night, he was *there*. He was outside the house, and I heard something, and then it seemed like... he was standing at my closet door, telling me to come out and play.'

'*Play?*'

'That's how he talked the last time. "*Missy! Missy! Time to come out and play, Missy.*" That's what I heard last night. Him standing at my closet door, calling to me like that.'

I had read her testimony and those interviews Nat Hall hadn't destroyed, but this was the first time I had heard about coming out to play. 'I got a deputy sheriff's report that says you saw him, that he threatened you.' Deputy Doo.

'That's probably my mother saying that. The woman's a hysteric. What can I say? Ten years ago the old gal lost *two* daughters. Can't be consoled.'

'Understandable. I think if I were her or your dad, I'd kill the guy.'

'Yeah, well, the parents are the kind of folks who want other people to do their dirty work.' She was quiet a moment. 'Things were crazy yesterday. I don't know who said what, but I'm telling you now. Will was there, I heard him, but I can't prove it. I didn't actually *see* him.'

113

'The sheriff went out to talk to Will Booker yesterday evening,' I told her almost casually. 'Booker didn't have an alibi until about six-thirty in the morning. After that, he's got friends who are willing to testify he was with them all morning. When exactly did you hear him talking to you?' I was helping her get her story together with the timeline. If Connie Merriweather found out about it, I would probably be on the cover of *Time* next week.

'I can't really say. After I came home he showed up. I don't know how long he was there. I kind of lost it after I heard him talking to me like old times.'

'If you actually saw him, I just might get this guy back into prison – at least until there's a trial.'

'Only thing I care about is Will Booker stays the hell away from me!' She smiled prettily, 'And that's already been taken care of.'

'What are you talking about?'

'Nothing. Not a damn thing, sweet cheeks. Let's just say, God is in his heaven and all's right with the world.'

Chapter 25

Monday 1:15 p.m., March 22.

I CHECKED IN AT THE OFFICE, mostly to make an appearance. Garrat was out and could not be reached for the rest of the day; Massey was in court. Linda Sutherlin was getting coffee. WOW. A simple matter of perspective. I said something that passed for pleasant, she gave me a smile that looked to have been stolen from some old piece of Greek marble.

After that I went on to the Shamrock for lunch. I ordered a sarsaparilla and got a Coke with some lip. I held the pool table a while, then grabbed a little lunch. I had mixed feelings about Missy Worth, to put it nicely. She was lawless and violent, vulgar with her sweetness, and positively obscene with her flirtation. But she was also convinced that William Booker was the man who had killed her sister and her friends and left her for dead in a shallow grave. Thirteen days of conviction.

Whether he had found her early Sunday morning while I was in the drunk tank and the rest of the world was blissfully asleep or simply sent his spirit the way a shaman will do, just to remind her that he was out, I could not say. I doubted she was lying about what happened, but if I sat on a jury I would have to say there was an overwhelming lack of proof that Booker showed up at her door, and a lot to argue the girl was a lunatic.

But there were larger issues to ponder, chief among which was the fact that the state's sole witness in a case of 'he says / she says' had just gone into psychiatric care – for a psychotic episode. Garrat was off the hook. No public sacrifices needed. I was back and going to keep my job; Steve Massey was going hang on to what little professional dignity he possessed. And folks were still going to mention the name Pat Garrat when talk about the next governor's election got serious. Happy ending all around.

I went back to the office late in the day and cleaned up some other business and worked until well after dark writing up quite a few reports and expecting Garrat to return, though she never did. Around ten o'clock I was back at the Shamrock, drinking coffee when I decided to call Garrat at her farm. The farm was an estate on a few-hundred acres that her daddy had built when he was a young man. I got one of her security people on the phone, and then got switched over to the barns. Garrat was spending a late evening playing the country girl with some of her old corporate lawyer buddies from the capital. I told her to go back to business, we would talk in the morning, but she pressed me for information, so I went through my interview. Missy Worth believed Booker was there, claimed actually to have heard him, but she didn't see anything.'

'Is she willing to sign a complaint?'

'I didn't ask her.'

'Why not?'

'She's not that convincing, Pat. If she makes the charge in front of a judge, he'll throw it out.'

'Forget the lack of evidence for a minute. Was he there or not?'

I hesitated. How to answer? I wasn't ready to write off Missy's fears as pure nonsense. 'She *thinks* he was. She *felt* him. She *heard* him.'

'Not my question.'

'What are we getting from the physical evidence?' I asked.

'The police don't have anything, and they looked for prints everywhere. They canvassed the area. No strange cars, no pedestrians. But at three in the morning not a lot of witnesses were up and looking out their windows.'

'After I talked to Missy,' I said, 'I checked with one of the docs about auditory hallucinations. He couldn't speak directly to her case, but he said they're not that unusual in a typical case of post traumatic stress disorder.

'Nobody is going to say a word if you drop the case, Pat. Not at this point.'

'What if he was really there, Rick?'

'What do you want me to do?'

'Talk to the parents and maybe some family friends. Missy Worth has been in and out of hospitals for years, but so have a lot of people with addictive personalities. I want to know if this woman is troubled or crazy.'

Chapter 26

Tuesday 9:00 a.m., March 23.

I FOUND MISSY WORTH'S MOTHER at her university office the next morning. Missy had said to me that the Worth family had lost two girls. I was curious to know what she meant. According to her mother, Missy never really came home. After the trial, she made a habit of disappearing for two or three nights at a time, never calling to say she was all right. She was suspended from high school for a week for drinking at school. A few days after she returned from her suspension, she attacked her guidance counsellor. After that she was permanently expelled and launched into a series of jobs. Some lasted a few days, others a few hours.

I asked about substance abuse and got the unadorned facts. They had spent years trying to help, '...but the truth is,' she told me, 'you can't help someone who doesn't want to change...'

'And before?' I asked.

'If she was experimenting with drugs on occasion as people are saying now, we didn't know about it. We certainly didn't see any of the classic symptoms.'

'What about Mary?'

'What about her?'

'Drugs?'

'Never.'

When I tracked down Missy's father at the faculty club, I got more detail but the same portrait. Missy's father explained that Missy had acted out repeatedly after the abductions. I wasn't sure what that meant and said so.

'She would disappear with three or four men for a day or two. When they were out of drugs and booze and money, the men would leave her. Sometimes she tried to hitchhike back home. Sometimes she called us. We got her with some of the best psychologists in the country. We tried medication. It didn't matter. The minute she got free from us, she would go off the deep end and only come home when she had no other options.'

'So she spent several sessions at Catherine Howard?'

'We used different facilities, but I'd say... nearly a dozen serious attempts to get clean and sober. Finally, we realised *we* couldn't make it happen. She had to. We helped her get set up in town. We never gave up hoping she would change, but after a while we had to accept the life she chose for herself.'

'Does she ever come to visit?'

Ken Worth looked me straight in the eye. 'We don't have that kind of relationship, Mr Trueblood.'

I pressed him about the kind of girl Missy had been *before* the attack. These days we had a good deal of evidence suggesting a problem child, but neither parent was comfortable with Missy-the-delinquent. Missy was not a perfect child before Will Booker, he told me, but she wasn't into drugs, and she wasn't promiscuous. 'Look,' her father told me, 'Mary and Missy were normal healthy kids. The Missy who came home... I frankly didn't know and still don't.'

LATE IN THE AFTERNOON, I CAUGHT up with a friend of mine at the university. Dale Patterson was a beefy, bearded fellow who liked to affect the lumberjack on campus, but he was too soft for anything more than the boots and plaid shirts. I had used him professionally twice before I had started working for Garrat, and we were drinking buddies as well. Professionally, you couldn't beat him. For the price of a few beers the guy would tell you anything you wanted to know about criminal forensic psychology and he'd keep talking until his glass was empty.

As a long-time prof at the U, Dale had known Margaret and Ken Worth for years. Missy and Mary as well. A normal childhood? I asked. Dale laughed at me. 'Mary was aggressive. Missy was violent. Mary had a problem with a boy. Missy went through a whole bunch of them.'

'*Before* the attack?'

'She was a party favour at the local fraternity houses, Rick. This was *long* before anyone ever heard of Will Booker.'

'Missy was only seventeen when she was abducted.'

Dale lifted his eyebrows. 'She looked older.'

'Okay. Crazy girl.'

'Wild girl. Crazy came later.'

'Was there a tender side to her?' I asked.

'Sure. If she wanted something.' I told him about the flirtation I'd received Monday and then mentioned with a drinking buddy's wink that when this was all over I might just get lucky – if she was drunk enough. 'She wants your approval,' Dale answered, nodding. 'You're a channel to authority without being an authority figure yourself. With you she's willing to talk. Men and women with badges or suits – to hell with them.'

'I've got a badge and suit,' I protested. I showed him my tin and flapped my thirty year old sports coat at him. I was just a little pissed off about the respect I wasn't getting from a wanna-be-lumberjack. A prosecutor's investigator, after all, is a serious piece of business.

'This isn't Missy's first psychotic episode, Rick. You know that, I hope?'

'What are you talking about?'

'Oh, boy... her parents didn't tell you about the other incidents?'

'They told me about putting her into rehab and trying to get her dried out and off drugs.'

'I'm talking about *serious* stuff.'

I leaned forward nervously. 'How serious?'

'About two years after Booker, she had the first one. She wandered off after rehab and was missing for ten days before she showed up in Portland, Oregon. The cops out there had found her bare ass naked digging up a cemetery plot. She didn't have any ID, and she didn't know who she was. They tracked her through her fingerprints. Thank God for a criminal record, huh? Anyway, they medicated her for a while and she got it together again. There was another incident in Santa Fe a couple of years later where a state trooper found her walking down the centre lane of a highway stark naked. Nothing but rattlesnakes for company.'

I groaned.

'Same thing. Didn't know who she was.' I shook my head, imagining the effect of something like this in the middle of a trial. '*Whoever* abducted Missy did a real number on her, Rick.'

Chapter 27

Darkness.

BEFORE I LEFT HIM, Dale Patterson asked me about my face. A little run-in with the police, I told him. He pushed it some, and I had a startling snapshot of my folly come back with uncomfortable clarity. Somewhere between six and ten cops in a circle around me, none of them too close. I am like a bear in a pit. Caught, not tamed. The girl, my dancing partner, gone. Rain, lights. Dark shadows of a milling crowd beyond the lights. Witnesses to my folly, I expect.

There is a rookie uniform who is supposed to cuff me. At my feet, I have three Sam Brown belts stripped of all police paraphernalia. I have bloody knuckles. A warm, swollen lip. The urge for one more hero to try his luck against me. I stand waiting with my insane bit of trophy collecting at my feet. I'm in the middle of a quiet street. Swaying, drooling. Hoping the next kid comes before I pass out. When I put him on top of his own squad car and strip his belt off him, I walk back and drop my trophy with the others. Four belts in all. It is a record, and I howl in my glory.

Of course by then, it has to stop. The others step forward *en masse*. Order is restored. The dignity of the senior patrol officers assured. Handcuffs attached. Lessons applied. Bets paid off. I was tempted to relate the full story. Instead, I told Dale, 'I shoved a cop.'

Dale stared at me in awe, 'You pushed a cop?' I nodded, pretending some embarrassment. Dale shook his head solemnly, 'You are in serious need of help, my friend.'

Chapter 28

Tuesday 9:00 p.m., March 23.

THERE IS THE BLAST OF a motorcycle engine as Will comes out the front door of the public library. It registers indistinctly. The noise of urban life, but Will is also annoyed by it. He has heard it several times in the last two days. He looks for it. This time he is rewarded. A fellow rolling through the ally, crossing the street and coming into the library's circular drive. He comes up fast as Will watches him. Tamara is supposed to pick up Will, but she is late. Night has fallen. In the blessed dark, she will take a long, slow road home. Kissing and fondling now. The sweetness and compliance of the girl excites him.

The motorcycle comes to a stop a few feet before him, and Will watches the man settle his bike on its kickstand. His thoughts leave Tamara Merriweather. The huge-bellied man before him gives him a big oafish grin.

'They closed?' He is standing with his bike between them.

Will isn't sure about the library. He turns to look back at the doors. It is almost nine o'clock exactly, but he thinks the doors are still open.

The first blow comes over his shoulder, a lightning bolt of pain. Will crumples to his knees under its force. Before he even understands what has happened, the man strikes him again. This too over his back. The next two flail upon him in hard succession. Practically the same spot. Pain courses through him. A light flashes behind his eyes. Will sees a blackjack, not a fist. It saps him so that he collapses against the pavement. He tries to roll away from the attack. His back protected now, his arms reaching out to guard his chest, the next blows descend on his thighs. Left leg, right, left, right. The big muscles of his legs are hammered mercilessly, and Will's stomach wretches involuntarily with the pain.

The man puts his knee into Will's stomach and holds the blackjack against Will's throat. He pushes until Will's breath is cut off. Will sucks vainly for air, certain he will die in a matter of seconds. Then fathoming the man's intentions, Will tries to see past his own panic. He knows it is over, that he will live. This is a lesson. Nothing more. Will has had all the lessons the world can teach. He tries to see the face again, to know who has done this to him. Nothing else matters. The beard, the fat red cheeks, the eyes. The narrow pig eyes...

Profanity and a promise: '...you go near Missy again ...' more profanity '...this will feel like Sunday School!'

Will sees the eyes behind the slits perfectly now. He stares into them. The man stands. Huge belly, lumpish, powerful shoulders. Big thighs. But the eyes he will know even in hell. He seems to know Will has marked him and takes it for a threat. He answers with an angry kick into Will's gut. Will retches, tastes bile. He curls up, gasps for air. Blackness descending over him. A second, a third kick. Razors dancing in his lungs. He rocks back and forth. He hears the motorcycle start.

Will wants to sit up but can't. The next thing he knows Tamara Merriweather is screaming. Will blinks slowly and looks at her.

'Help me up,' he whispers. He tries to sit up but still can't. He looks past Tamara. He sees people standing in a tight semicircle before him. They are spectators at an accident. A siren sounds in the distance. A tall, thin, bald man comes past the watchers. He kneels close to Will. 'They're almost here,' he whispers. 'Just relax. You're going to be okay.'

Tamara stands dumbly off to the side as Will is lifted up and taken to the ambulance. Tears stain her white soft face. Will lies back, closes his eyes. The siren screams.

Chapter 29

Tuesday 11:00 p.m., March 23.

'TROUBLE, RICK. CALL me when you get in.'

I rubbed my face and swayed in the darkness of my living room. I was reasonably coherent, but that was assuming I would be talking to other drunks. I had left Dale Patterson, called Garrat with the news about Missy Worth's various psychotic episodes out west, which, she admitted, might be a problem even with a sympathetic jury, and then I had gone out determined to shoot sobriety dead.

I had won the fight fair and square. I thought about getting some coffee and food before calling Garrat. Maybe waiting until the next day. It was eleven. The last respectable hour. Could it wait? *Trouble.* Well, what wasn't? I picked up my home phone and tapped out Garrat's number at the farm. After going through her intermediaries I gave her my best imitation of sobriety. 'What's up?'

'Frank Cottrell called me an hour ago, Rick. Routine assault turns out to be an attack on Will Booker.'

'How bad?' I asked.

'You don't sound surprised.'

'I'm devastated, Pat. I take it the bastard is going to live?'

'He'll live.'

'Cottrell have any idea who did it?' Frank Cottrell was the chief of police for the city. He had been left out of this party because of jurisdictional matters, but he was in the middle of it now and no doubt happy about it. Only Frank Cottrell could envy kids playing in a toxic landfill.

'Connie Merriweather has convinced him the sheriff's office pulled this stunt.'

'Max didn't order something like this, Pat.'

'Nice of you to have such faith in Max, but can you prove it?'

'It might take me a couple of hours, but I expect I can.'

'You're serious?'

'Tell Cottrell he might want to hold off repeating the accusations until you talk with him tomorrow.'

My second trip over the river and into the wilds was fairly uneventful. Clint Doolittle was not at the Dog Daze End. One of his buddies, and everyone was a buddy at the Dog Daze, gave me the name of a tavern over the state line where I could find him. I caught up with Doo around one o'clock at the Silver Dollar. We danced around a while, and finally I said, 'I need a good rumour that a biker ran Will Booker through the wringer; otherwise, the sheriff's department is going to take the blame.'

This really touched the big guy's heart, and he told me in his own gentle English he really didn't care about how things went for Max. We moved on from there: what a sheriff's justified wrath could bring down on a dumb-ass biker and his gnarly-toothed friends.

'You want a rumour?' Doo asked me cautiously. He wasn't an entirely stupid guy, and I think he understood something of the mess we were in with Connie Merriweather's PR machine.

'A good one,' I answered.

'Anyone going to get arrested?'

'Not without a confession and a couple of eyewitnesses to confirm it.'

He grinned at this. 'Say I heard something. What do *I* get out of it?'

'A good citizen award.'

Doo contemplated this quietly, before nodding sagely. 'Okay. I *heard* someone was pissed at what happened to Missy. He decided to leave a message.'

'*Someone*?' I asked sceptically.

'It was some guy at the Dog Daze, but I was too drunk to see who it was. A bunch of other guys heard him talking too. But don't start asking around who it was. They were all too drunk to remember.'

'Did he have a scraggly beard and a big gut? Ugly as a dog's butt?'

Doo gave me a hard look then he told me in all honesty, 'He was a pretty damn good looking guy, if I remember rightly.'

Chapter 30

Wednesday 8:30 a.m., March 24.

I TOOK A SHOWER THE next morning with my eyes still trying to grab a couple more minutes of sleep and got to the office at eight-thirty, feeling like a real hero.

'What have you found for me?' Garrat growled the minute I walked into her office.

'I can give you half-a-dozen witnesses who heard some guy bragging that he taught Booker a lesson. Trouble is they were all too drunk to remember the guy's name.'

'Doolittle?'

I nodded. 'He as much as admitted it – unofficially.'

Garrat absorbed this as though it were yesterday's news. 'Good work.'

'But?'

Garrat's smile was anything but happy. 'But we have a bigger problem.'

Craig Smith

'The guy's dead?'

'We are. Sunday night, Max Dunn told Will Booker – in front of Connie Merriweather – he's going to play Russian roulette with Booker using *six* bullets in his revolver.'

'That's ridiculous, Pat. Max carries an automatic.'

'Save it for the bars, Rick.' She saw my look. 'I'm sorry.' She said this quickly, dropping her eyes as if genuinely embarrassed. She had bumped into a truth that was better left unspoken. I was a charity case – a washed up drunk from her father's generation. 'I didn't mean it that way. It's just... damn him, anyway!'

'Who? Max or Connie Merriweather?'

'Take your pick.'

'Did Max really say it?'

'Said it and proud of himself.'

I closed my eyes. We had lost Will Booker. Maybe. 'I've got a theory, Pat.'

'I'm listening.'

'When you go out to North Shore Point, the first thing you notice is you can't even see the lake from the road. Now if Booker's out cruising for an opportunity, what makes him stop there?'

'He saw cars.'

'*Three* cars.'

'It's a party. That's apparently what he wanted.'

'He knew who was there, Pat. Finding those kids was no accident.'

Garrat considered the argument from a trial lawyer's perspective – how it would play with a jury – then shook her head. 'Maybe he knows. Maybe he follows them. Maybe he sees the cars and checks things out from somewhere across the lake, then goes back to take them. Too many possibilities to make any particular one stick.'

'What if Missy Worth is having an affair with the guy?'

Garrat laughed. 'How late were you out last night?'

'Think about it. A relationship with Booker gives Missy Worth a reason to lie about a lot of the details in her original testimony. For a long time, you remember, Missy didn't say anything to Nat Hall or Herm Hammer; complete amnesia, but pretty soon she finds out Nat Hall doesn't know about her relationship; doesn't even suspect it. All Nat wants is the guy who killed her friends and to hell with the facts; so she gives him what he asks for and never bothers to tell anyone the rest – that she and the others were meeting Booker at the lake.'

'It would take away any doubt about her ID...'

'If we can establish a relationship prior to an attack all the rest washes. Lunatic or not, Missy's ID is solid. Her testimony is unassailable. Booker goes back to Graysville prison.'

'Have you found something?'

'The original investigation focuses on Booker. Where

he goes, what he talks about, whether or not anyone else had a creepy experience with the guy: the usual background search on a solid suspect. The *second* investigation, the one Bernie Samples conducts for the *Star* –'

'You mean the one Connie Merriweather fed to Samples.'

'Whatever. That one looks at the abuses Sheriff Hall carried out. What I'm saying is this: if Missy Worth was a wild girl with lots of contacts at the university, maybe she ran into Will and struck up an acquaintance.'

'She was seventeen, Rick.'

'Her sister was taking classes at the U and Missy apparently was well known at some of the fraternity houses. The thing is maybe someone remembers something. Maybe Missy is willing to try the truth on for size – if we ask her nicely. And maybe it wasn't about sex. Maybe Will Booker was her dope dealer. He was peddling a little grass to make ends meet, wasn't he? All I'm saying is we at least ought to try to see if there's a connection between the two of them. This kind of stuff could just be sitting there waiting for someone to ask the right question.'

'You don't have a thing, do you?' I studied Garrat's eyes for a moment, before I shook my head sorrowfully. 'Rick, Missy Worth spent last Sunday morning hiding in a closet because she *thought* Will Booker was standing on the other side of the door. Now we'll just forget that Will Booker was in church at the time with over a thousand leading citizens – all registered voters, by the way. And we'll make believe that nothing like this has ever happened before. What's a little post traumatic stress disorder among friends? What I'm thinking about – the thing I just can't get out of my mind – is Max Dunn trying to explain to a jury how you can play Russian roulette with a fully loaded revolver.' She seemed to come to a decision after she said this. 'I'm thirty-one, the youngest County Prosecutor since my old man stormed this office when he was a boy. I've got friends who want me to rise and not too many enemies in this world besides Connie Merriweather. I'll put it bluntly, just between you, me and the fence post, and I'll deny it if you ever repeat this. I see a big horizon out there for me. Nobody expects me to win every battle – especially a battle I'm not responsible for – and I wanted this case win-lose-or-draw. But it's gone. Max kicked it away Sunday night. Worse than that he's convinced that what he did was a good thing. I could have taken a loss. I expected it, to tell you the truth, but I can't go to court and get laughed at. I can't even send Steve Massey in for that.'

'You were ready to lose?'

Garrat considered her options, then shrugged. 'If we got Missy Worth rehabilitated as a witness, I meant to take it all the way. I wanted a jury to decide if what she said was credible.'

'I misread this thing, Pat.'

'Yeah, well, maybe you did, and maybe you hardened my resolve with your little speech and walk-out last week. It doesn't matter at this point.'

'You're dropping the charges?'

She cocked her shoulder the way her daddy had always done it when he had to lose one. 'Quick retreats in cases like these are fairly standard. First reaction is say you mean to fight to the bitter end. A week later, you talk about the victim wanting to get on with her life, federal judges who are too quick to hear habeas corpus petitions, evidentiary problems arising from the lapse of years, and my favourite: the mistakes of my predecessor. We're on to new cases by lunchtime.'

I looked away angrily. 'It's your call,' I told her.

'Talk to me, Rick! Tell me I'm a coward. Tell me this guy's going to kill again if we don't stop him. Tell me we can get a conviction if we just try a little harder!'

'Hell, Pat,' I said, letting the steam go, 'Will Booker is an innocent man. Everyone knows that.'

Part IV

The Devil's Wager

...put forth thine hand now, and touch all that he hath, and he will curse thee to thy face.

And the Lord said unto Satan, Behold, all that he hath is in thy power.

Job 1: 11-12.

Chapter 31

Wednesday 12:30 p.m., March 24.

ALL DAY THE OLD MAN WATCHES game shows, talk TV, and news. Will studies the grey sky, or he reads scripture. Of poor Job who kept faith. He speaks once to the man the night before about Job. He tells him about wagers and sorrows. The story falls on deaf ears.

Will tries to sleep but the discomfort is constant. Back and thighs swollen. The IV in his hand fills him with a poison. They have promised to release him the following morning. And home to bed for a week. The hours to freedom drag. At lunch the old man asks him, 'You hear that?' Will looks up from his plate. He stares at the old man without answering. 'Hell's fire! They're letting that killer go! Can you believe it?' Will stares into the television. His own image answers. A woman's voice explains that just over an hour ago the prosecutor announced her decision. The Pat Garrat who did not shoot Billy the Kid. 'He looks a little like you, don't he?' Will does not answer. For once the television interests him. He tries to grasp what this means. A complete lack of physical evidence. An unwillingness on the part of the prosecution's lone eyewitness to testify. *Missy.*

No choice but to dismiss. It is over. There is nothing more to know or understand. Will is a free man.

Chapter 32

Wednesday 2:30 p.m., March 24.

WILL SPENDS THE EARLY AFTERNOON waiting
for Pastor. Expects him any minute. Come for his stroke
of vanity.

Will is not ready for the daughter. Tamara, tall and
heavy with her milky flesh and grey-blue-grey eyes, her
pale pink lips that he has kissed so many times now,
her fine golden hair. 'Will, I heard!'

Will lifts a finger to his lips. Tamara hesitates. Will
rolls his eyes toward the old man who still watches
television.

She whispers, 'You're free!'

'I just saw it,' he answers quietly, nodding toward
the television.

'You said when you're free...' Will studies her face.
Something has changed. Something has broken through.
Then he understands. Tamara would be his bride on

143

this day. Yes, he thinks, that is it. The hour has come for the devil's wager with the Almighty. This moment and no other. It is why God has set him free. The sure and certain sign he must proceed.

'We can go anywhere we want,' he tells her. 'Do whatever we please.'

'I can't wait.'

'I won't sin, Tammy, but I want you the minute a preacher says amen over us.'

'I feel the same way!'

'Are you ready to get married?' he asks.

'Yes.' Her voice rises. Again he hushes her with a finger to his lips.

'Right now? This minute?' There is a dare to his tone, the faintest bit of challenge in his eyes.

'But you can't, Will. They won't let you go!'

'I can leave if I want,' Will tells her. 'I'm a free man, Tammy. Remember?'

'But the bruises? And this thing...' She looks at the IV stand and the tube that runs to the needle that pierces his flesh.

'They're going to let me out tomorrow anyway. Why not hurry things along a little?' He lets her think about this, before he adds, 'We don't have to get married. Maybe you've got your eye on someone better.'

'Oh, Will, there's no one but you, and there's nothing I want more than to be yours!'

He looks forlornly at the ceiling. 'What about your

parents?' Tamara considers her parents briefly. It is a hard choice for her, and Will breaks in before she can work through her doubts. 'What are they going to say when we come back and tell them we got married?' His laughter has such innocence to it that she has to laugh. They're not running away forever. Just for a day or so. In the end Daddy will relent and Mamma Rachel will follow his lead.

In her eyes Will can see the wonder of being loved for the first time. Against that everything pales. From the beginning of time that truth is everything. 'Once your parents understand how much we love each other, they'll be happy for us, Tammy. You know that, don't you?' Her face reflects a dawning of consciousness, the thought of surviving without daddy's money, and Will moves in quickly. 'I have some money saved up, Tammy. I mean it's not much, but it's enough to get us started. Then I'll get work, I don't care what. We'll get by fine, and I'll go to school like I always wanted. Become a lawyer and help others.'

A solemn moment. 'Maybe we should wait, Will. It's all happening so fast!'

He looks away, his eyes taking in the bright dancing colours of the television screen. 'Whatever you want,' he answers coolly. 'If you don't love me, I don't want to force you.'

And that is all it takes. 'Could you really leave now?'

He sits up, grinning. His back resists. His blue, swollen

thighs send arcs of pain through him. He meets her gaze and laughs with a bit of bravado. 'In a New York minute.'

She giggles, then whispers his name. She wants it. She is only afraid to take the chance!

'I love you so much,' he tells her, 'I can't think straight until you are mine. I say we just get up and walk out of here now. We head down the road and find a little church in some little town and get married so we can start our honeymoon! After that no one can come between us ever again.'

Her face flushes at the thought. 'I don't know. I don't think we should, Will. Not just yet, I mean. Not right now!'

Will ignores the protest. It is as feeble as the girl's good sense. 'We'll have to go to the house first,' he explains. 'Get some clothes packed. You'll take me that far, won't you, Tammy? I mean if you want to change your mind once we get to the house, you can. I won't make you do anything you don't want to. I just... I can't sit around here anymore. I want to be free!'

Tamara looks about nervously. 'Will, I think we ought to wait until they let you out.'

'What are they going to do if I leave early, Tammy, arrest me?'

'Are you really okay?'

Will stands up painfully, testing his legs uncertainly. He is not good. The medicine saps him. The pain throbs through his muscles. He tears the tape away. He pulls the needle of the IV out of his hand. He studies the dark drop of blood which answers. He is dizzy and nauseous, but he puts on his robe and slippers. He asks her casually, 'Is your mother home?' Mamma Rachel will have to die, of course...

'She works today.'

'What about Tabit?'

'Where are your clothes, Will? You can't leave like this!'

'Will Tabit be home this afternoon?'

'I don't know. Probably.'

'Come on,' he tells her. At the door he stops to give the old man a wink. 'We're going take a little walk, Pop. Be back in a few minutes.'

Chapter 33

Wednesday 3:03 p.m., March 24.

CONNIE CHECKED HIS WATCH when he saw Will's bed was empty. The old man in the other bed looked away from his television set long enough to explain, 'He's taking a walk with some pretty little girl. He'll be back in a few minutes.' Connie went to a chair next to Will's bed and saw the IV needle hanging from the stand, the tape still attached to it. He reached to touch it, shook his head quietly, then took Will's Bible off the bedside stand. He wanted to find the psalm of David, about the glory of a man long oppressed who is set free by the blessing of God. 'Got a question for you!'

Connie looked up as the pages shifted under his fingers. The old man with his thin, haggard face was pointing at his own neck, but Connie understood the gesture at once. He was curious about Connie's dog collar. 'You're a preacher, ain't you?'

Connie closed Will's Bible and put it back on the table gently. 'That's right.'

'So do you believe in the hogwash you preach or do you just say it to make people feel good?'

Connie chuckled. 'Believe it? Friend, I *live* it!'

'My mother was a churchgoer.' Connie nodded agreeably at this. 'Give that woman a spare minute, she'd be praying and weeping to God like he could actually do something for her!'

'Maybe it's just that you don't know what He did for her. Some of God's gifts are very private. Not proof for the infidel but fodder for the faithful.' From Connie's boyhood, that one. A small white pillbox church in a green valley but preaching that had set his heart afire! Before his faithless years had set in.

'This here Job, he's in the Bible, ain't he?' Connie smiled for answer. 'Now he never did nothing but good… ain't that right, just damn near as perfect as a man can get?'

'The Lord called Job a perfect and upright man,' Connie answered solemnly.

'Well then, all I can say is the Lord did him dirty.'

'How is that?' Connie asked him.

'This boy you come to see? He asked me last night if I knew the story, and I said I'd heard of it, but I didn't remember none of it *particularly*. So he told it to me flat out. Now that boy's a talker if he decides he's going to bother! Kind of surprised me, to tell you

149

the truth. Sits here not saying diddle, then starts in on this Job fellow like they was best friends. Kind of an interesting story, too.' The old man's eye twinkled wickedly, 'But it don't put God in very good company, Preacher. Said the Devil sat down with God and they made themselves a *wager*! Then this boy told me all the things that happened to poor Job because of it. How he lost his money, his farm, his kids, his health... I don't know what all! Now Preacher, you straighten me out if I'm wrong, but it looks to me like if that's what being *loved* by God is all about, I'm damn glad we ain't even friends!'

Connie reared back in his chair and smiled serenely. He had come for a celebration of God's infinite mercy, but it turned out the Lord had given him work to do. Will had started this old man on the road to Glory, and it was Connie's job to bring him on home!

Chapter 34

Wednesday 3:35 p.m., March 24.

TABIT MERRIWEATHER CAME off the bus and crossed the road. She was not in a very good mood, as it happened. Her sister had vanished just before fifth hour, leaving Tabit to find her own way home. Tabit hated the bus. It made her feel like a kid! Then there were troubles with Miss Boetcher. She was determined her sophomore English class should read *A Separate Peace*. Not some of it, but every line, thank you, and who cared about a bunch of dead people anyway! And real life, getting some money, that was turning into a nightmare. It would not come from her parents, so she was going to have to earn it, but being sixteen you were last in line for every job they advertised. Supposed to have an interview next week. Sell ice cream. Perfect. Except she wasn't sure what she was supposed to say so they would give her the job. How would you describe yourself, Tabit? People person. I love people. I think scooping ice cream for people would make me feel I was doing something to make the world a better place. She shook her head miserably. Oh, well, just one more job she was not going to get.

Tabit checked the mail and pulled several envelopes out. Nothing for her of course. She tucked them under her arm and went up the drive. Still raining. Always raining. Build an ark, better. Tammy's car was not in the driveway, so she would still be at the hospital. The girl was in love, as if Will couldn't do better. Tabit stuck her key in the lock and turned it. The bolt snapped but the door held firm when she pushed. She had locked it, which meant Tammy had come home and then left and forgot to lock the door. So what was new? Eighteen-going-on-six. Tabit turned the key again and pushed the door open.

That was when the hand took her. Tabit felt it before she saw it, and what she felt was cold and strong. Before she could even set her feet, she found herself jerked through the door and thrown skittering across the entryway. She saw the mirror but could do nothing more than raise her hand. She hit the glass with her forearm. She heard the glass break, felt a dull thud as she hit her head. She saw her blood. Then saw Will closing the front door.

'What are you doing!' she cried angrily. Will bolted the door from the inside and pocketed the key. That scared her, but not as much as the look he gave her. Tabit did not speak again; her scream was nothing more than a single, primal shriek as she turned to run.

Chapter 35

Wednesday 3:58 p.m., March 24.

TAMARA SITS PRETTILY AT HER chair bound by thick cords of clothesline and gagged with a pair of socks from one of her drawers and tape from Pastor's workbench. Will pulls the tape and the socks from Tamara's mouth.

'Did you hurt her?' Tamara's voice screeches with hysteria and Will takes the girl's shoulders. He stares into her eyes. He must bring her down; he needs her. 'I told you, Tammy, I won't hurt her as long as you help me.'

'I don't know what you want!' Blubbering snot and tears.

'First, I want you to quit screaming. If you scream again, I'm going to go downstairs and kill her. Do you understand me?'

Tamara's face is red with grief and fear, but she nods her head, choking back her sobs.

'I want to keep Tabit alive, Tammy. I don't want to kill her. Just don't make me. Do you understand?' She nods again. 'And I don't want to hurt *you*.'

'Will! Why are you doing this?' Pleading, confused.

'Your voice!' he hisses.

She whispers his name as he frees the last of her bindings. A child begging through her tears. '*Will, please!*'

'If you help me, if you're good, I'll let you both go. Just don't disappoint me, Tammy.' His muscles aching, the nausea still throttling him, Will struggles to stay standing, even as he tells her over and over as they walk down the stairs that she has to save her sister; she has to help him if she wants them both to live. She is a believer in his power, so walks like a lamb to the blood-drenched altar. In the garage Will grabs a shovel and canvas tarp. He puts both in the backseat. He gets more rope from a long line, cutting it into equal lengths, rolling each piece up so it fits into his jeans pocket. After running several strips of tape along his jeans so he can get to it quickly, Will brings the roll along. He sees a long screwdriver in a rack and pulls it out. A weapon of sorts. *Sufficient for the day.*

HE SEES TAMARA SCANNING the windows of the neighbours' houses as they back out of the drive. 'They won't help you, Tammy. What they will do is they will just get you and Tabit killed.' At once, she stares down

154

at her plump knees. 'Now I want you to quit crying,' he tells her. His voice is soothing, reasonable, calm.

'I can't!' she sobs.

Will turns out toward the country at his first opportunity. They go along the gravel road they took before. After a time, he asks, 'Do you know where we are?' Tamara looks about, then shakes her head. Her eyes are bloody with her tears; her nose drips snot. The roof of the abandoned barn appears over the roadside weeds as they come closer. 'I kissed you here, Tammy.' Sobs rattle out of her. 'I'm not going to hurt you,' he tells her. 'I have something here I need. We have to get it before I can go on.' No cars are coming, and they slip into the drive, pulling back behind some heavy weeds so they are invisible from the road. Will tells her to get out. When he takes the shovel from the backseat Tamara thinks he means to bury her and falls to the dirt taking his knees, begging for her life. Will watches calmly. When her sobbing rises to the point of screams, he leans forward, taking her hair and pulling it to get her attention. 'My money,' he tells her simply. 'It's here. I have to get it. I'm not going to hurt you.' He pushes her toward the open meadow. 'I want you to get through this, Tammy. I want you to live. Just go along with me on this. I promise you everything is going to be fine.'

They go thirty paces due south of the barn. Will finds his spot and breaks the sod eagerly. Two feet under the soggy ground is a black plastic garbage bag. He punctures the plastic with his screwdriver. He probes about until he finds the Bernardelli. A seven shot, small enough to fit in his hand. He loads it and takes the extra ammunition. Before he can look at the rest of his treasure, he hears a car coming down the gravel road. He dives into the girl and takes her into the weeds. She yaps wildly in fear, but he crawls up and takes her mouth with his hand. He is close to her now. They lie together like lovers in the wet grass. They listen as the car roars by. When it is gone, he studies Tamara's eyes. 'I need your help, Tammy.' Tamara doesn't answer, but she is listening. 'What we're going to do, we're going to get me another car. That's all I want. A car people won't know I'm driving. Can you help me do that?'

Her eyes wide and frightened, Tamara nods her head.

Chapter 36

THE SHADOW OF A WOMAN moves in the picture window as Will brings Tamara's Chrysler Le Baron to a stop in front of the garage door of Ben Lyons's grand house in the suburbs. Will waves at the woman inside. Smiles. He tells Tamara, 'Get out and go to the front door. I'm right behind you, Tammy. Don't disappoint me.'

She hesitates. 'Do it!' he tells her, and Tamara opens the door. She could take off. She could run for the neighbours, but she doesn't know the neighbours. She *knows* Mrs Lyons. She is in front of the Le Baron when Tamara breaks into a run suddenly. Heading right for Mrs Lyons. Mrs Lyons hurries to open the door for her. Will shifts the roll of tape from his right hand to his left and reaches into his jacket pocket for his Bernardelli. He still grins at Mrs Lyons, who stares back at him in perfect wonder.

Tamara starts talking the moment she gets to the door. She pushes into the house and screams, 'HE'S GOT A GUN!'

Will steps toward them still smiling. Mrs Lyons holds the door, looking at the girl, then at Will. Her mouth is open when he sets the gun to it. Will fires two shots. Her head kicks back. She falls inside the entryway. Will bends and scoops her legs out of the way as he closes the door. He takes Tamara by the hair and pulls her to the floor beside the dead woman. He pulls her hands together, tapes them with a strip that he peels off his jeans. Now her mouth and finally her ankles. Seconds pass. Tamara has no fight in her. Will walks back into the huge house and sees Penny Lyons coming out of her bedroom. Penny screams when she sees he has a gun, but Will has her down on the floor instantly. He holds the gun against her face so she can see it. 'Don't make me kill you, Penny. I don't want to do that. Do you understand?'

Her eyes fill with horror, but slowly she nods. 'Is there anyone in the house besides you?'

A hoarse, terrified whisper, 'My mother.'

'Anyone else?'

'No.'

Will binds her wrists and ankles. When he finishes trussing her, he gags her and pulls her back to her bedroom, careful to close her blinds. He leaves her on the floor staring up at him with her wide dark eyes.

He tells her he has to do this. He apologises. Then he returns to the front room, pulls the curtain shut and surveys his workmanship. Tamara stares dully at the floor directly before the fallen Mrs Lyons. The girl looks to be in shock, her eyes wide, dilated, glassy. At least she is not fighting.

Will walks through the house to make sure of his surroundings. He sees a dog in the backyard: a German shepherd. He's jumping and barking. Knows something is wrong. Will feels a moment of panic but lets it pass without giving into it. He finds the garage, then the switch which operates the door. He opens the big door and walks casually toward the Le Baron. The keys are still in it. He starts the engine and drives it in next to a fat sleek van. He shuts the door with the automatic switch. He gets the tarp out. He can cover the windows of the garage door or the car itself. He decides the car is better and tosses it over the Le Baron. Next he drives his screwdriver into the garage door track, testing the door to make sure it holds.

Chapter 37

Wednesday 5:15 p.m., March 24.

THE MICE IN THE MOTOR SCREECHED as they always did when Rachel Merriweather's New Yorker rumbled to life. Connie just loved his Chryslers! Of course he was always saying the older ones were better. Classic! Not to mention cheaper. He never mentioned that! God bless him. She smiled even as she steered the big boat out of its tight quarters. Rachel checked her watch. A quarter past five. She had called just before she left work. Five o'clock, and the girls not home yet. Rachel shook her head. They were at *that* age. Lord saves us from teenagers! Such sweet kids though. And good girls still, but it was that time in their lives when everything was a fight. Everything so hard to do, so impossible to understand. And boys...

She would sooner juggle hand grenades than let one of them near her babies, but what was she going to do? Tammy had put up this poster of some new teen throb. Jeans slung down over his hips, rippling muscles over his belly, eyes staring out dreamily, hair in wet curls, and that *lump* in his pants! Rachel sighed. Her little girl all grown up. Or wanting to be. And Tabit. Quiet as a midnight kiss. What you didn't see in that one was what you worried about! Her posters were so philosophical it was scary. Rachel was sure they were only months away from opening their front door and finding a hippie-Goth-beatnik, or whatever they called themselves these days, asking for Tabit.

And Connie bringing Will into the house! At least that was almost over! This thing with the attack on Will and Tammy almost getting in the middle of it, she had told Connie, 'End of the week. Get him anywhere, but get him out!' And Connie had agreed. Definitely, certainly, positively. Working on it. She just needed to make sure he followed through. Tonight, they were okay because he was still at the hospital. Which meant Thursday and Friday nights and maybe Saturday night. She could put up with anything for three or four nights. But that was it. By Sunday if they had to put Will in the Holiday Inn, they were going to do it!

Rachel hadn't really minded Will. Sweet boy, actually, and such a nice voice, too. She could see why Connie felt the way he did. Solemn and... what was it? That kind of mock-cultured effect that self-educated people get. Everything done a little too carefully.

Precision always double-checked, the nervous grammar. Those *ain't*s that slipped through sometimes. And Connie was right. Never a Christian more faithful. The way he read scripture every spare moment he had! She had known ministers who did not work half so hard on their studies. You would think he found Jesus yesterday, God bless him. But of course there was that prison. Ten years without the touch or smell of woman and then Connie bringing him into our home...

'*A godly man, Rachel.*'

'*Abraham was a godly man, and look what he spawned!*'

Rachel shook her head fondly. Connie loved his God so much he sometimes did not pay attention to what the other side was up to!

THE WAY HOME CAME with thoughts about the countryside that was about to bloom and a worry or two for the weather. Clouds, a bit of drizzle, an endless field of gray that had gone on for weeks.

Hope Palm Sunday turns it around. Easter for sure. A blue sky for Easter. 'That would be wonderful, Lord.' Rachel thought about Easter a while, then slipped back, as she always did, to her private worries, her prayers, her anger and her thanksgiving. All trouble and joy coming from one source. Not God, not directly anyway, but the man she had met oh, it was too many years ago to count. Tall and trim in those days. Not that extra load around his waist back then! A load of books under his arm, every philosopher under the sun, just so he wasn't a Christian, and the look... well back then they didn't have the lumps in their pants, thank you. Cut the cloth differently. But the look was pretty much all *this girl* could notice from one day to the next! Such a handsome man, that Connie Merriweather! And the big lug looking when she wasn't, at least when he thought she wasn't. Finally, some talk. It was so hard back then. Maybe it was always hard and just didn't seem so after you had been through it. What's your name? I've seen you around. All the nonsense you had to go through just to find out if it was more than spring fever in September. A cup of coffee at the Student Union. Oh, my, he was a handsome young man, though! And good as a gold watch. But on the issue of God...

'Well, I have to be honest. I've looked at this every way a man can look at something, and there's nothing to it. There is just no God.'

'Thank you for the coffee. I have to be going.'

'What's the matter? What did I say?'

She could still laugh at what she had told him then. Oh, boy! *'I thought you were special, Connie Merriweather. I guess I was wrong.'*

And that was it. Connie Merriweather was out of her life. For about six weeks. Then he saw her one day, and he had said to her...

Rachel turned into the driveway and felt a twinge of

uncertainty. The garage door was open. Connie's car was not inside. Tammy's Le Baron was not in the driveway. Open for anyone to walk in and take whatever! Rachel pulled up short of the garage, a few feet in front of where Tammy would park when she got home. She got out of her car cautiously. She was not sure it was safe! She walked across the soggy front lawn and then up the step to the front door. Locked. She opened it with a key. She saw the spilled mail on the floor. The mirror inside the entryway was broken. There was blood on it...

Instinct told her to retreat, but the blood pulled her inside. The girls. Were they home? She shouted each girl's name out once and found herself walking toward two pieces of cloth on the floor in the TV room. Oh God! Tabit's jacket and what looked like a piece of her blouse. Ripped. She picked up the jacket. Yes. Tabit's. But that didn't mean...

Rachel's mind reeled back toward morning. What had Tabit worn? She went back to the front hall, the stairway. She called both girls' names again. She started up the stairs but stopped at once. She was shaking. She tried to breathe, tried to calm herself. Nothing wrong, she whispered. Just go up and check to be sure, then call Connie. A perfectly simple explanation.

He had said to her, '*You know I used to believe all of it. I went to church and I prayed and I loved God, but then I realized it was just an old myth!*'

And she had told him...

Oh, God! In Tammy's room she saw tape and rope. She felt the room swirling. Only the jolt of terror for her children kept her standing. She tried to breathe but nothing happened. Is this how you feel when you die? She whispered a prayer. She covered her face with the palms of her hands; she took a long, shaky breath and summoned her common sense.

There was rope on the floor. A piece of tape. It meant nothing. A school project. The jacket and blouse, the broken mirror... that could have just been some rough-housing. They were kids! Just kids playing, and then walking away thoughtlessly. She stood, staggering toward the door and hallway. Check Tabit's room. Everything would make sense. It had to.

And she said to him... she told the strange boy whom even then she knew she would marry, '*I could never marry a man...*'

Nothing out of place, nothing at all wrong with Tabit's room. She walked across the hall. Will's room. All of it quite neat, of course. She stopped as she was closing the door and peeked back in. She walked into the room now and looked at everything carefully.

'*...never marry a man who didn't love Jesus.*' And then of course she had realised she'd said *marry*, and he had heard it too.

A pair of jeans missing...

She had bought them for Will herself. Now why would

someone come into the house and steal a pair of jeans? And leave a bathrobe that I had taken to the hospital yesterday? And slippers that... that Will had with him at the...

Rachel blinked. Had Will come back to the house? But that wasn't possible. He wasn't going to be released until...

It wasn't possible! He was...

No! Oh, dear Jesus, no! 'No!' Her voice echoed through the empty house. And then again, her face melting to agony, 'NO! NO! NO! NO!'

Part V

Treasure of Darkness

I will go before thee, and make the crooked places straight: I will break in pieces the gates of brass and cut in sunder the bars of iron: And I will give thee the treasures of darkness...

– Isaiah 45: 2-3.

Chapter 38

AT PRECISELY 6:15 BEN LYONS pulled into King's Court and drove along a curving road until he came to Wolverine Lane. Turning into his driveway, Ben hit his garage door opener. Nothing happened. A frown of irritation settled over his dark features. He tapped the button again. Ben shut the Bronco off and went up to try the door by hand.

It wasn't moving. He peeked in through one of the three small windows. What he saw did not make sense. There was a car parked in his slot with some kind of a tarp tossed over it. Ben turned and looked at the neighbours' houses. Across the way Lou Stillman's car was parked in his drive. Next door the Eilers were still gone. On the other side, it looked like the Frosts were home. He could see through a window that their television was on as usual, hear the low indistinct rumble

169

of a game show leaking out through their porch, both of them deaf as a couple of posts. Everything was as it always was. Except Ben's garage door was not opening, and it looked like there was a strange car in his garage!

The curtains were all closed. The lights were off. That was odd, too. Judy and Penny were supposed to be home. He checked his watch. It was almost dinnertime. He pulled his key out but the door was unlocked. Ben leaned into the house cautiously. He called to his wife. When there was no answer, he called again. 'Judy? Penny? Anybody here?' Something wasn't right. But what? Still in the doorway, Ben took a quick glance across the room. Nothing he could see, just a feeling. Something out of place. An odour, maybe.

Yes! There was something in the air he didn't like. Ben took another step and heard Penny sobbing. He went as far as the hallway and saw William Booker standing behind his daughter, a pistol pushed into her ear. For just an instant, Ben felt nothing. In that first split second even the terror wasn't quite real. Then of course he understood.

Ben Lyons had just stepped off the edge of the world.

Chapter 39

Wednesday 6:52 p.m., March 24.

BENNY'S DAD'S CAR WAS in front of the garage when Benny pulled into the driveway. The house was dark. Taking his gym bag and trotting to the front door, Benny felt a moment of uneasiness. Why was his dad's Bronco parked outside? What was going on? His dad should have been watching the evening news while his mother cooked dinner, and they weren't even here! The door was locked. Benny opened it and called out. There was a light on in the hallway, but no one answered him. Had something happened?

He stepped into the room further and called out again. 'Hey! Anyone home?'

'They're downstairs, Benny.'

Will Booker was standing in the hallway by Penny's bedroom. He was holding Benny's dad's pump shotgun. Its hollow bore pointed at Benny. Benny felt a jolt of adrenalin surge through him. He dropped his gym bag without intending to do it. He heard it hit the floor with a thump. The sound seemed to come after an interminable delay. He was shaking in surprise. He thought to run, but suddenly his legs were too heavy to move. 'I don't want to hurt you, Benny, but I will if I have to. Do you understand me?' Benny stared for a long moment at Will Booker, then nodded. 'Now what do you say we go down to the basement?'

The seventeen-year-old hesitated as he studied the situation. Will Booker seemed to know what he was thinking, seemed almost to be laughing at him because he could not fight. Not here, not now. He had no choice but to do what he was told. On the stairs, Benny thought about turning back. If he could get his hands up fast enough it might work. He was close enough for just a second, and he was strong enough. He knew that. This guy was small! He looked back with a quick glance, measuring the odds a second time, but it was already too late. 'Your dad wants to see you alive, Benny. Let's not disappoint him. What do you say?' They were alive. His dad at least. What about his mom and Penny? And where was Pete? At the bottom of the stairs they walked through the recreation room. 'There.' Will pointed toward his mom's storage closet. A key was in the deadbolt lock. Benny turned it. Benny swore quietly after he had opened the door. The light from the hallway broke over the tiny room. His dad, his sister, and Tammy

Merriweather were huddled together on the floor. 'Inside,' Will Booker told him.

When Benny could not quite commit himself to go into the room, his father spoke to him in a raspy, frightened voice. 'Do it, Benny. It's okay. Just come inside.'

The room had been cleared, but it was still tiny, and Benny stepped into the room, careful to avoid stepping on anyone. He studied the frightened eyes of his dad and sister and Tammy Merriweather for only a moment. Then he saw his dad was hurt.

In the next instant Will Booker brought the butt of the shotgun down against the side of his knee. Benny went to the concrete floor with a scream. Even as the pain arced through him the room went black. A jiggling of the deadbolt.

His father's voice came out of the darkness. 'Don't do anything, Benny. Don't say anything. Just stay down.' Benny lay silently in the dark fighting back his tears. He listened until the sounds beyond the door ceased. Will was still outside. Benny was sure of it. Would he just start firing the shotgun? Was that what this was about? Benny huddled close against the floor holding his knee. What was happening? How did this guy... just...?

'Benny? How bad are you hurt?' His father's voice came out of the blackness.

'I don't know.'

'Can you stand up?'

'I don't think so.'

'He broke my ankle. I was sitting here and he came in here for no reason and he slammed the gun down on my ankle.'

Benny listened numbly. He was in pain, but worse than that was the nagging regret that he had been given a chance and failed to take it. Now with his leg injured, if not broken, he was not sure if he would have a second opportunity, especially if his dad's ankle was broken as well.

On the stairs Will had been moving so carefully, almost like he was struggling with the steps. He had gotten closer to Benny than he should have. If Benny had just tried!

But he hadn't. Because he was afraid. 'Where's Mom?' he asked. His voice, he thought, sounded weak and childish.

For a terrible second nobody spoke. When his dad finally answered, he was sobbing. 'Oh God, Benny!' His dad's voice rattled oddly. It was a voice Benny had never heard. 'Tammy says Will shot her.'

Benny shivered and leaned his head back against the wall as his dad's soft hurried speech rushed over him. She was dead, he knew it, but for a moment he could feel nothing. Dead. Like that. No goodbye, just a whisper in the dark.

'A head wound – she *thinks*. Right, Tammy?'

'I think so. I didn't really get a good look.' Tammy Merriweather's voice was dry and timid.

'But you said she was alive?' his dad asked.

'Yes, sir. I saw her legs moving. She was hurt but she was still alive.'

'The point is, Benny, we don't *know* how bad it is.'

'He shot her *in the head*?' Benny asked. No tears yet, but he thought he might be sick to his stomach.

'I think so,' Tammy whispered.

Benny thought he ought to feel something, but only his irritation with Tammy Merriweather registered – as it always did. 'Did you see it or not?' When Tammy didn't answer him, he nearly shouted, 'Did you see it happen?'

'Keep your voice down,' Penny answered. Pissed, as usual, her voice cold, tired. She would not let them hear her fear.

'I want to know what she saw,' Benny answered, his voice softer, if not his tone.

Benny's dad spoke. 'We can't give up believing she's still alive, Benny. She could be alive, couldn't she, Tammy?' His dad was asking Tammy to lie. Benny heard it, yet he waited himself for her answer.

'She was alive last I saw her.'

Chapter 40

Wednesday 8:30 p.m., March 24.

THE MESSAGE LIGHT ON my phone was blinking when I got home. I punched it and heard Garrat's voice. 'Give me a call as soon as you're in. Emergency.'

When Garrat answered, I asked her, 'What's up?'

'My God, where have you been? Why isn't your cell phone on?'

'The battery is dead, Pat. I was out. I had dinner. Is that a problem?' It was almost the truth. My cell phone was in the glove compartment; I had grabbed a breaded tenderloin sandwich at one of my favourite hideaways and stayed for dessert.

'You haven't heard?'

Where I had gone the beer was cold, the TV was dead, and folks still thought Dick Nixon was about to make a comeback. 'What are you talking about?' I asked her.

'Will Booker has taken off with both Merriweather girls.'

I felt sick, cold, and deathly sober. It was a moment of such disorientation that it seemed I had just learned that Sarah was missing. Before I could gather my wits to answer, Garrat spoke again. 'Max is at the Merriweather house right now, Rick. Anyway you can get out there – in a reasonably sober condition?'

I thought about my thirst and about how tired I had been a couple of seconds before I had spoken to her. Suddenly those things did not matter. 'Sure,' I said. 'I'll be there in half-an-hour.'

FORTY-FIVE MINUTES LATER I passed a roadblock using my badge and ID and rolled up behind half-a-dozen county cars, a clique of federal government-issue sedans, some beat junkers that belonged to the under-paid print reporters, and three shiny new TV vans. As no one in the media seemed to recognise me, I got to the door without difficulty. An old sheriff's deputy I'd gotten drunk with a few times twenty years ago told me to go on in. Stepping through the entryway I found myself looking at a broken hall mirror stained with a bit of blood and covered in black fingerprint powder. In the next room a knot of men were locked in a tight circle. Out of their midst, I heard Max Dunn's big voice. 'Glad you could make it, Rick.'

I met his gaze, then looked back over my shoulder

at some suits in what looked to be the preacher's study. 'Feds?' I whispered.

'They've got the phones for now,' Max answered. He had just a flicker of nervousness in his eyes. This case was his. He did not want to lose it to the feds. 'If Booker is stupid enough to call, we could have this thing sorted out in a matter of minutes.' Max grinned his big horse teeth at me and winked. I decided Max had gotten religion on me when I wasn't looking.

'They're here at your invitation... or Merriweather's?'

'Ms Merriweather called them *after* she called me. Right now, they're happy to give us the case. This thing is ours until someone says *ransom* or *state line*.'

I did not say it, but I knew if the feds did not want it the odds for the girls surviving were desperately bad. Will Booker was an extremely competent madman, and those he had wanted to kill had perished – with the lone exception of Missy Worth. We knew this from hard experience and so did the Feds from watching us the last time.

'What about the media?' I asked. 'Have you given them anything?'

'They know the basics. The boys in suits, *in their advisory capacity*, say I should get them involved, but I dearly hate TV people, Rick.'

I answered with a friendly grin, 'At least the feeling is mutual, but I'd say, this time, you want to use them all you can. Get them to help out. Make a plea for everyone to start looking for our boy William, that kind of thing. And pictures: they can put Booker and the faces of those kids on TV every ten minutes if they feel like it... and if you make it worth their while.'

Max was nodding, but he was not buying it. 'That's what they told me.' He glanced in the direction of the FBI agents.

The TV people had burned Max every time they put a camera on him. At least that was his perspective. 'Then, too,' I added, 'these are the same folks who were telling the world yesterday that the sheriff's office had framed an innocent man. Kind of nice to shove that down their throats. Of course maybe that's just *my* thinking.'

I could see genuine pleasure coming back into Max Dunn's dark eyes. 'You think they'll let me push it down their throats, Rick?'

'These people would run their own funeral for good ratings, Max.' When he nodded agreeably at the image, I told him, 'The worst we can do by going public is maybe give the kids some hope, if they're able to watch.'

Max looked at the stairs almost morosely. 'The parents, too, I expect.'

'They're here?' I asked in surprise.

I'm not sure where I imagined them to be, but as they had not been with the rest of us, I could only assume they had gone to stay with friends or down to their church.

They're in one of the bedrooms upstairs with a half dozen people from their church. The old boy was wailing a while back, Rick.' Max thought about it for a second and shook his head. 'I never heard anything as spooky come out of a human being in my whole life.'

I pointed at the mirror. 'Anything else to see?'

'We don't know who hit the mirror; probably get a report on the blood tonight, but our bet is Tabitha Merriweather, the younger of the two girls.'

'How old?'

'Just turned sixteen a couple of months ago.' I tried to shut off my feelings, but it was hopeless. Will Booker had managed to tear my soul loose. 'We found some unopened mail on the floor just inside the front door. We found a good latent print belonging to her on one of the envelopes. Her jacket and a piece of her blouse were over here.' Max pointed to the front room. 'Ripped off her body, from the look of it.'

I studied the spot where he pointed. 'Did he rape her, Max?'

The sheriff hesitated, then shrugged. 'I don't know, Rick. We're still putting the evidence together.'

Chapter 41

Darkness.

TABIT MERRIWEATHER HAD been in the trunk so long the feeling in her hands and feet was gone. The rolled pair of socks in her mouth had grown soggy. She had begun to think of it as a tumour in the back of her throat. It was better that way. Almost natural. A part of her flesh, the fate God had given her to endure.

Like the cramp that had started in her arm. She had tried to roll over to take the pressure off, but it wasn't possible. All she could do was change the pressure in the vain hope that the muscle would somehow relax. It didn't. The muscle ached. Her hip hurt as well. After a while, she forgot to wonder why this was happening to her. She got so used to it she could almost believe it was the most natural thing in the world. Hour upon hour of it. Aching and grieving, wondering if this might be the good part. And if it was?

She told herself there was no use worrying about what she could not control. Best to keep something beautiful close to you. A thing her mother had told her once. She tried it, but all she could think about was Will's face as he closed and locked the door. At that moment, she had known with certainty he had killed those kids. No matter what her father believed. She had known too that she was going to die by his hand as well.

A door creaked open. Not the first time. Will had been in and out before, but this was different. His footsteps came directly toward her. So it begins, she thought, and struggled to pray, but before she could even think the words she would offer God, the key penetrated the lock abruptly and the lid came up. It was dark outside, dark within. His face was a blur of shadows. Only the voice assured her it was Will. 'Time to come out and play, Tabit.'

Chapter 42

BEN LYONS COMES OUT of the darkness first. The man crawls – his ankle truly broken. Boy after him, pulling himself across the floor with his arms – his knee now fat with swelling.

The three girls walk in a line behind Ben and Benny. They come to the carpeted part of the basement, the recreation room. Will lines them up in a semicircle, all of them sitting on the floor. He wants to see each of them fully. He keeps them spread out. He studies each face now. Tamara has lost her fear and hope. She looks five days into it, not five hours. Tear tracks stain her face. She still wants his words to be true, imagines this is only a terrible nightmare. He has promised to marry her, hasn't he? Even now, she would go off with him if he bothered to flatter her a little. It is why she bores him. No sense of betrayal, no soul at all that he can see.

The others are different. Unbroken yet. They are full of wrath and terror. They own the fury of dogs, if they could only surrender to their rage. And so they are dangerous. At least until he breaks them. Will holds a cordless phone out toward Ben Lyons but very carefully. 'Your store manager's home number,' he whispers.

'Which one?'

Will blinks. 'The manager, the man who reports directly to you.'

'Which store?'

'The person you call if you have to leave town.' Will has not anticipated this. Suddenly he is unsure of the whole idea.

'I don't know. It's never come up.'

Will sees now what Ben is doing. He walks down until he stands before the three girls, the tip of the shotgun waving before them innocently. 'Are you sure you want to play games with me, Ben?'

'I call Tony Corrigan if I have to leave.'

'Dial his number.'

Ben Lyons pretends to hit several numbers, and Will walks toward him quickly. 'The phone! Give it to me!'

Ben's face pales before the barrel of the gun. He has no choice. He hands the phone over. A voice answers, 'Nine-one-one.' He had called the police!

Will snaps it off and walks to the three girls. 'Ladies,' he whispers, 'Ben just killed one of you.'

When Ben Lyons shouts in protest, Will steps back toward him quickly, striking his face hard with the butt of the gun. Blood flows out of his nose. Now Will twirls the weapon down so that the barrel points into Boy's face. Boy's eyes flash hot with fear. Ben holds his nose. The blood on his hands and covering his mouth excites Will. He begs the life of his son like a man praying to God. Will nods calmly, like a man convinced of a thing. He walks toward the girls again. 'You can have Benny, if he's the one you want, Ben. I'll take Penny so the rest of you will understand me.'

Tamara looks at Penny Lyons, but she says nothing. Tabit cannot help herself; she glances at the girl too. Neither dares to protest or volunteer to take her place. Will lets Penny see that she is the one they all have chosen. They all give her to him. Not a second thought about it either. Only the pleading of a foolish father: 'For God's sake, Will!'

It is a prayer as pious as Sunday morning. Will responds to it by walking back to Boy. 'Make up your mind, Ben. Is it Benny you want to see die?'

Ben screams his protest, 'No! My God, Will, why does someone have to die?'

'*You* played the game, Ben. This is the price when you lose. I won't take your favourite though. Not this time. But someone has to pay.'

'Then take *my* life!'

'I make the rules. You make the choice.'

185

Ben Lyons won't choose. So Will tells him with a friendly shrug as he levels the gun into Boy's face, 'We do it by the Bible then. First born male.'

'No! Not Benny!' He is crying freely now, because his choice is made. He knows it, the same as Boy and Penny know it.'

'Your little girl, then?' he asks gently, making the point for the rest of them. Ben Lyons shakes his head, still weeping, but he does not speak. Penny watches the choice being made. Her face pales; that is all she does. It is why Will loves her.

He holds the shotgun before her face for a long moment. He hears Ben weeping for the death he chooses. Will lets Penny understand that her father has done this to her, then lifts the gun barrel from her eyes. He smiles as he does it. 'Not *my* favourite,' he whispers.

WILL KNOWS SHE WILL love him for this kindness. Maybe not at first, but in time this will be what she remembers.

'The name was Tony Corrigan?' Will waits patiently while the man weeps and curses him in whispers. 'Call Tony and tell him you have to leave town tonight,' he says finally. 'You don't know for how long, but you will call him early next week. You say anything else, you pass a message of any kind and everyone dies – starting with Benny.'

Ben Lyons collects himself. 'I have to have a reason, Will. I have to be going someplace.'

'Tell him it's a death in the family. He'll believe it. You sound terrible. Just don't tell him who – or where you're going. And don't play with me, Ben. Not this time.'

Ben's look darkens. He hits the numbers. When Will takes the phone, he hears a woman answer. 'Corrigans.'

Will hands the phone back to Ben Lyons. He remains standing over Benny; it is all the threat he needs. Ben handles it perfectly. It's quite sudden. No, nothing to be done. He'll call next week. He hangs up before Tony Corrigan can ask anything more.

'Principal at school,' Will tells him. 'Mr Ahrens, I believe his name is.' Ben Lyons has to look the number up. When he finishes this call, Will asks, 'Does Judy have a job?'

Ben's eyes flash, 'Is Judy okay?'

'Judy is upstairs, Ben. I won't lie to you. She's hurt...'

'She's alive?'

'I'll bring her down when she's able to take the stairs on her own. Don't worry about it.'

'I want to see her!'

Will smiles coolly. 'Does she have a job, Ben?'

Ben Lyons shakes his head, eyes wet. 'She works at our two stores when we're shorthanded...'

'I'm going to need a day or so here,' he tells them. 'Through the weekend at the most. 'Four days. After

187

that, I'm taking off. Nobody needs to get hurt. Just stay in the room I've set up for you, and you have my word, you'll all live through this.'

'I want Judy with us,' Ben tells him. 'Let Penny and Tabit –'

'As soon as she can walk on her own,' Will answers.

'Is she conscious, can she talk?'

'She's not conscious, Ben. It's a head wound. I want to be honest with you. I don't know if she's going to make it.'

'You bastard! We have to get her help!'

'Don't worry about Judy, Ben,' Will answers gently. There is a bit of chiding in his tone. 'Worry about getting everyone in *this* room through the next couple of days. That's within your power. The rest, friend, is up to God and me.'

'We need food.' This from Boy. 'You can't lock us up without food and water!'

'Tomorrow morning I'll bring you some water.'

'What about using the bathroom?' Ben asks.

'I put a bucket in there already. That's going to have to do.'

WILL MOVES ON TO MORE important matters. First their clothing. They have to take it off. When it is stacked neatly in five little piles and they have only their underwear to cover their nakedness, Will sends Ben and Boy crawling back toward the room. The three girls walk behind them. At the door, Will holds Penny Lyons back. Penny's eyes widen in surprise. Her lips fall open in confusion. From inside the darkness Ben Lyons roars in protest, but that is all. His eyes lock onto his little girl. Then the darkness swallows him.

Will listens to Ben Lyons demanding that Penny come in with the rest of them. He is too loud. Will pulls his Bernardelli from his hip pocket and fires twice into the wall. Silence answers. He slips a towel across the bottom of the door, plunging them into perfect darkness, because that is the essence of infinity, as close as a kiss.

Will takes Penny into her brother's bedroom. Will has stripped it of its pornographic posters. He has made the bed with soldierly neatness. Penny comes without quarrelling; only a bit of shiver as he turns her so she will face him. He lets her sit primly on the bed, watching the terror forming in her eyes.

'I'm not going to hurt you, Penny,' he tells her.

'Please! I've never…' Her voice is a whisper, a sigh. Her tears are fat drops that hang on the edge of her eyelids.

'No!' he answers. He puts his finger under her chin. 'That's not what I want. Now listen to me. Just listen…'

Chapter 43

Night.

AFTER I LEFT THE MERRIWEATHER house I drove for a while. I stopped for gas at a highway service station. I got a can of Coke, a piece of pie in wax paper and then headed back into the countryside. It was an old habit I hadn't tried on in years. The state trooper in me that hadn't quite washed out when Sarah disappeared. Checking driveways, looking at cars, watching windows. I knew I was wasting my time and energy, but I couldn't go home. I couldn't sleep. I could only think of the last time Will Booker had struck. The way the community had been forced to watch the thing unfolding by horrible degrees. Like no crime in the history of Shiloh Springs. Two boys dead at the abduction site, then the days passing. First one girl, then the second turning up. Both buried in shallow graves. Then a long wait, two sisters imprisoned somewhere. No one finding a lead. The whole community holding its breath. Finally the word had come that one girl had survived, even as we learned her sister was gone, the body never found.

In those days I had been running Century Secure, doing a lively business with various factories, stores and offices. I was blissfully unaware of personal tragedy that comes with a crime. Completely disconnected from criminal law enforcement. Unless I needed the cops to bust some folks for my clients I did not have any business with them.

All the same, William Booker had scared me the way only a nightmare can. He had been too close to ignore, proof no place was safe. Of course I hadn't done anything about it. I had left it to Nat Hall and the state troopers and the city police and the FBI, in their advisory capacity. I remember thinking this is what happens all the time, somewhere, but not here. Not in Shiloh Springs. I remember pushing it all away until Will Booker had been caught, and then of course, like everyone, I wanted his blood. He had lost his rights as far as I was concerned. If I had known about the Russian roulette, I would have cheered old Nat Hall and voted for him no matter what office he was running for. Of course later, when my passions had cooled down, I was as shocked and outraged as every other hypocrite in town.

I know I watched the fate of Will Booker as a perfect spectator. I know my heart was elsewhere. I was making money, securing the workplace for corporations. Living a decent life with my wife. Attending my daughter's college graduation and coming up with a bit of extra cash to help her with law school. And going to the same school as little Patty Garrat! As good as a Garrat! *'And when you see her in your classes,'* I told Sarah, *'tell her you used to play together in the governor's mansion!'*

Not bad times, only not enough of them. A short two years after Will Booker proved it could happen in Shiloh Springs, I got a call at work. My wife Nicole. The police in Attica had just phoned, she said. Sarah was missing. Missing? *'Took a walk at sunset and didn't come back...'*

There's not much I don't recall about what came next, starting with getting my revolver out for the first time in years and ending with it in my mouth on several dark nights a couple of years later. Always holding off the trigger because I hoped, before I died, I would kill the monster who hurt my Sarah. It was a hell of a reason to live, but the only one I had. Which says worlds about the marriage I had loved right up to the moment of that phone call.

I don't know how much I saw of the countryside the night the Merriweather girls vanished. I was adrift in other nights. I know my eyes scoured driveways, alleys, country roads, culverts, and dark lanes that led into lonely pastureland. But all the while my heart was seeking Sarah. It was not introspection. I was beyond introspection. I was in the night that does not finish. I was looking for ghosts. I was rescuing my own lost child. My Sarah. Losing my marriage again with the grim determination of a man who doesn't deserve to be loved.

WHEN I SAW ANOTHER GREY DAWN breaking out of the night sky I turned around and drove back to the city. The snow began shortly after that. It fell fast but without a wind, the flakes fat.

By the time I ended up at my big broken down urban palace a thick blanket of snow had covered the street and topped the houses and cars. And still it came. I took a shower, then dressed about as well as I ever do, and headed over to the 24 hour joint where I ordered sausage and eggs and seven or eight cups of coffee. The snow was two feet deep when I came outside again, and it was still coming down. It was beautiful, the last hurrah of winter, and as I walked back to my house I saw the usual sights of winter. People were out getting their cars ready, stamping their feet, waving at neighbours, sometimes just smiling.

I stopped at St. Jude's on the way to the office, thinking to pray, but as I waited on my knees for something to say, I could only think about the beauty of a fresh, heavy snow and all the ugliness it hides.

Chapter 44

Thursday 5:30 a.m., March 25.

CONNIE MERRIWEATHER OPENED his eyes and blinked dully at the walls. He looked at his watch. It was 5:30. He was pretty sure he had slept most of an hour. He shifted about in the big chair, then stood and walked toward his office. Two federal agents were there, waiting. They were reading old *Mission* magazines. Through the window Connie could see the snow coming down, thick but not yet deep.

'How long before they call – usually?' Connie asked the one who looked up.

The senior agent, a man close to Connie's age, cleared his throat. 'Sometimes it takes a few hours; sometimes it's a few days.'

'And we just wait?'

For a moment, Connie was certain the agent wasn't going to answer, but after a look that seemed to take

Connie's measure, he answered, 'Yes, sir. At this point there is nothing to do but wait.'

Wait and pray. Connie had spent the better part of a lifetime doing just that. Death watches, failing marriages, drug and alcohol addiction: it didn't matter. In the end, you did what you could. Then you waited and you prayed. Sometimes the prayers were for God to move the world. Sometimes you prayed just to give you the courage to take what the devil dished out.

Connie began to break apart from the inside at this thought, and before he lost control completely, he forced himself toward other matters. 'You care for some coffee?' He found himself looking at the gun one of the men had as he waited for the two men to respond. Its potential for violence gave him odd comfort.

'Thanks, we're okay. Your wife got us some.'

Connie looked back in the direction of the kitchen. Rachel. When he had finally gotten home last night Rachel had thrown herself at him. Screaming, swinging her fists at him, her face knotted in fury, she had called him a *damn fool*. Then had come her coldness. His betrayal was too deep to forgive, and so she had no more words for him.

Connie wandered back to the kitchen and found Rachel with four women and two men. They were all from the church; all but Louise Robbins had stayed with them through the night. Louise had come while he was asleep. Someone had left, but he couldn't

195

remember who. Through the kitchen window, Connie could see a deputy in his patrol car parked in front of Bryce Appleberry's place, his car covered in snow. The angle of the houses gave the deputy a clear view to the Merriweathers' back door. Connie tried to catch Rachel's gaze, but she left the room. Well, he *was* a damn fool!

Bob Soloway asked Connie if he had been able to sleep. Connie poured a cup of coffee and answered that he slept maybe an hour. He stood for a moment looking at them. He thought about throwing his cup someplace. Bellowing his rage again. Instead, his eyes brimmed up suddenly, and his whole body began to shake. Louise Robbins came to him quickly, taking him in her arms. Her eyes were as wet as his, her voice tremulous. 'Oh, Connie,' she whispered, 'it's going to be…' She stopped herself, gathering in all the strength she had, '…I just pray God protects them.'

Connie felt something odd running across his hand. He looked down curiously to see scolding hot coffee splashing over his fist.

Chapter 45

Thursday 8:30 a.m., March 25.

I FOUND GARRAT IN HER office when I got to work. She had everything from Max and probably three other sources, but she wanted me to go through what I had seen. I told her, then described what I had given Max in terms of advice. I finished my report with a review of the hard evidence we already had in hand. It was music to a prosecutor's ears. She was paranoid, all the same.

'Sounds like we have enough to convict – *assuming we don't lose the evidence.*'

I gave her what she was waiting for. 'I'll oversee everything personally, Pat. Daily if necessary.'

'Hourly, Rick. And statements,' she said. 'I want copies of those on my desk by lunch. If we don't like what we see, you get out and do the follow-ups immediately. Date-stamp everything you do. I want this evidence so pure even a senile appellate judge can follow it. You hear me?' She wasn't mad at me or anyone else – with maybe the exception of William Booker, Judge Buford Lynch and that damn fool Connie Merriweather. She was just afraid that we would somehow lose our man again, assuming we ever caught him. Partly it was because the guy was slippery or at least lucky. Mostly it was because all her worldly ambitions hung on the successful prosecution of William Booker.

'What about the murder charges?' I asked her. 'Too late?'

Garrat's eyes flashed hot. She had already filed with the court, she told me. 'We lost him on the murders.'

She said nothing more, and I thought about what must be going through her head. The kind of charges a good prosecutor could stack on Will Booker at this point, assuming we caught him before he killed anyone. It wasn't pretty. Anything less than life in prison without possibility of parole and there would be talk that Pat Garrat was not equal to her reputation. 'Maybe we ought to let the feds steal this from us,' I offered gently. 'Max could scream bloody murder – you know, take some of the heat off us.'

Her eyes went cold, 'When we catch this guy, Rick, I'll build a cage for him! Don't you worry about that!'

'You care if I start digging around in the case, assuming I have some extra time?'

Garrat looked surprised. 'You want in on the hunt?'

I had never admitted to Garrat how I had ruined myself because of my search for another madman, but she knew. Everyone who knew me knew. 'No prayer is ever answered that isn't first prayed,' I said.

'Look, I think I understand where you're coming from –'

'I don't want to be disrespectful, but I doubt it.'

Garrat locked her gaze on me, then finally nodded in agreement. 'It's not in your job description, Rick. Finding those girls is police business. Prosecuting Mr Booker once he's caught is our responsibility. Let's not get confused about that.' She saw my face screwing up with an answer, and cut me off. 'I can't let you do it.'

'You're the boss,' I answered grimly.

I was at the door when Garrat called my name. I looked back expectantly. 'You really think you could find them?'

'Rolly Tincher is running this case, Pat.'

Garrat's eyebrows lifted. She knew exactly what I was saying. Rolly Tincher had been trained by Nat Hall. It was the kind of police work that got results without much effort. She turned her chair so she was facing the window. She was thinking about my offer. How it would play in the media if she got me involved in the hunt for the girls. How Max would resent the interference. The political risks weighed heavily against the slim advantage of my experience as a human bloodhound. The chances of either girl surviving were negligible. Max

Dunn's fury was guaranteed. Finally, she shook her head.

'I just can't do it, Rick. It's the sheriff's business until he gives us the case. If we get in the middle of this thing before there's an arrest, the press will make it look like we don't have confidence in the sheriff's office.'

'Do we?'

'Max has good people working for him.'

'Rolly Tincher isn't one of them.'

'Max and Rolly go back a long way.'

'That's the problem. Rolly has his position because he knows too much.'

'He's not a bad cop, Rick.'

'No, but he's lazy.'

'I'm sorry. I can't cross Max on this.'

I knew what she was saying. She was in trouble for her decision not to prosecute, even though everyone had thought it was a great idea yesterday. The best way to handle things at this point was to hide behind procedures. Respect the bureaucratic boundaries. Let Max Dunn take centre stage and hope everyone forgot that she had reversed her position seemingly without cause a mere four hours before Will Booker finally tore the mask off. I had lost my idealism when this one's daddy fell to an assassin's bullet while I lay on the floor already hit. The Governor was taken down by a one-time political ally with a choleric temper. A scandal had left his career in ruins. What he did not understand was that Pat Garrat had protected him for as long as he could.

When Garrat had finally walked away, the assassin felt betrayed. He took his revenge on the man he thought was responsible – the only man who had in fact defended him. I got hit throwing myself in front of the first two rounds.

WILL BOOKER WAS GOING to make his play as maniacs always do, and we would come in behind him, when it was over, as we always did: sheriff, coroner, and county prosecutor. We would all shake our heads at the terrible thing done to the innocents. We would all trumpet plenty of nonsense about justice once it no longer mattered. Will Booker would get a lawyer; his victims would get a prayer.

And neither Pat Garrat nor I would ever mention that we had had a desperate chance at the beginning of this thing – an old bloodhound turned loose on the devil's trail – and we had let it slip away from us.

For political reasons.

Chapter 46

Darkness.

A KNOCK AT THE DOOR. THE furtive whisper of Will Booker. 'It's time to come out and play, Penny!'

Mr Lyons swore at the sound of Will's voice. When the door opened, he shouted, 'Don't go, Penny!' Tabit rolled to her side and curled up. She was certain Will would start shooting again. There was candlelight in the hall, darkness beyond it.

The door closed behind Penny. Mr Lyons swore quietly as he had the last time Will had called her out. And the time before that. Then he got quiet, as they all had done each time she left. Penny had told them nothing happened. Will had just talked to her. She couldn't say what he talked about. She refused to answer when Mr Lyons pressed her. She was lying so the rest of them wouldn't know the truth, but they all knew the truth.

'I don't understand why Will wants *her*,' Tammy moaned.

Tabit didn't answer. No one did. Benny sighed, his voice cutting through the darkness angrily, 'We have to do something, Dad.'

'What? We can't even *walk*! We have nothing in here that we can use as a weapon...'

'Do we just let him do what he wants to Penny?'

Mr Lyons said nothing for nearly a minute. Like he wasn't there. And then quietly he told them, 'He'll make a mistake, Benny, and when he does...'

Chapter 47

Thursday 2:00 p.m., March 25.

JUST BEFORE LUNCH I got with the sheriff's office and collected the reports on the Merriweather girls that Garrat had asked for. We ordered pizza and did a lunch-conference in Garrat's office, going through the thing in tedious detail. We had witnesses seeing Will Booker leave the hospital before three. We had the kids in the school bus seeing Tabitha Merriweather go into her house a few minutes after three-thirty. We had the bathrobe Booker was wearing out of the hospital left inside the Merriweather house. We had the blood on the broken mirror matching Tabitha Merriweather, a good print belonging to Tabitha on one of the envelopes from the mailbox. We had Booker's prints on the tape that had bound Tammy Merriweather in her room. We had a bit of blood and clothing from Tabit on the carpet of the TV room but no evidence of rape.

When the meeting broke up, I took an underground passage to the city police department for a meeting about another case with the assistant chief of detectives, Bobby DeWitt. My arrest was still a good joke on that side of the plaza; so it was bound to come up after we had knocked around the gossip on the Merriweather abductions.

The rookies, he said, were still asking how an old man had taken them out so easily. I played dumb with DeWitt. Too drunk to remember what really happened, I said. 'All I know is I sure hurt the next day.' He bought it, but levelled his gaze on me with an intensity that I was not prepared for. 'If you ever got off the sauce, Rick, Max would love to make you his chief of detectives.'

'That's Rolly Tincher's job.'

'For a real detective Max could find Rolly a big office and nothing much to do.'

'Did he say that or are you just speculating?'

'Actually, he said it the morning he came over here and pulled you out of lockup.'

MY VANITY TOYED WITH ME on the short walk back across the plaza. I actually thought about walking into the sheriff's office. If I asked Max for a detective's badge I was pretty sure he would give me one. Before I got there my nerves betrayed me. I felt a monumental thirst coming on.

There was a witness in an assault case who did not live that far from the Shamrock, and I figured after I touched base with him it would not be the worst thing in the world for me to stop off and have a few. Guilt licked at me as I considered my plans for the afternoon. The problems Connie Merriweather's two teenage girls faced were not mine to solve. It was perfect nonsense for me to think about leaving Garrat for their sake.

I was almost out my office door, on a fool's errand, when the phone rang. It was Garrat. 'Max found something interesting, Rick.'

'How interesting?' I asked.

'His people found a body about an hour ago.'

'Oh, God,' I muttered. My gut went cold. For a second I thought I might be sick all over my desk.

'It's still tentative but they think it's Mary Worth.'

'*Who?*'

'The body they never found. Missy Worth's older sister.'

'Can you still prosecute for *that* murder, Pat?'

'Hammer indicted Booker for her kidnap, not the murder. We're back in business on a death penalty case as soon as we have a positive ID on the body. What I want you to do is to get out there and have a look around. We can't use any of the physical evidence we have from the old case, but there might be something useful at the scene. Just make sure Max is careful. Everything by the book!'

'I'm on it.'

'Max said something about getting the media out to the crime scene...'

'Great,' I muttered.

'Don't get involved with the TV people, Rick. Don't even let a camera find you!'

'I understand. Do you have directions?'

'The sheriff's dispatch can give you what you need.'

Chapter 48

Thursday 4:10 p.m., March 25.

MAX DUNN SAW ME AT a distance and came across the beaten down snow grinning like he was hosting a party. Mary Worth had been mourned if not buried by all of us too many years ago to feel much sorrow now. On the contrary, her body was a second chance for us to get the death penalty for a maniac who yesterday, by official proclamation, had never committed a felony. 'Is Garrat coming?'

I shook my head and surveyed the field. A knot of men and women hovered beside what I could only assume was Mary Worth's grave. 'How did you find it?' I asked.

'A woman named Julie Breen called up this morning. She lives down the road, attends Merriweather's church. Said she thought she might have seen the Merriweather car out here Sunday afternoon. She caught the news this morning and called us right away. Watch command sent a deputy out to look around. He found a hole that was filled up with snow, but it was clear *someone* had dug it fairly recently, and he called for the detectives. Turns out it was just a hole with a plastic sack in it.' Max took me to a small excavation that was maybe twenty paces distant from the gravesite. 'Booker came back to get something – we think probably the gun he used last time. For whatever reason, he didn't take everything that was here, and he didn't bother covering the hole after he got what he wanted.'

'So what did he leave behind?'

'All the evidence we needed at the last trial and didn't have. We've got an army jacket with blood on it and a couple of bullet holes in the pocket. The gold mine is what looks to be a sawed off baseball bat of some sort. It's covered with blood, Rick. It's what he used for his kills!'

I felt my pulse kicking up. 'Get prints?'

'Rolly's got everything in our lab as we speak. They'll use luminol on it because of all the dirt and rot. If there are any prints on that bat, with the luminol they are going to show up like neon.'

I looked at the small hole where Will Booker's treasure had been kept, then across the field to the larger excavation. 'What about the body?' I asked.

'That's the funny part. We're all over here with this evidence we wished to God we had found before Garrat

209

quit on this thing, and that's when it hit me.' Max pointed at the grave. 'I just didn't like the way the snow was kind of sunk down over there, so I put two men to digging, and there she was – about eighteen inches under!'

I walked to the shallow trench with Max and looked down at the skeletal remains of Mary Worth. She was on her back, ready to be pulled out of the grave, her arms neatly folded over what had been her torso. She had broken bones along both legs, one shoulder that had been bashed up thoroughly. Half of her skull was broken open. When I had seen enough, I stepped away. I felt a chill of outrage at the utter brutality of such a murder. I looked at the drifts of snow and blue sky – the first blue sky we had seen in weeks – and I tried not to think that the body I had just seen belonged to a girl who would not even be thirty for a couple more years – if she had lived. Younger than Sarah.

'When is the media coming?' I asked.

Max looked at his watch and smiled contentedly, 'They'll be here just in time for the evening news to pick it up. Not a half-second sooner.'

I checked my own watch. The evening news was set, but they would clear the programme for a body. Probably run over into network time with a story like this. A local politician's dream. 'Did you contact the family?'

'I sent a deputy out to the Worth house, another up to Catherine Howard for Missy. We called the FBI at the Merriweather house a few minutes ago. Didn't want them to hear it on the news. You know these damn vultures. They'll run a lead on it that will sound like we found one of our two kids from yesterday.'

I heard the thumping of a helicopter in the distance. A deputy stepped toward us. 'Sir.' That was all he said.

Max walked back toward the crowd at the grave and gave Doc Wolfe, the county coroner, a nod. 'Let's bring her up, Tommy!'

Tommy Wolfe straightened his bow tie and all but smiled. I watched the helicopter coming in fast, then studied the sudden lively interest at the pit's edge – all a great show.

I walked over and tapped the sheriff's shoulder. 'I'm out of here, Max! Will you give me a call if you find prints on the bat?'

Max grinned happily. 'If I get Will Booker's prints, buddy, I'll come buy you a beer!'

Chapter 49

Thursday 5:55 p.m., March 25.

I GAVE GARRAT EVERYTHING over the phone as I drove back to town. Her mood held. Not joy, really, but the grim satisfaction of one committed to a cause. We had our capital case.

After I pocketed my phone, I pulled into a diner on East 340 and sat down to have dinner. The TV was on. Some nonsense was playing. Before I had my salad finished, a news flash hit the screen. Foreplay to the evening news. The restaurant came alive with interest when they noticed the lead. As Max had predicted, they played to the natural assumption that the sheriff had found a Merriweather. I watched with the authority and wisdom of an insider. I had been there. I had seen the hole in the ground, the old bones. My entree came, and I tried vainly to suppress my look of superior wisdom even as the waitress talked to me about it. 'Terrible, isn't it?' She was talking about the Merriweather girls. I nodded at her sentiment and chewed my meat contentedly. We were watching the grave from a bird's-eye view, and I saw the deputies waving the helicopter off in a carefully orchestrated fury. At the corner of the screen, I saw a really handsome old bald gentleman in a good looking sports jacket walking away from the grave.

'A tragedy,' I said.

There was a quick cut to Max now. A microphone in his face, Kathy James holding it toward him aggressively. They were still in the field. Tommy Wolfe in his bow tie managed to walk behind them three times in the few seconds they talked. The body was now being identified as most likely belonging to Mary Worth. When I heard Max say the word *prints*, I stood up and walked forward to listen.

'Do you mean to say William Booker's prints are on the murder weapon?' Kathy James asked him.

Max nodded and grinned. It was a slight, quiet one, but it was there. A sheriff who's bagged his prey. *'In blood,'* he answered.

I stood in dumb awe for a minute. His people had worked fast! A nice set of bloody fingerprints on a murder weapon was the one piece of physical evidence any jury could hang onto when they got confused with everything else, which was inevitable when the lawyers started barking. Up from the grave! Case closed. And welcome to hell, Mr Booker!

I called Garrat with the news as I drove to the Dug Out, though she had already heard it. Finished with my obligations to the boss, I burst into the bar and ordered a shot and a beer chaser for myself, and a round for the house. A couple of hours later, coming off my natural high and starting to roll with the hard currency now, I got a call on my cell. It was Max. He sounded a little fuzzy himself, and I thought he had probably just remembered he'd promised to let me know about the prints and maybe, more importantly, buy me a beer.

'They found fingerprints on that club, Rick.'

'I saw it on TV, Max! Congratulations. You looked great on camera, by the way! Did you wear makeup for that?'

'Rick, listen to me.' Max had been drinking. 'We've got a serious problem.'

'Problem? What are you talking about?' I felt nervous suddenly. I thought about lost evidence, contamination, a print not quite sufficient for a trial judge to admit into evidence. I couldn't dream enough legal catastrophes to guess the truth, though. Not if I worked all night on the possibilities.

'Rick, I jumped the gun a little. See, we didn't have any of Booker's prints on hand right at the moment, and Rolly called me as soon as our people knew they had prints. The news people were on us and I figured, well, I mean...'

I felt myself going weak. 'Say it, Max. Tell me what in the hell you're talking about!'

'They're not his prints, Rick. Will Booker didn't touch that bat.'

Chapter 50

Darkness.

THE FLOOR CREAKS OVERHEAD as Ben tries to remember why that is interesting. Getting food for them, he thinks. Or taking care of Judy…

Then the fog of his thoughts cleared. *Upstairs.* Will was upstairs! He hadn't been upstairs since he'd brought Tabit in. Ben had listened for it, because if Will Booker went upstairs there was a chance. The floor groaned again, and Ben spoke with sudden authority, though his voice sounded like a dusty phonograph. 'He's upstairs, Benny!'

'So?'

Ben waited to answer. He was not sure suddenly. Then came the faintest creak of wood. 'Hear that! He's in the kitchen! Now listen to me! We've got to get out of this room. If we don't, he's going to kills us all!'

'*How?*'

'We get to our feet. We take the door down with our

216

shoulders. If we hit it hard, together, I don't think it can hold us. Once we get outside, we have to separate. You get into the bedroom across the hall; I'll go into the laundry room. I'll try to draw him to me. When he comes through the door for me, he'll have his back to you. Break his neck if you have to, Benny! Do you understand me?'

'No!' The voice belonged to Tammy Merriweather.

'He'll shoot you!' Benny answered.

'If he's shooting at me, he won't see you coming. It's the best chance we have!' Ben pulled himself up to his feet. 'We can do this!' he told them. 'We *have* to do this before he starts killing us! Penny, you and Tammy and Tabit just stay here. He won't hurt you if he's worried about Benny and me.'

'WILL!' Tammy Merriweather's shrill cry cut through Ben like the blade of a knife.

'Quiet!' Ben hissed.

'WILL, THEY'RE TRYING TO BREAK OUT!'

'No!' Ben cried.

'WILL! WILL! They're breaking out!'

Ben fell back against the wall and slipped to the floor, whispering to Benny to get down as well. It was too late to get out. He could hear Booker on the stairs.

'EVERYONE OUT NOW!' he shouted as he came. A moment later, they heard the key turn the lock. The door stayed closed. 'Come out now, Ben, or I start shooting through the wall with the big gun!'

'We're coming,' Ben answered. He could hardly breathe he was so sick with fear. He knew Will would have to punish them now. Benny or Penny...

Tabit opened the door, and Ben could see Will in the flickering shadows caused by the candlelight on the floor. '*Everyone* out!' Will shouted. He was scared, dancing from foot to foot. The shotgun shifted from Ben to Benny now as they came. Will backed down the hall, careful to keep his distance from Ben and his son. The three girls followed behind them.

They came into the basement recreation room. Will placed them as they had been before. Benny next to Ben, the three girls farther away.

Will paced nervously before them. His eyes were bright, manic. Ben hadn't seen him like this since the phone call to the police had excited him to threaten to kill Benny and Penny. It terrified him because he knew this time Will was going to take a life.

The cool control, the whispering confidence: it was gone. What Ben saw now was the unadorned man: pure madness.

'I didn't want to do this. You pushed me to it!' He left the room for a split second and returned with a bloodied baseball bat. Was it Judy's blood? The thought came with a clutching of Ben's heart. A certainty that he had not admitted until now.

Will told Penny to stand. The girl did as she was told, her mouth open, her dark eyes wide, unblinking.

218

'You'll do it for me, won't you?' As he said this, Will handed Penny the bat and pointed at Tammy Merriweather. 'Right where she sits – take her!'

Ben could hardly believe what he was seeing. Will walked away from Penny and waited. Penny held the bat and looked down at Tammy Merriweather.

'Kill her, Penny. Hit her and don't stop until she's dead or so help me God everyone dies tonight!'

'Will?' Tammy's voice creaked in fear and confusion.

'Now, Penny! DO IT NOW!'

Ben Lyons shifted uncomfortably.

Will spun toward him, pulling his handgun and pointing it suddenly at Ben. 'I'll start with your dad, and I won't stop until it's just you and me!'

Tammy was weeping and calling Will's name plaintively.

'She's a traitor, Penny! She betrayed you!'

He walked toward Tabit, pointing the gun at her skull. Ben was sure Tabit Merriweather was about to die, but Will did not pull the trigger. 'Do you want me to show you how it's done?'

Penny wept as both Tabit and Tammy wailed for mercy.

Will shifted his gun again, now pointing at Benny. 'Take her, or I shoot Benny! Your choice!'

Ben spoke. 'Will, for the love of God!'

Will shifted the gun sights to Ben and shot him in the chest. 'Shut up, Ben!'

Ben grabbed his chest and stared in utter wonder at the madman. Then he looked at his daughter. 'Penny, put the bat down! You don't have to do this! Just put the bat down!'

A second shot hit him, and Ben fell back.

'Next is Benny!' Will shouted. 'You can save him if you want, Penny! All you have to do is kill the traitor!'

Ben heard only the gasps of the others as he struggled vainly to breathe. Then came the surf-sound of blood roaring in his ears, the vision of Will Booker standing over him, his little gun pointing into his face. The *coup de grace*. Ben waited. Ready, knowing it was the end.

TABIT AND TAMMY ARE wailing. Penny has dropped the bat to the floor. Ben Lyons's gasps are ragged, loud. Will considers the man, the wounds, then the others. Penny watches with a pale face, her arms wrapped around her chest, her lips hanging open in surprise. Her eyes wet. Penny is not like Tamara, who weeps, nor Tabit, who holds her face in her hands, her breath failing her as she gags. Nor like Boy who wants to join his father in a hero's grave.

Will shifts the gun to Boy. 'You want it too, Benny?'

Will feels the blackness coming over him. The ache of his wounds reviving. He hasn't much time left. He can barely stand before them. Boy sees it, too. His eyes are hot, eager. Will cannot give him the chance. Will

220

points the gun down until it is almost touching Boy's forehead. In his rage, Boy fails even to tremble. Instead, he swears at Will with filthy words. Does not even lower his gaze.

Penny pleads, 'Please, Will, no!'

Will drops the gun to his side in response. They all think it is over. Boy draws a solid breath of relief. Will smiles at him – right before he lifts the gun up again and pulls the trigger.

Part VI

Comes and Old Man

An old man cometh up; and he is covered with a mantle.

I Samuel 28: 14.

Chapter 51

Thursday 9:40 p.m., March 25.

I STARTED MY COUNTY CAR AND drove east toward Garrat's farm on white roads. I pushed past the guardhouse with a wave of my hand maybe twenty-five minutes later and rolled up to the barn.

Garrat was inside riding a big bay stallion in an arena that looked close to seventy yards long. The place was lit up like noon, but it was cold. I stood with her manager and watched her turning the big horse in the tight smooth circles of dressage. Garrat rode in a beat up hunt outfit, jodhpurs, high boots, a worn wool riding coat, and a knocked about cap of felt and steel. She had the look of a woman who did this four or five times a week, a couple-three horses a night. It had been her father's passion as well.

The barn manager had about ten years on me, a liver ready for life support. He was a short, physically tough man with meaty cheeks, a couple of chins. He had eyes that measured by inches. We didn't use each other's name or bother with hello. He'd been around the farm for about forty years and had a good way with horses and the folks who worked with them. He pretty much lumped the rest of the world into his own private dung heap. He was devoted to Pat Garrat and Wild Turkey whiskey, not necessarily in that order. I was competition for Garrat's affection; we both knew that. I didn't try for his good opinion or even angle a smile out of the old bastard. We stood together and his small watery eyes never left the centre of the big arena. Finally he told me, 'Beautiful, huh?'

I didn't know if he meant the riding, the horse, or the woman. I grunted in agreement and watched as Garrat cantered the horse. The animal moved with such a compact stride it hardly took any ground at all. I had seen rocking chairs that didn't look as comfortable. As Garrat came down the line she finally saw me. She said nothing, rode the horse a long way past the gate, stopped and walked the horse out a few more strides. The bay let his head nudge lazily toward the silt floor of the arena. Settling her shoulders quietly without a word or a touch of the reins, Garrat stopped the big horse cold. She slipped off the stallion easily and led him back to the gate. She gave the reins to the manager, who took the horse right back into the arena, walking it toward the other end as we talked.

I had been to the farm plenty but never uninvited. Garrat was certain I was going to tell her one of the Merriweather girls had just been found dead. When I told her about the prints on the bat not matching Booker's, her face tipped to the side thoughtfully, a mix of relief and frustration as she offered the sum of her reaction: 'Son-of-a-bitch!'

'We'll connect him to the jacket we found in the bag with his DNA,' I said, 'but for the moment we've got –'

My phone rang and I pulled it from my sports coat. It was Max. 'We just got a match on those prints, Rick. You're never going to guess –'

'Missy Worth,' I said.

Garrat looked at me curiously. After a long pause, Max asked me, 'Now how in the hell did you know that?'

'Just a minute,' I answered and covered the speaker. 'The prints on the bat belong to Missy Worth. You want to talk to Max about it or wait until tomorrow?'

Garrat stared at me blankly, absorbing the meaning slowly. Finally, she shook her head. 'Eight o'clock tomorrow morning. My office.'

I passed it on to Max and thanked him. 'How did you know, Rick?'

'Lucky guess,' I said and switched him off.

Garrat kicked the arena gate angrily. From the other end of the arena her stallion lifted his head at the sound.

Garrat's barn manager kept his eyes on the dirt, as I pretty much did too. Garrat didn't need to explain herself to me. Max Dunn, as happy as a kid at his own birthday party, had just fallen on the cake. 'What are you going to do?' I asked when she didn't saying anything.

She looked at me curiously. 'What would the old man do, Rick?'

I looked out at the arena and shook my head. I didn't have any advice to give. Garrat had stood up to fight when everyone had thought she should walk away; then she'd given up on the thing a few short hours before her opinion proved correct. She had Will Booker for any number of crimes, but her capital case was now irreparably compromised. The state's star witness had just become a suspect in the narrative the defence attorney would undoubtedly tell. Will Booker might have lost his world class lawyer when he disappeared with the Merriweather girls, but even a public defender could make a run at this one. And no one beyond the courthouse steps would ever forgive a prosecutor who could not return Booker to his Death Row cell.

A sympathetic view would have put Pat Garrat's political destiny in the balance, but the truth was bad luck and Max Dunn had finished all talk of higher ambitions. What would the old man have done in her position? I had no wisdom to give her, though she waited with a patience I had never seen in her before.

And then it came to me, one of those awful nights

that hit us all eventually. Governor Garrat assailed on all sides, support running away like a routed army – and what had he done? I tipped my head out toward the big bay stallion. 'The governor would climb back up on that horse out there and just ride, Pat.'

She smiled, a girl who had loved her daddy but was too young when he passed on to understand him entirely. 'What good would that do him?'

'Your daddy did his best thinking on top of a horse. I think there were nights he rode five horses sore and went back for another. Next morning, he'd be ready to take on the world.' I felt a tear boiling up in my old eyes and silently cursed my renegade sentiments. Seventeen years dead ought to kill off the emotions for an old friend, and did for most, but not for the governor. It didn't seem to have hardly got a good start.

The barn manager was coming back down the line toward us. 'You want him back or should I run him on the line, Ms Garrat?'

'I'll take him,' she answered. Taking the reins, she turned back toward me, 'Max just *had* to get on TV, didn't he?'

'It seemed like a sure thing,' I said with a sorrowful shrug.

Garrat leaped up on the stallion's back without the benefit of her stirrups. 'The only sure things in life are death and taxes. A good politician like Max ought to know that.'

I watched Garrat for nearly half-an-hour before I left. She worked like a professional rider training for events, though she hadn't ridden competitively since her childhood. This was what passed for fun in the Garrat clan. The focus of the woman was comprehensive: for the moment, all that existed was that horse.

The rest of the world was just a surface to ride over.

I WAVED AT GARRAT'S security guard as I left the farm and then rolled out into the country. I drove all that night along snowy country roads. I found lanes that weren't on any maps, cabins and sheds long abandoned. I looked into every dark place that whispered to me. I stopped and got out of the car more than once. I smelled the sweet black air for death. I listened for the faint cry of living girls. I studied the snowfields for footprints.

No fool like an old man.

Chapter 52

Friday 8:00 a.m., March 26.

I HAD TIME FOR A SHOWER, a cup of coffee and a change of clothes when I finally got home. I was out the door and driving my three minute commute to work in time for Garrat's eight o'clock meeting.

Garrat used her conference table for her meeting. Steve Massey was there, Max Dunn and Max's chief of detectives, Rolly Tincher. Tincher was about the same age as his boss, an inch or two taller, and seventy pounds heavier. Sitting down winded the guy. Both Tincher and Max wore tweed sports jackets. Their shoulder holsters bulged beneath their jackets with sleek pewter-finished Colt .45 automatics. The jackets came off the minute Garrat pointed toward her conference table. This was a tactical manoeuvre, I decided, though probably an unconscious one. Max was in trouble. He needed to discourage a really nasty mauling. Guns showing tended to quiet the girls. Most girls anyway. I doubted guns much affected Pat Garrat. In her world the servants had always worn guns. The people with power, real power, never did.

The meeting began with Garrat asking about the kidnapping of the Merriweather girls. The sheriff had nothing good to report, nothing at all, really. City, county, and state police were scouring the area for any sign of the girls or their car, he said. Road blocks had been set up throughout the region, the net expanding now to a seven state search. It was cop talk for 'we lost him.' Was there anything her office could do to help? Max shook his head. 'I think we've got it covered, Pat. FBI is minding their manners, watching the phones and the mail, holding hands with the Merriweathers. I've got a deputy parked outside the reverend's house, keeping an eye on things.' An eye on the FBI, he meant.

Even as he finished his report, Max had the look of bracing himself for nasty winds: the matter, once again, of having operated his mouth without benefit of fore-thought.

'Then let's figure out what we're going to do about these fingerprints,' Garrat told us all pleasantly.

'First of all,' Max announced, 'I want to apologise for talking to the press before we verified whose prints we had. I'm taking full responsibility for releasing any information before we had confirmed whose prints were on that bat. The mistake is mine and mine alone.'

'Nobody here wants to point fingers,' Garrat answered easily. 'The only thing I'm interested in at this point is whether or not to proceed with an investigation against Missy Worth.'

Max Dunn's expression went from tense expectancy to incredulity. 'Investigation for what, Pat?'

Garrat smiled prettily. 'Murder in the first.'

Max opened his hands in a gesture of conciliation. 'We're still looking at a *victim* here.'

Garrat gave me a quick look, but I couldn't read it. Conspiratorial? A plea for help? A friendly face? I had no idea where she was going. 'Missy Worth was never a suspect, Max, never looked at for possible involvement. I think before we make excuses for her fingerprints showing up on our murder weapon we need to get some answers.'

Max Dunn nearly exploded at this. 'You don't seriously think she was involved?'

Garrat looked at me. 'Rick has a theory.'

I cleared my throat, going slowly in case Garrat wanted to present it. 'There's some indication,' I said, 'that Booker knew his victims in advance. If that's the case, we don't know but that Missy and he had a relationship – maybe even planned the whole thing.'

Garrat spoke while Max and Rolly Tincher were still trying to get their jaws hinged back together. 'He put her in a grave and shot her through the dirt, Max. The slugs barely penetrated her flesh. Everyone just assumed he over-estimated the gun's power. Maybe he didn't. We could be looking at a partnership that only blew up when Missy lost her nerve and started telling Nat Hall and Herm Hammer what they wanted to hear.'

I nodded as though this made perfect sense. I was running on faith now. None of us had anything else to go on. But Max wasn't buying any of it and said so with a sullen fury. 'Going after victims is bad business,' he said solemnly. Bad politics, he meant.

Garrat's expression was one of quiet dismay. 'Rick?'

I blinked and managed to meet Garrat's questioning gaze. What did she want? Max was right, but I knew better than to say that. When in doubt, agree with the boss. 'I think we have to pursue it,' I said with as much conviction as I could muster.

Garrat looked gratified. 'I don't want this thing with the fingerprints to develop into what happened with Booker ten years ago, Max. I don't want it to even *seem* like we're headed down that road. I say we either pursue Missy Worth as an accomplice to murder or you go forward and correct yourself. You spoke too soon… full responsibility, etcetera, etcetera. Just what you told us here.'

Max, who had been gaining ground up to this point, suddenly had the look of wishing he could circle his wagons. He grabbed at his holster uncomfortably and cleared his throat. 'I'm not sure I'm quite ready to do that. Publicly, I mean. We'll have DNA on that jacket in a couple of weeks. At that point it might be better to bring up the thing about the prints not being good enough to admit into evidence.'

Garrat pondered this quietly for a moment before shaking her head. 'The trouble is the prints are good. If we diddle around and start telling white lies it looks like we're trying to fix the evidence again. When that gets out, and it has to come out sometime, *I'm* going to be implicated in the lie. That doesn't work for me, Max.'

'It wasn't a lie, Pat. It was a mistake!'

'It *was* a mistake. If we don't correct it this morning it becomes a lie – mine as well as yours.'

'Are you telling me that if I don't go to the press this morning, you will?' Max was hot. He expected cover from an ally – not this.

Garrat ignored the emotion and explained her proposition. 'If you were just going along with my office yesterday – with the aim of misleading Missy Worth before we interviewed her – I suppose we could let this thing drag out a few weeks and release a correction when absolutely no one would notice or care...'

'You mean you *asked* me to say they were Booker's prints?'

'Let's call it a cooperative decision, Max. Something we both understood we had to do.'

Max Dunn smiled like he had just been kissed by a beauty queen. 'I could live with that!'

Garrat turned to me almost as an afterthought. 'Rick, I want you to go after Missy Worth. Don't be afraid to push those prints at her. Let her know Max and I wanted to protect her from the media by claiming the prints we found belonged to Booker, but she had better know that if she does not cooperate fully, and I mean right now, I'm going for an indictment on three counts of murder. Then I want you to try to establish whatever patterns in the two cases that seem reasonable.' She looked up at Max. 'Max, are we going to have a problem if Rick noses around the Merriweather situation before you have handed us the case?'

Max was certain there weren't going to be any problems at all. 'Anything you want from my people, Rick, just say the word. You've got a free hand, buddy!' He finished his offer with a friendly wink, 'Might even throw in a get-out-of-jail-free-card for you, if you need one.'

Chapter 53

Friday 8:35 a.m., March 26.

AS SOON AS MAX Dunn and his chief of detectives beat a hasty retreat, Garrat gave Massey his orders in detail – what he was to say to the media and what he was to keep to himself. When she had finished, Massey asked about Garrat's decision to drop the charges on the very day he took off with two more victims. 'They're going to bring it up,' he said. 'You know they will the moment we have a news conference.'

'Tell them,' I growled, 'if they want to talk about history they should interview Connie Merriweather. It's not Pat Garrat's fault we dropped the charges! It's his!'

Garrat shook her head. 'Don't you dare mention Merriweather's name in that context, Steve.'

'So what do I tell them?'

'Tell them to interview Buford Lynch. He could have ordered a new trial without turning that monster loose.'

When Massey was gone, I took a seat by Garrat's big desk and told her, 'Max is right, you know. If we go after Missy Worth at this point we're going to look like cheap shot artists – even to Missy.'

'We've finally got some leverage on that woman, Rick. Let's use it. She knows something she hasn't told us. I want you to get it from her.'

'She's not afraid of jail, Pat.'

Garrat shook her head. 'This is not about jail. It's about linking her to the deaths of her sister and friends. You need to wake her up and make her see what her silence is going to cost.'

'I'll do what I can,' I said.

'No. I want you to get everything from that woman. I want you to hang her over a cliff if you have to!'

I was assuming Garrat meant that metaphorically. On my best day, I doubt I could have held Missy longer than a few seconds.

I WAS AT THE DOOR when Garrat called to me. I stopped and looked back at her.

'I got you in the game, Rick. It's what you wanted. Do whatever you need to do; chase down any lead you want. Max won't say a word at this point, but for the love of God find those girls before it's too late.'

Chapter 54

Darkness.

UPSTAIRS, WILL DOES NOT creep about as before but moves freely, fearlessly. Tabit and Penny and Tamara cower below. Boy with a broken leg and a bullet in his other knee is failing. Ben, who is where Will left him, is conscious, but the fight in him is gone. His lungs are bleeding. He is dying.

Will looks across the backyard. He checks to either side of the house. Nothing moving. No one coming. He goes down the stairs slowly, the ache in his muscles and bones making him nauseous. In the basement he sees Ben on his back, hears the sucking of his wound.

The man rolls his head and looks at Will. 'Please...' Will does not know if he pleads for death or life.

He walks on. He finds the others waiting for him in the darkness. He whispers for Penny to come with him. She comes to him fearfully. Will looks past her and sees

Tabit in the shadows holding her sister. Tamara weeps like a bride in an empty church. Boy alone looks at him. Boy does not speak. The pain has not yet taken all the hero out of him; he stares so Will and God will know what he would do if he still had two good legs and half a chance. But of course he doesn't.

'Shut the door,' Will tells Penny. When she has done this, Will tells her, 'I want to show you something, Penny.'

Ben Lyons is on his back, eyes still open. A soft sucking slurp breaks out of him with each breath. 'He's dying,' Will tells the girl. She stares numbly at her father. Eyes dry, she is mystified, not sad. Ben's eyes shift dumbly over his daughter's face. He is a man looking at a stranger. Will draws the Bernardelli from his pocket and puts it in Penny's hand.

He moves her wrist until the gun points down into her father's face. 'If you kill him for me, Penny, I'll let the rest of you live.' Father stares at daughter in wild, mute confusion. Penny still does not weep. 'Tell her, Ben,' Will whispers. 'Tell her it's for the best.' Ben's eyes begin to tear up. He turns away to stare at the wall. It is as close to giving permission as he can manage.

'*Now*, Penny,' Will whispers, 'and I promise you, it's over. You'll walk out of her with the others. I'll get in the car and drive away, and no one will ever have to know what you've done. The others won't even know, and I'll never tell. He's dying anyway. Why not save the living and bury the dead?'

She pushes against Will, wanting to lift the gun up to him, but Will holds her tightly. Left arm over her back, right hand to her right wrist. This is what she wants, to kill daddy, but first she must pretend to fight him. 'He *hates* you, Penny. You know I'm right. Always Benny. Everything for Benny. *Twins* in name only. You knew it long before he gave you to me so Benny could live.'

He feels her weakening, hears her weep. She would collapse if she could, but Will holds her to the truth like a hand to the flame. 'Does he ever tell you how much he loves you, Penny?' She nods, lying to Will about Ben's affection, but as she does it, her tears float on her eyelids. Her shoulders tremble. Not resisting what Will asks of her, but because she longs to do it. 'Does he ever tell you how *proud* of you he is, Penny?'

Will feels something move in her. He watches her eyes cooling. He feels her tender, formless body stiffen. Today is the day she has dreamed of – though she has never admitted such a desire even to herself. Today she has her revenge.

Holding her, Will feels the drawing of her breath, her muscles locking down. Ben feels it too. He *knows* he is about to die. He knows too it is for good reason! He shifts his gaze to Penny, his eyes filling with tears. 'Penny, please!'

'Do it!' Will hisses.

The gun clicks, and all three of them flinch. But that is all the sound there is. A Bernardelli holds only seven bullets.

241

Chapter 55

Friday 9:40 a.m., March 26.

'DID YOU BRING ME a beer?'

I sat down across from Missy Worth in a small room they used for counselling the patients. 'Have you heard?' I asked.

Her face went numb. 'A deputy came by yesterday. The parents came in last night. With it all over the news, it's kind of hard not to hear about it, even in here.' She hesitated awkwardly. 'So how soon will they know if it's really Mary?'

'If we get enough dental we ought to have it this morning. Otherwise, they'll have to try for a DNA match. That usually takes a few weeks.'

Missy Worth lost her focus for a moment. I could only guess that she was somewhere in the night ten years ago. 'The news said Will's prints were on some kind of club they found.'

'We asked the sheriff to lie about the prints until we could get your version of what happened.'

Missy Worth's face drained of colour but she managed to look at me with all the sincerity of a used car salesman. 'My *version*? What are you talking about?'

'Missy, I need to read you your rights before this goes any further.' She swore as I pulled one of Max's business cards out of my shirt pocket and read off the back of it, '*You have the right to remain silent…*'

It is a short speech full of good advice that no cop wants a suspect to take. A good con eventually learns to heed the words the high court insists that we read, but most are too impatient to find out what the cops know. They waive their rights, thinking they can lie their way through the tough spots. Of course, if they were predisposed to listen to good advice, they would have avoided the crime in the first place. I read Missy her rights for no other purpose than to get her attention, and it worked beautifully.

'I want a lawyer,' she told me flatly.

I smiled evenly, 'He's going to tell you to keep your mouth shut.'

'Then that's what I'd better do.'

'You clam up now and the prosecutor is going to charge you right alongside Will. Only choice you'll have is whether you two stand trial together or separately. You might not do time, but then again, you might get the needle. Hard to know what a jury is going to do

243

with bloody fingerprints on the murder weapon and a long history of violence.'

A little fear can trip a lot of switches, and I let this settle a good ten seconds.

'On the other hand,' I added, 'if you cooperate, Garrat will deal. Maybe a suspended sentence, maybe nothing at all. Depends on how fast you decide you want to be a good citizen.' Missy didn't answer me with much enthusiasm, so I pushed her a little. 'What you've got to realise here is we've got two kids in jeopardy, and you're the only person in the world with a clue as to what's really going on.'

'I don't know what's going on!' She tried to stare right through me as she told me this.

'You lied about not knowing Will before the attack. I want to know why.'

'I want my lawyer.'

'You think a lawyer can talk your fingerprints off that bat, Missy? You think getting two girls killed because you wouldn't cooperate is going to win a jury's sympathy?'

'I got nothing to do with that preacher's two kids!'

The prosecutor thinks you might have set things up, that maybe the other night Will Booker showed up at your door and told you he wanted some help and you gave it to him.'

'That's crazy! I never even talked to the guy. I told you, I didn't even see him!'

244

'Garrat thinks you're lying about that too. She's looked at your record; says the only thing that could scare *you* as bad as you were last Sunday is a long heart-to-heart with your old partner.'

'*Partner*?'

'I've got to tell you, Missy, people are going to be looking for blood after this thing finishes. Once they get like that, they'll believe whatever the prosecutor tells them.'

'I've got nothing to do with what's happening with those girls!'

'Garrat says she'll take you to trial herself.'

'I can't believe this.' Missy was shaking her head. 'I didn't set anyone up!'

'So tell me what really happened ten years ago. Maybe I can change Garrat's mind on this thing.'

Her big face set itself like a piece of plaster: cold and white, hard and vulnerable. 'It happened like I said.'

I didn't even blink.

'Okay, some of it was...' Missy stopped. 'She's got to deal with me. And I want it in writing. I'm not saying nothing until I get a deal!'

'I've got to take her something if I'm going to get her to offer you a deal, Missy.'

Missy was quiet for nearly three minutes. I never stopped looking at her, never gave her the chance to evade me. Finally, she shook her head. 'I didn't know him, like you think. Lisa did. She scored some grass from him a couple of times. Had *a thing* for him, I guess. We were meeting him that night at North Shore to do some coke. That's all I know that I didn't already tell.'

'Had you ever seen Will before that night at North Shore Point?'

'Me? I knew what he looked like, but like I said, I never met him. Lisa went to see him at the Student Union Grill one time. I was with her. I didn't talk to him. He sold her some grass; said something about getting some coke at the end of the week. If we all wanted to get high with him, all we had to do was meet him at North Shore that Friday.'

'Did he know the boys were coming along?'

Her eyes shifted so that she was staring at me suddenly. Times past were long gone. The gal I was looking at knew the system: when to give it out and when to hold it back. 'You got your good faith, sweet cheeks. Now go tell your boss I want my lawyer *and* I want immunity – in writing. Then I'll tell you the rest.'

'Is the rest worth hearing?'

She reached for her cigarettes and pulled one free. She lit it and watched its glow. I'd seen walls more likely to make a confession.

Chapter 56

GARRAT WAS IN CITY HALL meeting with the mayor when I found her. 'Our girl wants immunity before she gives us anything,' I said once I had pulled her out to the corridor. Garrat shook her head angrily, but I stopped her before she answered. 'I found out one thing, though.' Her pretty blues flashed expectantly. 'They were all meeting Booker at North Shore Point, Pat.'

'Like you thought.'

I nodded. 'He was apparently coming on to Lisa Chenoweth. Sold her a bag of dope at the Student Union.'

'Assuming we can convince a jury this isn't just another story –'

'We can run it down now that we know where to look; that's not a problem. The thing is she's got more. I don't know what it is, but she claims she's not talking without immunity.'

'Is it going to help us find the Merriweather girls?'

I let one shoulder kick up. Who knew?

'I'll send Massey over and see what we can work up, but to hell with getting her a lawyer; I don't need this thing about the fingerprints getting out just yet. In the meantime, why don't you get with Connie Merriweather.

I shook my head. 'I'm headed to Graysville Prison. Talk to some of the cons; make some offers. Besides we already got a report on the Merriweathers from the sheriff's department. There's nothing there.'

'Max and the preacher had a pretty good fight Sunday night, Rick. I'm guessing it coloured the interviews on both sides.'

'Rolly did the primary interview,' I told her.

'Rolly couldn't get a tape recorder to talk, Rick. Work the guy. Take your time with him. If you want to know what Will Booker is all about, Merriweather is your man. I guarantee you he knows more than any con at Graysville.'

'Merriweather got eight years of lies, Pat.'

'You don't want to talk to the man?'

'I'm afraid I'll wring his neck.'

'I expect right now he would thank you for the kindness. Look, it will cost you an hour or two. If nothing pans out there, you can still get over to Graysville this afternoon. I'll even call the warden for you.'

'I'll make you a deal,' I offered with a grin. 'I'll go swap sweet nothings with the preacher if you work Missy Worth *personally*.'

'You don't think Massey can handle her?'

I gave a lonesome shrug, 'All I know is Missy Worth told me she didn't think you had the guts to come see her.'

'Really?'

'Something about that prissy county prosecutor...'

'*Prissy?*'

Chapter 57

Darkness.

'WHAT DID HE WANT?' TABIT ASKED.

Penny Lyons didn't answer.

'Penny...?' Again she did not respond. Tabit shivered and felt Tammy pulling closer to her, taking the role of the younger sister as she often did when things went badly. Tabit was sick with fear and Tammy's clinging forced her to be braver than she felt. She wanted Tammy to let go of her. She wanted to cry her own tears!

Tabit could not erase the image of Mr Lyons being shot. She saw the shells spinning in lonely arcs to the floor, the spray of blood like a mist off his chest. Then she remembered Will shooting Benny in the knee. The way he had smiled just before he did it!

Something beautiful, she whispered for only God to hear. Something to carry her to the end, she meant. But all that came to answer her prayer was the most horrible thing she had ever witnessed. She closed her eyes to the darkness and pulled her sister close, suddenly as hungry for touch as Tammy. She thought to pray, because there was nothing left to do *but* pray. When she tried there were no words for God. No words. No beautiful thing. No peace. No God at all. Not if he let such things as this happen.

'Dad's alive,' Penny announced.

A voice out of the dark, a sigh of pain. Benny's voice. 'Did he say anything?'

'He said he loved us,' Penny answered with a whisper. 'He said he loves *all* of us. He says we have to hang on.'

Chapter 58

Friday 11:30 a.m., March 26.

I WAVED AT THE SHERIFF'S deputy with a lone finger rising off my steering wheel. He was parked on a side street at the back of the Merriweather house. I drove on around to the front and put a tire in some deep snow close to the Merriweather lawn. Two other cars were parked the same way. Both of them FBI-issue.

I went directly to the front door. A federal agent opened it and made quite a show of checking my credentials. Then he said he would go see if the reverend could talk. A moment later, he came back, followed by a trim middle-aged woman. I decided she must be Mrs Merriweather.

'Pastor's resting,' she offered simply as the agent vanished into the shadows to wait with his partner for Will Booker's call for a ransom.

I tried out her name and was informed coolly that

she was not Mrs Merriweather. That gave me a little encouragement and I said, 'Tell him it's important.'

'He's already talked to the sheriff. I don't see that he needs to go through all this again.'

'And you are?'

'Louise Robbins.'

'Ms Robbins, get Dr Merriweather out here or I'll go in and wake him up myself.' From the look on her face, I might have said I'd kick his ass. Louise Robbins disappeared in something of a huff. A few minutes later Connie Merriweather appeared. He was alone, blinking, disoriented. It was late in the morning, working toward the lunch hour, actually, and I realized I'd probably interrupted the man's first sleep since his kids had been snatched.

'What is it?' he asked.

Connie Merriweather was about as friendly as Louise Robbins. I introduced myself as congenially as circumstances allowed and shook the big man's hand. The guy towered over me, too. I figured six feet, eight inches, but he could have been taller. 'Sorry to intrude, Dr Merriweather. I know it's a trying time for you and your wife, but I'd like to talk to you about Will Booker.'

'I've been through this with Detective Tincher.'

'Yes, sir, I know that, and I expect you'd do it a thousand times more if you thought it would help us find your two girls.'

Connie Merriweather thought about this. 'Come on back to the kitchen.'

The kitchen held a tight, worn group of folks from the minister's church. They looked to be living on stale coffee and desperate prayers. Introductions were quick and cool. I was an outsider, come to stir the pain up again. The prosecutor's own. To their thinking that was still the enemy camp. 'I suppose the first thing *Miss* Garrat wants to hear,' Merriweather offered with a grim smile, 'is that she was right, and I was wrong.'

'What Ms Garrat wants is what we all want: your girls back home safely. You can help by giving me as much information as you can think of.'

Connie Merriweather shook his head. 'I don't have any information.'

'The daughter he left the hospital with…'

'Tammy.'

'She's the older of the two?'

Merriweather nodded. 'She's eighteen.'

'And the younger girl is Tabitha?'

'Tabit. Says Tabitha is a witch.' There was a fond smile with this, and I liked the man with a suddenness I hadn't expected. A fool for his cause, but a man all the same. A father with losses I could calculate all too well. 'She turned sixteen a few months ago.'

Tears came to the preacher's eyes but the voice didn't quite break. I felt sick at my stomach watching his misery. I was sure I had been as bad when Sarah had vanished. Break anything, weep, swear, roar. But nothing changes because of it. A missing child is a rock that won't break.

'Do you have any pictures of the girls?' I asked.

'The sheriff has been provided with pictures,' one of the men answered sharply. He had a name, but I'd already forgotten it. I didn't back down. I'd seen the pictures they had provided the sheriff, but I wanted Connie Merriweather to show me his girls. I wanted to know just what they were like, from his perspective. Getting a man to show you pictures of his kids will tell you what speeches never can.

'There's a good one of them both in the family room,' Merriweather announced. 'I can't let it go, but if you'd like to see it...' The preacher looked at another of the men sitting at the table, and the fellow rose to get the photograph. 'The church has been here from the start,' the minister explained, almost as an afterthought. It was something to fill the gap, at the same time a way to give the others around the table a thank you.

'I bet you've had a lot of phone calls from friends,' I said, 'people dropping by...' I remembered my own house packed to the brim sometimes, empty at others. Strangers wandering around, the perfect chaos of it.

'Actually, the deacons organized a few people to come around to the house in shifts. And we put the word out to keep the phone lines free, in case Will wants to call.'

I looked at the others. Not the closest friends, but there on assignment.

'We have a prayer line,' one of the men told me, as if he imagined I was curious. 'Everyone has three or four people to call. We can get the word out pretty fast when we want to!'

'We're a big church,' Connie Merriweather told me, 'but we're close. Like a family, I mean.' He looked at his parishioners, friends for years, if I read the look right. 'We've got a couple hundred people at the church day and night reciting prayers and singing hymns.'

'It's more like five hundred this morning, Pastor,' Louise Robbins announced primly.

Merriweather nodded, and then dropped his gaze. 'Rachel went down this morning for the first time,' he told me. 'I'll go this afternoon.' He thought about it quietly, then added, 'First time.'

The man returned with a photo and Merriweather took it from him. 'I shot that last fall at a retreat,' Merriweather announced fondly. His eyes swept over the thing. 'Just a snap shot, but it was so good we had it...' Merriweather hesitated, gathering his control, then seemed to forget to finish his thought.

I considered the two girls without comment. So young. So perfectly innocent, and I wondered again how a man could be so stupid and proud and stubborn as to put them in harm's way. The older, Tammy, was a big, soft girl with chalky eyes and straw-blonde hair. A double chin, rosy cheeks, a kid's smile. Even at eighteen, despite her weight, she had no real breasts to speak of: a little cherub, right out of a Rubens painting, giggling on cloud tops. The other, Tabit, was trim and pretty. She had her father's dark features and the same sharp little nose. Small breasts, tight hips caught in a candid little wiggle, a smile that was full of an uncommon grace for one so young. A sexuality beyond her years.

'Did Will show interest in either girl?' I asked, lifting my gaze up suddenly on the preacher.

Connie Merriweather shook his head. 'He was a perfect gentleman, Mr Trueblood. Never a look that was out of place. Nothing that anyone could... no. Nothing. If I'd even thought...'

'What about the girls? Did either of them show interest in him?'

'No.' This was too quick, and Merriweather seemed to reconsider. 'Well, I don't know if that's true. Rachel seemed to think Tammy had a schoolgirl crush on Will.'

I took this without comment. Tammy was the one at the hospital when Booker disappeared. She was also the kid Will Booker had been with when Clint Doolittle attacked him. Predator that he was, Will Booker hadn't tried for *pretty*.

'Do you have children, Mr Trueblood?' Merriweather asked me.

The question startled me, and I answered him before I had time to consider a dodge. 'I had a girl.'

The eyes narrowed, softened. 'The law student down in Attica?'

I nodded and looked out the window to the blue sky beyond. 'Sarah.'

'The name Trueblood was familiar. I thought...' he hesitated. 'I'm sorry.'

'It was years ago,' I said. Eight and counting. Nothing had changed for me, but I knew the rest of the world had moved on. I pretended time had healed my loss some. It was the kind of lie that made it easier for people to deal with me.

Merriweather's eyes went wet and distant. 'Her death happened not long after Will was imprisoned,' he said thoughtfully. 'I always thought there might be a connection between your daughter's murder and what happened with the kids Will was convicted of killing.'

'I read the theories,' I said. I kept my voice flat, neutral. I didn't tell him what I thought at the time, the hatred I had had for him; how I had felt like he was contaminating my girl's life with his far-flung theories in defence of a killer. Sarah deserved better than to end up as an alibi for William Booker.

'You must know what this is like,' the big man told me quietly, his voice trembling.

I didn't answer him. All death is private. A lost child is like no other. I had some idea of his pain. He had some idea of mine. There are many mansions in heaven. A lot of tiny rooms in hell.

Chapter 59

Friday 11:50 a.m., March 26.

'YOU KNOW,' MERRIWEATHER TOLD me after we had talked a while about the day of the abduction of his two girls, 'I keep thinking I could have done something...'

'Pastor...' A hand reaching out to shut him up.

But Connie Merriweather shook his head. 'The old man sharing Will's room told me Will had taken a walk with some pretty girl. I thought he meant... well, I didn't know what he meant. If I had just asked!' He shook his head miserably, tears taking his eyes again.

'Was the old man at the hospital in your congregation?' I asked. I was having trouble understanding the sequence of events, especially Merriweather's long talk with some old codger. But for that, Merriweather might have stopped this thing before it began.

'A parishioner? No. He was... what I like to call

pre-saved. Primed and ready for the Lord. Just needing a little push. Wanted to talk Bible. Seems Will had...' The big man blinked and gave me the most miserable smile I have ever witnessed. 'Will was talking to him about the Book of Job, Mr Trueblood. Do you know it?'

'I know Job suffered,' I said. 'I haven't read the story for a long time.'

The preacher looked at me like I was lying, but he didn't call me on it. I *had* read it. I had read the whole Bible cover-to-cover after Sarah's death. I just didn't want to be quizzed on it. 'The old man thought it was strange that God and the devil would sit down and hash things out face-to-face, even make a wager.'

'That *is* a bit unusual, isn't it?' I asked.

'Singular,' the minister answered. 'Nowhere else in scripture do they even talk with one another.'

'Any idea why the Book of Job would interest Booker?'

'Will knows his Bible, Mr Trueblood. The last ten years, it's all he's studied; the only thing he'll read. He won't even watch television. As for a computer, he won't touch one of those!'

'Yes, sir. But was he especially fond of Job?'

'Not especially,' Merriweather answered. 'But you have to realize Will thinks *biblically*, if that makes sense to you.'

'I'm afraid it doesn't.'

Merriweather gave a quick, strained look at one of

the others. This was something they had discussed among themselves but hadn't bothered giving Max Dunn or Rolly Tincher. 'The wager Satan made with the Lord is about Job's faith – whether he'll keep it or lose it when ruin hits.'

I frowned, not quite getting it. 'You think this is all some kind of test?'

'The whole point, as far as Will's concerned.' He smiled gently. It was a look I had seen at funeral homes.

'The point being...?' I asked.

'Connie...'

Merriweather was crying again, but his voice held together reasonably. 'The first thing that happens after the wager, Mr Trueblood, is a mighty wind comes and blows a building down. It kills all of Job's children.'

Chapter 60

Friday 12:05 p.m., March 26.

PAT GARRAT'S SECRETARY called ahead to arrange
an interview. When Garrat arrived, Missy Worth was
sullen. She was missing lunch and made a point of
mentioning it. Then, lighting a cigarette, cool as an old
con doing twenty: 'I told that bald guy that works for
you I want a lawyer.'

Garrat sat down without greeting the woman. 'His
name is Rick Trueblood.'

'Whatever. I still want a lawyer.'

'He wants me to cut you a deal, but I'm not sure
that's in my best interest.' The hollow dark eyes came
into quick focus. Old what's-his-name wasn't such a
bad Joe, maybe.

'If you want me to talk, I have to get immunity. In
writing. Approved by my lawyer.'

Full of confidence, this one. Holding hostages with

her silence. Garrat's smile was as thin as piano wire. 'Enjoy your lunch, because when you are done with it, the next one is going to be courtesy of the sheriff.'

Garrat had made it to the door when Missy Worth called out. Garrat stopped, turned and faced the younger woman. 'What?' she asked.

'You need to work on your sense of humour,' Missy told her sourly.

Garrat returned to the woman but didn't sit down. 'Let's get something straight right now. I'm the county prosecutor, not your girlfriend and not someone else's flunky. If you want to play games with me, I'll bring ten tons of grief down on your sorry head. You think you know how things work? Spent a few nights in jail, call your bail bondsman by his first name? Go ahead and play your games, Missy, but I'll tell you right now, you don't know what a murder indictment is going to do to you. First of all, forget about ever getting out. You'll sit in the county jail until I can find room in my schedule to take you to trial. You can write your job off. If you're financing anything... like a motorcycle, maybe? By the time you get out, assuming I don't get you convicted, it will be repossessed. You got friends? Forget them. Oh, they'll be allowed to come visit, but they won't make it. They never do when it comes to murder. Best you get with a murder indictment is your mother – unless you're accused of killing your own sister. That leaves you batting your eyes at your court-appointed attorney, and if you think I've got a lousy sense of humour, wait until you try one of those kids in legal services.'

'You made your point.'

'I don't think I have. I don't think you know what kind of hole you've fallen into, lady.'

Missy Worth held Garrat's gaze only a few seconds before she turned away. She pulled at her cigarette and blew the smoke out angrily. 'I need a deal,' she answered. 'I don't want to serve time.'

'Here's *my* deal. Tell me the truth right now. That's your only chance of avoiding an indictment for murder.'

'I want my lawyer here so you don't pull any tricks!'

'No lawyer. Just you and me. I can't use it against you. You know that as well as I do. I refused you a lawyer. Anything you tell me now will never get to court, but if you turn me down so help me God I'll see you get a lawyer, because you'll need one. I'll have you indicted for obstruction, conspiracy, and murder-in-the-first before the sun goes down.'

'Look, we knew Will was coming out to the lake. We were going to get high with him. He drove up, but he didn't come down the hill. Ricky and Chuck went up to see what the problem was, and that was when he killed them. Then he came down the hill, like I said. He broke Lisa's leg when she tried to run, and he took us all to that farm. After that I don't remember much of it.'

'You're wasting my time, lady.' Garrat started for the door.

'Do you want to know what I remember?' Her hand on the doorknob, Garrat stopped and studied the big woman. Missy Worth took a drag of her cigarette and blew it into her lap quickly. The sound was strangely like laughter. 'What I remember is Will telling me how pretty I was. How the others didn't like me because they knew I was going to be prettier than any of them. Stuff like that.'

Garrat stepped back into the centre of the small room, 'While he was raping you?'

Her eyes shifted nervously, 'I lied about the rape.'

'Why would you do that?'

'Sheriff Hall came up with all that. I mean... once they knew I wasn't a virgin they asked me if he had raped me. I lied. I mean at least I didn't have to explain about all that.'

'He didn't rape *any* of you?'

'What he did, he *talked* to me. He told me stuff. Okay?'

Garrat shook her head in confusion, 'It's not okay. I don't understand what you're telling me. What did he talk to you about?'

'He would say things like the others didn't understand me, they didn't like me, they only put up with me because of Mary...'

Missy seemed to draw into herself strangely, to get

265

smaller and more timid as she confided this. She did not look at Garrat as she spoke.

'He did the same thing with the others?'

She shook her head; her eyes had gone off to other times. 'It was just me. He never talked to anyone but me.'

'Why?'

'I don't know!'

'What was the point? What did he want from you?'

'He wanted me to kill them!'

Garrat sat down. 'Wanted *you* to kill them?'

Missy Worth stared at the wall, her voice breaking like a child's as tears poured across her cheeks, 'He said if I would just kill... just *one*. If I killed one of them... I could... *we* could all go free. We wouldn't all have to die. Just that *one*...'

'Look at me, Missy.' The eyes found Garrat. '*You* killed the others?'

Missy Worth shook her head, but she wasn't denying it. 'I can't do time. I don't want to do time. He made me do it!'

'Listen to me. I need to know exactly what is happening with the two girls he has taken.'

'I don't know!'

'He's got two girls, Missy. Two *sisters*. Like you and Mary. Now I want you to tell me what he's doing with them!'

Missy had the look of someone reporting a nightmare;

the terror of it had faded but that did not mean it would not come again. 'One of them... he's talking to her. Telling her she's got to do it, got to kill her sister...'

'He's not raping her?'

'Will's not interested in that. He's just talking. Telling her things. Trying to... I don't know. Trying to steal her soul!'

'Threats? Violence?'

'Not against the one he's talking to! I mean... he just keeps asking her to do it. He says she's pretty, says things about... what the others have said about her.'

'What others?'

Missy looked up, not understanding the question. 'I mean... that's what he told me.'

'Did he let you live, Missy? Was that the deal?'

'He said he would, but then...'

'He put you in the ground?'

She nodded, the tears coming in warm gushes. 'AND THEN HE SHOT ME!'

'Listen to me. I need to know if he hurt you before that. You said he made you do it. Did he hurt you when you resisted him, force you somehow?'

Missy Worth shook her head.

'He didn't hurt you?'

'HE JUST TALKS! He talks until she can't... she can't think straight anymore. She's so hungry and tired and cold and if she just does what he says she can go home!'

'That's what he told you. Just kill *one* of them?'

267

Missy nodded.

'And you hit her with the bat?'

Missy could only nod.

'*You* buried her?'

Nodding.

'And the next one?'

Missy Worth's head rocked forward, her tears still falling, 'He kept telling me the others would live, but when I gave him Lisa he wanted Kathy. And then he made me give him Mary! I DIDN'T KNOW HE WOULD JUST KEEP ASKING!' Now a whisper, 'I thought I could save us! *Some* of us, anyway...'

Chapter 61

Friday 12:30 p.m., March 26.

IS THIS ALL FOR THE GIRLS?' I asked, pointing at the cars in the church parking lot. I estimated something over three hundred vehicles on a Friday lunch hour.

The minister nodded. 'They tell me there are some folks here who showed up Wednesday night and have been here ever since. I'm just sorry I didn't come sooner. This is where I belong.'

I shut off my car engine. 'Now look,' I said, 'I don't quite get this bit about the wager between God and the devil. Did you ever talk to Will about it?'

'I can't remember if we did. All I can recall is that Will had some questions about Job's *perfection.*'

'When was this?'

'This winter, maybe. February, I expect it was...'

'Just a few weeks ago?'

Merriweather hesitated. 'I think that's about right.'

'By then he knew he was going to get out?'

'It was looking very good by that point. Look, we talked Bible by the hour, Mr Trueblood; I don't remember everything we covered. You see, Will was concerned about his legal situation, but it didn't matter to him as much as knowing the Lord. He always had some kind of question for me. Always wanted to talk Bible!'

'So what was the issue with *perfection*?'

'Only Christ is without sin, so Will wanted to know why Job was called *perfect*. It's mostly a translation problem with the particular Bible Will uses, and that's about how I dealt with it.' He heaved a sigh. 'Then I believe I told him what I tell everyone, that the wager is the same wager God makes with the devil for every soul. The whole thing – all of life – is about us keeping faith in the face of tragedy and heartache and loss.'

'I thought Job was about suffering.'

'That's Job's perspective, certainly, but the truth is, what happens to Job will eventually happen to all of us: a time comes when evil things happen to us for no good reason. Not caused by our own sins, but just life! The more faithful we are to our Lord, the more unjust it seems, and, naturally, the more alone we feel because of it. That's when we keep our faith or we lose it. The dark night of the soul, Mr Trueblood. I expect you know about that.'

'So what happens?'

'Oh, in the end Job keeps his faith.'

'I mean with Connie Merriweather. Does *he* keep *his* faith?'

The smile that had crossed his face as he preached his homily now began to quiver, and in the preacher's dark eyes, I could see something of a debate going on, whether to tell me the truth or pass out the platitudes. As I was a stranger, I think Connie Merriweather elected to go all the way. He pointed at the steeple over us. 'You see this church, Mr Trueblood?' I gave it a cursory look to be polite. It was a big showy piece of brick and glass that made me uncomfortable with its vanity. 'I've lost it,' he told me simply. 'They're all with me now. My God, they're suffering almost as much as Rachel and I. But no matter what, I'll be gone inside a year. We won't quibble about whose choice it's going to be. I'll just be gone. Now I'm not a pessimist, but I can't imagine Will letting Tabit and Tammy live. He'll... he'll give me just exactly what the devil gave Job. *All* his children dead. If that happens, Rachel will never forgive me, so I'll lose her as well. I know that, the same as Will knows it. Truth is I've lost her already. She can't bear the sight of me. I can't really blame her. The other night, once I understood what had happened and what Will meant to do, I cursed God and all his angels in heaven.'

I looked away, sorry I had asked. I had wanted to

hurt the man with my question about his faith, especially after his dark-night-of-the-soul remark that he had aimed so purposefully at me, but I wanted no man to hurt as this one was.

'And then I woke up and saw the truth.' I forced myself to look at the preacher now, because I was sure he was going to tell me the truth was that there is no God, but Connie Merriweather was a thousand miles away, 'God didn't do this to me. Will Booker and *I* made this mess. Curse God?' The preacher almost laughed, 'The truth is God's all I have left.'

Chapter 62

Friday 12:40 p.m., March 26.

WITH OVER A HUNDRED PEOPLE milling about in the church commons on a continuous basis, there was food for the asking. At the sight of it I realized how hungry I was. I left Merriweather to his friends and parishioners and found a nice enough woman offering me a plate and no sermon attached.

While I dished up my lunch, Connie Merriweather moved through the crowd, shaking hands, hugging folks, listening and nodding and laughing and crying. He wasn't telling anyone anything for the moment, but I knew his breed enough to expect a speech by and by. Before he committed it, I wolfed down some slaw and beans and got my bearings. I had come inside the church chiefly so I could talk with Rachel Merriweather. When I asked about her, one of the ladies pointed her out to me. As it happened, I should have been able to guess which one she was. Rachel Merriweather was the woman who was always physically as far from the preacher as anyone in the room. When Connie Merriweather finally stepped up on a little platform to make his speech, she was the only one in the room who walked out.

I followed her, hearing at my back the amplified voice of Connie Merriweather, who had cursed God and believed they were still buddies because he had said he was sorry. 'I've preached Christian charity my whole life,' he announced, 'but I don't think I ever understood it until now.' He was a talker, that one. Good enough to build a church this big and fool enough to keep talking until he had torn it back down again.

I was in a long narrow hall and gaining on Mrs Merriweather when I called her name. 'I wonder if I could have a word with you,' I said when she stopped and turned to face me. I put my badge and ID away after she studied it and let her lead me to a small room where she said we wouldn't be interrupted. The tag on the door called it a study. It felt more like something you find in the new prisons. It was sterile and full of institutional furniture that will look like junk faster than bread stales.

Rachel Merriweather was close to her husband's age, somewhere just under fifty, a trim youthful looking woman all the same. She was tired, angry, frightened... and beautiful. 'What exactly do you want?' she asked me.

'Your husband said you were worried about Tammy having a crush on Will Booker.'

The woman smiled. I had no idea if it was because she had expected something else from me or if the thought of her daughter had triggered the reaction. It was a sad, gentle smile. 'Tammy's an awfully pretty girl but she has a weight problem, Mr Trueblood. A bit like her father. *Big-boned* we used to say.'

Big-boned myself, I answered her quickly, 'Some of us still call it that.'

'In Tammy's case, bulimic is probably closer to it. Did Connie tell you that?'

'You think Will played to her vulnerabilities?'

'I don't think she would exercise much judgement if someone gave her the slightest bit of attention, if that's what you mean.' She thought about it quietly. 'I tried to tell Connie that, but all he could think about was Will.'

'You felt differently about Will's innocence, I take it?'

Rachel looked at me without accusation or judgment, 'Are you a believer, Mr Trueblood?'

'I'm of the opinion we hold the world up and God holds us,' I said.

She smiled gently, 'I've never quite heard it put that way. Most people either believe or they don't, but I think very few believers actually *know* their Lord. Will had such faith and love of God, I think it moved all of us to trust him more than we should have.'

'You don't think it was an act?'

'I see *acts* all the time. For Will, God is as real as you and I. It's just that...' Rachel Merriweather closed her eyes, '...he is a very sick young man.'

I hurried her past this, for both of our sakes. 'What can you tell me about Tabit?'

'Tabit's more careful than her sister.' Again the gentle, tender smile. 'Will fascinated her, but she isn't so impetuous. I wasn't worried about her falling under his spell. She's not really emotional at all. Well, that's not right. Her emotions aren't on the surface. She's deeper than her sister. Deeper than any of us, I think sometimes.'

'Strong faith?'

'Both of our girls walk with the Lord, Mr Trueblood. It's what's going to get them through this.'

Chapter 63

Friday 1:07 p.m., March 26.

THE BULK OF MY INTERVIEW with Rachel
Merriweather involved pragmatic issues, all of which Rolly
Tincher had already covered, but I took her through a
series of questions anyway. I knew Rolly would focus on
the preacher, thinking because he had such a loud voice
he would know a lot more than his pretty wife. My bet
was Rachel Merriweather missed nothing, and I kept
asking her questions until I had confirmed my theory.

As we headed back to the commons, a woman came
toward us and called out to me, 'Oh, there you are! I
said you had left. You had a call.'

I PULLED MY PHONE OUT AND TURNED it on.
Garrat. She wanted to see me as soon as possible. When
I found her she was alone in her office, staring out her
window. 'What have you got?' I asked.

'Missy Worth did it.'

I laughed; I really thought she was making a joke. 'What are you talking about?'

'After Booker killed the two boys and took the girls off to that farm, he spent the next thirteen days talking Missy into killing her friends.'

'My God.'

'She was locked in a room, Rick. She got next to nothing to drink and eat. She never saw the sun. He pulled her out and bargained with her, pleaded, lied, whatever it took, until murder just finally made sense. The first murder was the girl whose leg he had broken. They were supposed to be set free after that. She killed the next one to save her sister. And then she killed her sister to save herself.'

I thought about the broken skull of her sister. Missy Worth had crushed it with that blood-splattered club Max Dunn had dug up. 'What are you going to do – charge her?' I asked her.

'I'm thinking about what this means for the Merriweather girls.'

'You think one of them is holding a bat on the other one right now?'

'We know Booker can kill people, but that's not what made him grab these two girls. He wants one of them to turn on the other. He wants to set up a situation that he can control with just his promises. He wants to turn one victim against the other. That's what this is about.'

'Connie Merriweather tells me he thinks this is about the Book of Job.'

'Excuse me?'

'Booker was talking to an old man at the hospital about Job the night before he took off.'

'Help me out here, Rick. It's been a while.'

'According to Merriweather, God and the devil make a wager over Job's soul. They want to know if Job will curse God if things get bad enough. The first thing the devil does, he kills all of Job's children.'

'Not what I wanted to hear.'

I lifted my hands, palm upwards, a weariness I had not known for years sapping me suddenly. 'Religious fanatic acts out a divine vision, then takes his own life. It just has that kind of feel about it.'

'We have to call Max.'

Chapter 64

Friday 4:05 p.m., March 26.

THE MINUTE MAX Dunn found out what we had, he called the city and state police, then more reluctantly the local FBI special agent in charge. Emergency meeting.

Garrat brought Steve Massey, Linda Sutherlin, and me to the meeting, which was just down the hall from the prosecutor's offices. Max had Rolly Tincher sit with him as well as his chief deputy and SWAT commander, Joe Roby. Roby was in his late forties, a lean, tough man with steel coloured hair that he kept cropped short. He had eyes that look fitted for gun sights. His counterpart with the city was at the meeting as well. Cass McCreary was a tall honey-blonde woman nearly forty years old, though no one would guess it looking at her. McCreary had begun her career in Shiloh Springs sixteen years ago as a decoy. She could still pass on the streets for a kid selling it to keep body and soul together but these days she ran intelligence for the city and was a key player in the state's task force on drugs. She also commanded the city's SWAT team. If we had a save anywhere in Shiloh County, both Roby's and McCreary's teams would be involved.

Chief Cottrell made the meeting as well as his assistant chief of detectives Bobby DeWitt. By chance, the state police detective assisting the investigation wasn't available. The post had sent Lt. Commander Jerry Powell in his place. I had served with Powell for a number of years. It was a comfort seeing him involved in this thing. Powell was a straight-shooter, blessed with that most rare of all qualities, good common sense.

The wild card in this brew was the FBI's new agent-in-charge at Shiloh Springs. Winston Fortney was not the intrusive Fed we had all feared. He was a corpulent man with a quick smile and a pleasant manner, the last fellow in the world you'd pick to be a cop, let alone FBI. He was more like a life insurance salesman with all the ragged edges trimmed and tucked. I liked him at once, but I had to keep reminding myself that he had the power to turn Will Booker into a federal case, leaving us all off the dance card.

Our meeting convened at just after four o'clock that afternoon. Max Dunn apologized for the inconvenience of such a hurried meeting but said the information we had gathered was critical. 'With any luck it just maybe helps us put the puzzle together.' As the sheriff related to the others what Garrat and I had given him, the expectancy he had stirred in them turned to horror. 'Son of a bitch!' Roby hissed. 'You're saying he gets his victims to do the killing for him?'

'It's what he did last time,' Garrat answered.

Agent Fortney nodded. 'A variation of the Stockholm syndrome. The hostage begins to identify with the hostage-taker rather than the police. All sense of perspective is lost. Finally she thinks her salvation is linked to his.'

Frank Cottrell nodded and mentioned the Hearst case, explicating the thing as if none of us had ever heard of Patty Hearst.

'There's a difference here,' I said. 'In the classic scenario, the rage is turned out toward the police, the government, and the population in general. They're not there to help, they're the cause of the problem... that kind of thing. Will Booker turned Missy Worth against *one* girl. He made her the reason he couldn't let the others go. Not so much siding with Booker as letting loose her own rage at her captivity. After the first murder he used Missy's guilt to leverage the next kill. By the time it came to Mary, Missy was terrified of dying the way the others had. So she gave up her own sister on Booker's promise that he would set her free.'

'Something else we need to look at, too,' Garrat told us. 'It seems Will Booker was talking about the Book of Job the evening before he took off with the two girls.' She described the devil's wager with God, and then told them flatly, 'According to Connie Merriweather, the first thing that happened was the devil killed all of Job's children.'

Bobby DeWitt, our resident born-again, smiled at us all condescendingly. 'It's not the *first* thing that happens, Pat.'

'I'm quoting Merriweather, Bobby.'

'Well, he's wrong.'

'*Again*,' I said.

Linda Sutherlin smiled. I don't think my humour registered with the others, because Max roared over my line, 'Well, let's see what happens *first*; somebody get a Bible!'

Somebody was Rolly Tincher. He waddled out of the sheriff's conference room and called to someone in the sheriff's main office that he needed a damn Bible. I saw Bobby DeWitt dip his chin and close his eyes. I expect he wanted to be spared the bolt of lightning God should have sent down on us.

Less than a minute later Rolly came back into the room. 'Ain't nobody's got a Bible, Max. You want a patrol car to find one?'

'I've got one in my office,' DeWitt answered. 'I'll go get it. It's a Gideon,' he offered, as if we might refuse him on that count, then he almost blushed, 'I stole it from a motel room before I found the Lord.'

'Booker reads King James,' I said.

'King James *Revised*?'

Max shook his head like a man about to draw his weapon. 'Just get the thing, Bobby!'

Cottrell nodded his permission and DeWitt took off.

While he was gone, Garrat outlined Merriweather's theory of a test of faith, including the ruin that came to Job. Agent Fortney suggested it was possible the two scenarios were both in operation here. 'One sister takes the other's life; then Booker finishes it by killing the second one. Not much different from what he did with Missy Worth and the three girls.'

'The past seven years,' I said, 'Will Booker has hardly had his nose out of that book. I've read the experts: I know what they all say about *signatures*, but I think realistically there's a good chance Booker is operating under a new set of rules these days.'

Powell nodded thoughtfully. 'The old is passed away.'

'Plus,' I said, 'the last time we had four victims locked up. With just the two girls the whole dynamic has to be different.'

'Maybe he's got a houseful and we just don't know it,' Roby answered.

'There's a happy thought!' Max Dunn grumbled.

Chapter 65

Friday 4:23 p.m., March 26.

BOBBY DEWITT WAS WINDED from what was undoubtedly a hard run through the underground passage. 'Got it!' he called. He held a black book toward us cheerfully, then sat down and began flipping pages. 'Here,' he said after a moment. *'And there came a messenger unto Job, and said, The oxen were ploughing and the asses feeding beside them, and the Sabeans fell upon them and took them away; yea, they have slain the servants with the edge of the sword; and I only am escaped alone to tell thee.'*

Max grimaced. 'So we look for some dead cows and mules, is that it?'

DeWitt held us hand up, and read on. *'While he was yet speaking, there came also another, and said, The fire of God is fallen from heaven, and hath burned up the sheep, and the servants, and consumed them; and*

I only am escaped alone to tell thee. While he was yet speaking there came also another, and said, The Chaldeans made out three bands and fell upon the camels, and have carried them away, yea, and slain the servants with the edge of the sword; and I only am escaped alone to tell.' He looked up, 'Then you have the children.' He read it for us: *'Thy sons and thy daughters were eating and drinking wine in their eldest brother's house, and Behold, there came a great wind from the wilderness and smote the four corners of the house, and it fell upon the young men, and they are dead, and I only am escaped alone to tell thee.'*

Max shook his head. 'So basically, the preacher was right. It all happens at once. His kids gone on day-one. How was it again? A mighty wind?'

'A collapsed building,' DeWitt answered, then shrugged apologetically. 'Sorry, I thought it might be important. I knew the kids didn't die first. I remembered that much.'

'Camels, sheep... and oxen...' Cottrell intoned, as if trying to recall where one might find such animals in Shiloh Springs.

'And servants,' I said. 'Don't forget the servants.' I looked at Linda Sutherlin, who had already given me a smile, 'Nobody ever remembers the faithful servants.'

She gave me another, then crossed her legs, flashing her MOM, and of course I had to imagine reading it upside down. WOW.

'Maybe we'd better take a look around the country for collapsed buildings,' McCreary offered.

Rolly nodded, 'I'll put it out on the wire tonight.'

Cottrell took the Bible from his subordinate and studied it while we waited, then he looked up and offered for all of us, '...*and I only am escaped alone to tell thee.*' He nodded at our dumb looks. 'It's Missy Worth.'

We all looked down at the table, none of us willing to tell the Shiloh Springs chief of police his chronology was screwy by about ten years.

'According to Merriweather,' I answered at last, 'the story of Job is about faith. If you take everything away from a man, the question is, will he curse God or keep his faith. Now these two have been meeting for almost seven years. From our perspective, Merriweather has been this royal pain in the butt, but the two of them together have spent most of their time talking Bible, not law. The minute it finally looked like he might get out, this winter, Booker seemed to focus his attention on the Book of Job. Specifically he asked about Job's *perfection*. He either wants to show Merriweather the truth about himself, that he's not perfect, or he wants to find out for himself how much faith the old boy has. Either way, the girls don't seem real important. This is about Merriweather.'

'So he stays close?' Jerry Powell answered. 'Because he wants to watch?'

'A good chance of it,' I answered.

287

'If he stays in the area,' Roby answered, 'his problem is where to hide the car.'

'That car is not on the streets anywhere in the county,' Max Dunn answered. 'I'll wager my badge on it.'

'He hides it in someone's garage,' I offered.

Rolly Tincher grumbled. 'This guy gets out of prison and sits in his room at Merriweather's house for what... five-six days? One trip to the mall, where he goes to two stores for some clothes and then he goes home again; a trip to the public library, church on Sunday, and then the hospital. When does he get a chance to scout out a garage?'

'It was *three* trips to the library, Rolly,' I said.

'Merriweather said he went to the library,' Rolly Tincher answered with a heavy shrug of his shoulders. 'That's all I know.'

'Rachel Merriweather told me it was Sunday afternoon, Monday evening, and Tuesday evening, the night he was attacked.'

We all grew quiet, all of us thinking the same thing. It was Max Dunn who finally voiced it.

'So what in the hell do you figure was so interesting about the library?'

Chapter 66

Friday 4:24 p.m., March 26.

ROLLY TINCHER SHOOK HIS head. 'No one we talked to at the library even saw the guy. Course that doesn't mean he wasn't there; it just means no one saw him.' A smile to let us know we were off on a wild goose chase.

'It's possible,' I said, 'that Booker didn't even go inside. He could have spent the time looking for his hideout.'

'And he didn't have a car...' Max turned on Rolly suddenly. 'He didn't drive, did he?'

'Didn't have a valid driver's license.'

'He got his rides from the preacher or Tammy Merriweather,' I told them.

Rolly shot me a look, which I answered in full. Max Dunn leaned back in his chair thinking about Booker. 'So let's start at the library,' he said, 'and then move out in four directions and start looking into garages. It's a hell of a job but I mean it's *something*!'

Jerry Powell leaned forward in surprise. 'You mean go door-to-door?'

Max shook his head, 'We're only interested in finding some kind of garage or shed where he could keep the car. For that we can just go down the alleys taking a peek. You put thirty-or-forty plain-clothes people out after sundown, and I mean look in every damn garage window and you're going to find that car if it's there!' He grew animated with a sudden thought. 'You got the river on the west. One squad could handle everything in that direction. Public housing, no garages! Industry out there is all behind fences, not more than a couple dozen private garages in the whole area. Points north, you've got the university. Security and maintenance have already swept their garages and anywhere else you could hide a car. They even went through their tunnels looking for the kids. So we go on north of that maybe a mile or two at the most. And houses east and south, right up and down the alleys out to the suburbs!'

'What about garages or buildings that are shut up?' Cass McCreary responded. 'If you can't see into a building you're going to have a problem.'

'For the buildings we can't see into we can bring a team in tomorrow morning and find out from the neighbours what going on! If we don't like the answers, we'll get nosey!'

'The one thing you can't do,' Massey warned, 'is you can't pry doors open or break windows for a better look. I mean really you shouldn't even be able to step on people's property.'

'We're just having a look at what we can see from the alley – which is public access. It's no different from grabbing garbage bags and checking them without a warrant. We're not going on private property!'

Cass McCreary said, 'Maybe we should look at bus lines, too. If he didn't want to walk, busses are cheap and easy, and the drivers know their regulars, so they might notice a new face.'

Max gave Rolly Tincher a look. 'Might as well look at taxi drivers too. Anybody gave this guy a ride last week, it would be nice to know it.'

'If you don't mind,' I said, 'I'll take another look inside the library.'

Rolly grinned. 'You're wasting your time, Rick.'

'Did you talk to *everyone*?'

'We talked to enough of them.'

'It's just possible he met someone there. It's the only time we have him without one of the Merriweathers escorting him. I just want to be sure.'

Winston Fortney opened his hands. 'You could say the same for the hospital.'

'We checked it,' Tincher answered.

'Meaning?'

'Meaning we talked to the nurses, interviewed the old

guy he was rooming with, went down the hall, asked folks if they'd had any contact with the guy. We *checked*!'

Powell scratched a note to himself. 'I can get three, maybe four state police detectives on the hospital tonight. Look at personnel: see if anyone's missing for the last few days, then look at patients. Find out if someone has an empty house because they're staying in the hospital, ask if maybe there's a family that hasn't been by to visit a patient since Wednesday night.' He looked at Rolly. 'Just to be sure.'

'What about the church?' Massey asked.

Tincher answered with real defensiveness on this one. 'The church we've looked at hard. The guy shook hands with folks. Period.'

'Anyone missing?' Garrat asked.

Tincher shook his head. 'Everyone's accounted for. First thing we did was to get their prayer line up and going, called everyone and his sainted brother.'

Max looked around the table, his eyes settling on agent Fortney. 'You hang with us a few more days on the phones, keep the house covered in case he comes back?'

'As long as you need us.'

He looked at me. 'You need a hand with the librarians, Rick? I know those sorts can get pretty wild sometimes…'

'I'll call for backup, if I do.'

Max put both hands on the table: 'Well then folks… there's nothing left to do but lose some more sleep!'

Chapter 67

Friday 4:45 p.m., March 26.

IN THE HALL BEYOND the sheriff's office, our meeting finished, Garrat and Massey walked together, while Linda Sutherlin and I trailed several feet behind. Massey was talking excitedly, something about prosecuting Missy Worth.

When we hit the office, I asked Garrat if she had a minute. As Sutherlin and Massey went on, I heard Massey suggest dinner. Sutherlin answered him without rancour. 'I'd rather attend my own crucifixion.'

Massey handled the rejection with his usual aplomb. 'Another time, maybe.'

'What was Massey saying about prosecuting Missy Worth?' I asked Garrat when I had shut the door to her office.

Garrat rolled her eyes. 'He thinks it is something I need to look at if our only capital case is Mary Worth.

Otherwise Booker can claim he didn't do it – and he's right.'

'Did he say what he's going to use for evidence after her confession gets tossed?'

'He'll think about crossing that bridge after he's burned it.'

'I want you to make me a promise, Pat.'

Hand up, stopping me, 'I'm not touching her, Rick. She's a victim in this thing.'

'The promise I want is that you'll take this to trial yourself, if and when we catch this guy.'

'Let's catch him first.'

'We'll get him,' I said. 'Sooner or later, if he hasn't killed himself, he's going to be ours. I want the promise now.'

'Why now? Why not let me think about it and look at the situation.'

I shook my head. 'I want to know whether to kill the son of a bitch with my bare hands or bring him to you.'

She smiled. 'You can bring him in alive, Rick. I'll take lead on it – just for you.'

'Promise?'

'I promise.'

I smiled with a new thought. 'Do you suppose Lynn Griswold will still be his lawyer?'

'If he is,' she said, 'it will be Griswold's first defeat.'

Chapter 68

Darkness.

WILL WALKS TO BEN LYONS, whose eyes are closed. Ben's breathing is ragged, wet. He sleeps. 'Ben!' The eyes open. 'How are you feeling?' Hissing pain for answer.

Penny will not kill him. Will brings her to him time after time. The gun is reloaded, but she will not touch it, will not give to God and Will what they demand. All the same, Ben is close to death. God takes him soon. One way or the other.

Will studies the crusted wound, the twin bloodied lumps in the fat muscle. He bends over the man, touches his face in compassion. The man's big hand takes Will's wrist in a tight grip, and Will is trapped. His pistol is in his pocket, but he can't reach it with his left hand. He feels the grip of the big man tighten. Will's bones are almost breaking. Even dying Ben Lyons possesses the power to kill, and Will knows he has made a terrible mistake. The hissing comes again; only now Will understands it: 'Water!'

Will nods. 'I'll get some water for you,' he says. The hand releases him, and Will stands. He studies the grey face, the wounds. Water might keep him alive a bit longer. He goes to the prison cell and tells Tabit to come out. When she does, he points her toward the laundry room and tells her to give Ben a drink of water.

After helping Ben to drink, Tabit asks Will for blankets and food and water for the rest. Will sends her into the cell with more water, watching them as they drink. Only when she has finished serving the others does she take some herself. He tells her he will get them food soon. He locks the door and goes upstairs. The climb is hard for him. His muscles ache. His exhaustion is terrible. He finds bread but will not eat it himself. He takes them two thin slices apiece. Then he finds one threadbare wool blanket in a closet. Tabit asks for more when he delivers it, but he tells her they have more than they need. It is more than his grandfather ever gave *him*. Will had been locked away so long on some occasions he thought he must die of hunger – three, four days, a week, even ten days once. In the end, the suffering had only made him stronger. That's what his grandfather told him, anyway.

Before he can leave, Tabit asks to bring Mr Lyons back to their room. Will almost refuses her but he decides that since Penny will not cooperate he might as well send Ben back to them. 'If you can pull him across the carpet,' he answers, 'you can have him.'

Tabit organises it; Tamara and Penny assist. They slip the blanket under Ben and struggle to drag him across the carpet. They haven't the strength to do it easily, but in time the man is taken close enough that his son crawls out of the room and helps them. Boy has two ruined knees; his wounds taking all his strength, but still he pulls his father's weight as best he can.

Penny glances up at Will when she sees him studying her brother. She worries for Boy. Will wonders if she would sacrifice Tabit or Tamara to save Boy.

Tabit is the dangerous one; she gets stronger as the hours pass. Despite being the youngest, she begins to lead the others. He ought to offer Tabit to Penny, but Tamara is the traitor. Who would not kill a traitor for the sake of a loved one?

Chapter 69

Friday 4:56 p.m., March 26.

I FOUND WHAT PASSED FOR the boss in a back room of the library. I asked him if he knew who William Booker was. He did. He had been working the night Booker was attacked in front of the library. He had waited with him until the ambulance arrived.

Mr Wirtzmyer was a tall, thin, bald man with a long, lonesome face. He was my age – pushing toward sixty, if not a year or two beyond. He possessed the quiet habits of a lifetime of libraries: a walk that seemed to slink, hands that had never known a callous, a voice that barely rose above a whisper. He looked to be suffering from a surfeit of virtues, a life lived so grey and frail the colour had left his blood. 'Too bad he didn't die right there,' Wirtzmyer offered softly. I nodded agreeably at the sentiment and took a second look at the guy. I had made a bad call. Wirtzmyer was a librarian with Vikings for ancestors.

'We think he was either talking to someone here or he was looking for something in the area,' I said. 'It might help us find him if we can figure out which.'

'If he checked out a book or tape, I can find out what it was.'

I shook my head. 'We know he didn't bring anything back to the Merriweather house. I'd appreciate your checking anyway, but I've got a feeling whatever he wanted he found right here. My first question is a bit awkward.' The old fellow seemed to brace himself. 'Have you had any absences since Wednesday? Maybe a regular who hasn't shown up for the past couple of days?'

The librarian saw at once what I was driving at. His face lost what little blood he possessed. He thought about it. He wouldn't know about the regulars so much, he said. But the workers might. I pushed it. 'Any staff absences?'

'No, I think we're all on schedule.' He babbled a bit more. One absence, yes, but then back to work today.

'I wonder if I might talk to your people?'

The librarian thought about this. 'Do you have a picture to help them recall his face?' I tossed him one of Will's prison issue portraits. He considered it, then looked at me sorrowfully. 'Not everyone is here, of course.'

'Let's start with the people we have,' I said. 'Maybe we'll get lucky.'

After we determined Booker had not applied for a library card, we went around the library talking to the employees. I kept my mouth shut and let Wirtzmyer ask the questions. He was a thorough man and seemed to understand exactly what I was after. When he showed them Booker's picture, the librarian took each shake of the head as hard as I did.

'I have two girls myself,' Mr Wirtzmyer said as he walked me out the front door. 'I sure hope you find him in time.'

Once in my car, I looked at my list of off duty library employees and quickly sketched out a plan. The first two turned out to be easy to find. They were home. Friendly enough. Excited to be a part of things. Then came the thoughtful shrug I had seen the others give. No one missing that they could think of. Neither had seen Booker inside. I was fairly sure by this point that Max's people were going to turn up a bus or taxi driver who had given Will Booker a ride somewhere, but I pushed to the end of my list anyway. Call it an old cop's diehard determination: every lead chased down no matter how thin. We are the statistical leaders in lottery participation, after all, which is what passes for a faith in miracles these days.

'A friend's house,' a mother told me about one young man. I got there and the mother of the friend said they had just taken off for the park to go sledding.

Every Dark Place

I found the kid in the midst of a group of maybe a hundred people in the twilight. A bonfire illuminated the hilltop and kept off the chill. This kid hadn't seen Booker either, but he was a good guy. He let me ride with him on his sled back down the hill to my car.

Chapter 70

Friday 8:40 p.m., March 26.

I TRACKED IRENE FOLLET through three of my own favourite haunts, getting a contact high. One of her co-workers had told me she was helping a friend celebrate something or another. 'A happy hour gone bad,' the bartender at the Dug Out told me, when I asked if he had seen her. 'Try the Shamrock,' he said. 'I think she lives around there somewhere.'

'Can you tell me what she looks like?' I asked.

'Got a t-shirt on. You can't miss it.'

'Why is that?'

A quiet smile, 'You'll see.'

I knew most everyone who frequented the Shamrock, but with quite a few people I didn't have a name, so when I stepped into my favourite tavern, I looked for distinctive t-shirts. The first t-shirt I saw was kind of goofy, so I asked the woman, 'Are you Irene Follet?'

She pointed back to a table full of maniacs, and I went on. Irene Follet was in her early-to-mid-forties, a woman who still wore sneakers and blue jeans and plain, unadorned t-shirts. I saw at once what the bartender had meant though. Her figure did wonders for the faded yellow t-shirt she wore. Absolute wonders. She had green eyes, red curly hair, and pale freckled skin. I knew the face and had admired her figure more than any other on several occasions. But I had never spoken to the woman. Once or twice I had caught a coy smile tossed in my direction, but I'd never approached her. She was usually a part of a group, people I didn't really know.

'Irene Follet?' I asked. 'I'm Rick Trueblood. I'm an investigator with the county prosecutor's office.'

That was when she laughed.

Not many people laugh when you say *prosecutor*, so I looked around the table wondering what was so funny. 'Am I missing something?'

'Apparently.' Giggling now, looking me in the eye like I was a perfect idiot.

'I've seen you around,' I said, 'but I don't remember ever being introduced...'

Coy, having some fun now. 'You don't remember dancing with me last Saturday night?'

Something about the voice, the straight white teeth, the way her square shoulders moved so easily. And the t-shirt in all its glory...

303

'Oh, no,' I said. 'Was that *you*?'

Irene turned to the others at the table, five of them in all, every one of them toasted. 'I never saw anyone get as upset as this guy just because someone wanted to cut in while he was dancing!'

'Oh, God...' I muttered.

'Little trouble with the old blackouts, Rick?'

Her girlfriend laughed, 'The dreaded-blackouts! Been there, done it... just can't remember what it was!'

They bounced this back and forth a little, leaving me feeling like a damn fool, but Irene Follet was handling it okay. Like maybe she'd had some fun. 'They didn't hassle you any, did they?' I asked. 'The cops, I mean? Maybe take you down to the jail?'

This got some *oohs* and *ahhs* from her friends, a quiet little grin from Irene that I couldn't read. 'They pretty much had their hands full with you,' she said, when her friends had quieted. 'To tell you the truth,' she added, 'I thought they were going to have to *shoot* you!'

'You watched it?'

'I left when the SWAT team arrived.'

'That wasn't the SWAT team. They called all the rookies out. They were taking bets on whether any of them could cuff me.'

'Anyone win?'

I grinned, 'They did if they were betting on me.' I got some razzing from her friends about my bravado, but Irene kind of liked it. 'Listen,' I said, 'if I embarrassed you the other night... or said anything inappropriate...'

'Hey, I thought marriage sounded like a great idea!'

'I didn't ask you to marry me, did I? Tell me I didn't propose marriage.'

The friend beside her liked this. 'Breach of promise! Lawsuit! Lawsuit!'

Irene was kinder: 'Hey, if you don't remember me accepting, I don't remember you asking. How's that?'

'I can live with that.'

'You're an awfully good dancer, though, and that's important... *in a future husband.*'

'I'd love to buy you a drink so, you know, we could try to remember old times, but right now I'm on official business, I'm afraid. Something of an emergency actually. You work in the library, right?'

'Ten years. But some days it feels like thirty. Is this about my overdue books?'

I pulled Will Booker's photo out of my sports jacket. 'I'm looking for anyone who saw this guy in the library. You didn't happen to see him, did you?'

'I remember him.'

'Out front?'

She shook her head. 'He was inside. Special collections. My area.'

'Do you know who this guy is?'

One of her friends made a sound of recognition, and I held my hand up, checking him.

'Not a clue. Kind of cute, though.'

'You're kidding me,' her friend answered. 'He's like all over TV!'

'I don't watch TV. I don't own one. Who is he?'

'You heard about the minister's kids?' I asked.

'I heard about that.'

'Everybody's heard about that,' the friend shouted, taking a huge gulp of beer. 'Talk about getting what you deserve! That preacher...!'

'It wasn't the preacher who got kidnapped,' I told the guy. Then to Irene Follet. 'This is William Booker, the guy who took off with the preacher's two daughters.'

Irene studied the picture again, 'Well, he was in the library. Looked like a pretty quiet guy in there.'

'You're lucky to be alive,' her friend answered.

'How many times did he show up?' I asked.

She shook her head after a moment of reflection, 'I don't know. A couple times? Three?'

'Was he alone? Talking to anyone? Do you remember?'

'I helped him out with the microfilm Sunday. Then I saw him reading it. That's all I know.'

'What was he looking at on microfilm?'

'I didn't pay any attention.'

'Do you remember anything else? Was he with anyone?'

'He was alone every time I saw him, but I remember he was reading a lot of different books.'

'Did you see which ones?'

'I remember the area where he got some of them. If that does anything for you.'

I looked at my watch. Four minutes till nine. 'It might. What are you doing right now, Irene?'

'Goofing around.' She looked at her friends, grinning. 'Working on a blackout.'

'You want to show me exactly where you saw this guy? I can bring you right back afterwards.'

She shrugged, 'Why not?'

Chapter 71

Friday 9:06 p.m., March 26.

I CALLED WIRTZMYER AS SOON as we were outside. Once I was in the car I called Garrat and told her we might have a lead. Then I got hold of Max Dunn as I drove.

'He was there?' Max shouted.

'My witness saw him *inside* two, maybe three times.'

'It was three times,' Irene Follet announced.

'The thing is,' I told Max, 'there is no way we can put him inside the library the whole time, so he could still have gone out looking for a hideout.'

'We're going to finish the search no matter what,' Max answered.

'Is there any way you could spare some people?'

'What do you need, buddy?'

'The library is closed for the night, Max. I thought we might treat the place like a crime scene and get some people in there. Find his prints. Figure out what he was reading.'

'I can give you Roby's squad. They've swept the river from here to Bethel Falls and looking to help somewhere.'

When I had finished with Max, Irene Follet said, 'Did you say *crime scene?*'

'Yeah. Everything but a body. I want to take a look at anything he touched,' I said.

'Don't they use some kind of powder to get fingerprints?'

'There are different ways to locate prints, but powder is simple and easy. Plus, the average sheriff's deputy can lift a print – assuming the surface is decent.'

'Messy?'

'A little, I guess. I mean it's a powder...'

'Oscar is going to have kittens.'

'Oscar?'

'Mr Wirtzmyer.'

'He seemed like a nice enough man.'

'That's because you didn't tell him you were going to make a mess.'

IT WAS A FEW MINUTES PAST nine when we arrived at the front door of the library. The place was locked up tight, but Wirtzmyer was waiting for us. He saw Irene Follet next to me and asked her excitedly, 'Do you remember seeing him?'

'Three visits to Special Collections.'

Wirtzmyer looked at me. 'That explains it. You see, if he was in there, nobody else would have noticed him. Special Collections has its own room.'

In the parking lot two sheriff's cars pulled up with lights flashing. 'I'm afraid I have another favour to ask you,' I told Wirtzmyer.

He studied the activity in the parking lot, then looked at me almost accusingly. 'I'm not going to be happy about this, am I?'

Joe Roby came toward us on the run, three men following him. I introduced Roby to Wirtzmyer and Irene Follet, '...our witness.'

As we walked back toward Special Collections, Irene whispered for only me to hear, '*our witness and my fiancé...*'

SPECIAL COLLECTIONS WAS fairly extensive, with an office made of glass walls and a couple of study niches tucked in here and there. Irene pointed to a lonely corner hidden away from view, 'He was there mostly, I think, but also at the microfilm machine a few times.'

One of the deputies walked to the drawers where the microfilm was stored and began dusting. Joe Roby asked Irene, 'Did you see him get any books?'

'He had books every time I saw him. Lots of books. Most of them from over here...'

Wirtzmyer nodded sagely, and I looked at him. 'Maps and Directories,' he told me.

From the cabinets the deputy called, 'Got something, Joe!' We walked over and saw a smudged mark on one of the handles. 'Could be his,' the deputy explained, holding up a copy of Booker's prints that every deputy was now carrying because of the fiasco with the prints on the bat. 'Wouldn't hold up in court, but I'll bet he opened this drawer.' The drawer carried the local newspaper on film; the dates were from ten to fifteen years ago. 'Do you want me to lift it?'

'Just open the drawer,' Joe answered. 'Maybe we can figure out which reel he was looking at.'

I pointed at one box almost at once. 'Try that one,' I said.

Joe Roby looked at me curiously but told the deputy to dust it. When he got a print, he compared it to Booker's, and looked at Roby. 'It's his. A good one, too.'

'Go ahead and lift that one,' Joe Roby told him. Then he spun around on me, 'How did you do that, Rick?'

Irene was impressed too, and I hated to give away my secret, but I thought I'd better. 'This is the local paper from ten years ago.'

'That's when he was raising hell around here...'

'Booker was in here reading about himself, Joe.'

The deputy asked Roby. 'Keep going?'

'Max said *everything*.' The deputy nodded, and began

the process of extracting all the boxes from the drawer, meticulously checking each one of them.

I walked over to Maps and Directories and watched another officer moving down the shelves, pulling each volume, dusting it, and checking anything he got against Booker's prints, then moving on. The books he left behind were stacked on the floor in filthy piles.

'What I want to know,' Wirtzmyer asked me quietly but with grave concern, 'is who is responsible for cleaning up after you finish?'

I looked at Joe Roby, and I could see he didn't care to answer the question either.

'Civilians,' I said.

Wirtzmyer's face twitched, but that was all.

I looked back at Roby, 'I'll get our witness back to her friends, if you don't need her anymore.'

'Take your time,' he answered. 'We're going to be here a while.' The detective looked at Wirtzmyer, 'There's no sense all of us losing a Friday night, sir. If you leave me a set of keys, I'll make sure we lock up when we're done.'

Wirtzmyer stiffened, 'I'll be back in my office. You need anything, just let me know. And do try to be as neat as you can.'

Chapter 72

Friday 9:21 p.m., March 26.

STANDING OUTSIDE IN THE SNOW, Irene Follet told me, 'Could you just take me home?'

'Sure. You live close to the Shamrock, don't you?'

'Just around the corner.'

'Prime real estate,' I told her.

I headed east down Ohio as far as Fourteenth before turning north. As we drove, we talked about people we both knew, bars we liked, bars we stayed out of. She asked about the life of a prosecutor's investigator. Was it as boring as it sounded? I wanted to know what a special collections coordinator did all day.

She gave me a coy smile, 'I usually keep an eye peeled for flashers. Anything to stay awake. But mostly, I just walk the genealogy buffs through the material. Thrill a minute.'

'Are you ever going to do anything else?'

'I do something else. I'm a poet.'

'Yeah? Ever publish anything?'

'Six books.'

'Six *books*! That's a lot! You must be doing all right...'

She laughed. 'Yeah, I'm really rich. I just don't like to show off my millions.'

'They pay you for them, don't they?'

'Have you ever read a poem that you didn't have to, Rick?'

I felt like a Philistine. 'I can't say that I have.'

'That puts you in a very large majority.'

'So why do it?'

She offered that smile of hers again, very private, very beautiful, 'Because I'm good at it.'

I pulled up in front of a big house on Fourteenth a block north of the Shamrock. Like a lot of the big houses in town, the thing had been chopped up into apartments.

'You want to come in? Maybe have a cup of coffee? The guy said it was going to be a long night, and you look tired.' She had no idea how tired. I hadn't slept since the kids had been taken. I had hardly been back to the house, except to shower and change clothes. I figured if I sat down I just might pass out.

'I'd love to, but I need to get back.'

'Well, you know where I live now.'

She leaned over and kissed my lips. It was a soft, quick kiss, but no mistaking her meaning, especially not with the long look that followed. 'Don't forget me this time. Huh?'

'I won't.'

She started to open her door, then stopped herself. 'Do you know why Methodists don't make love standing up, Rick?'

I smiled. 'I can't say that I do.'

'They're afraid it might lead to dancing.'

And then she was gone. I watched her climb up a wooden stairway at the side of the house. I saw the light go on in her place and marked the window where she lived, so I'd know how to find her. I even thought about following her. Get some coffee, have a talk about nothing in particular, steal just one more kiss, and maybe just ask for one more dance...

But I couldn't. I had a maniac to track down.

Chapter 73

Friday 10:09 p.m., March 26.

'WE GOT THREE MORE PRINTS, Rick!' Joe Roby announced when he opened the door for me. 'Two on microfilm boxes, one on a city directory.'

I had stopped on the way back and was eating a sandwich and sipping a Coke. I swallowed and looked at the man curiously. 'City Directory?' I asked.

'Current year. We tried the pages but we couldn't get anything more than a few smudges here and there. The pages are too porous.'

I followed Roby back to Special Collections and looked at the book. There were four sections to it. Businesses, with business owners listed; then the metro residents were listed three ways: by address, by phone number, and by name. A lot of the people had their professions listed and quite a few entries included family members. A madman's shopping list.

316

'You can get a lot of information about someone here,' I said, pointing at the directory.

'These days most people just Google it.'

'From everything we know about this guy Booker never touched a computer.'

'Too bad for us.'

'If he was using this he could have had a phone number or maybe an address. From that he could find out everyone who lived there.'

'What does that get him, Rick?'

'If you've got names, you can call folks and set up an appointment, like to show a vacuum cleaner or sell them insurance, maybe deliver some bogus prize – you know, get them to open the door without a fuss.'

'An appointment? That's something we hadn't thought of.'

'Rolly Tincher has already checked the calls from the Merriweather house,' I told him. 'Same with the phone in his hospital room. But he could have made a call here, couldn't he?'

'According to the sign out front,' Roby answered, 'there are public phones downstairs. Of course, these days he might have borrowed someone's phone...'

'Let's check the phones; any calls going out, we'd better do a drive-by on the property.'

Roby pulled his cell phone out, while I wandered over to look at the microfilm boxes. Bernie Samples' series on Booker's case in federal court was in one of the boxes with Booker's prints on it. Long winded florid swill about crooked cops, an ambitious prosecutor, an innocent man… and the preacher who wouldn't give up. I'd seen it all as it came out and had no inclination to go through it again. This was about Will Booker's vanity. The other box, though, was a long reel of microfilm and no reason that I could see why he wanted to read it. Had he touched it to move it aside? I didn't think so. It was the most current. It was maybe just a read-through for current events, or maybe there was something in it he wanted. I had nothing better to do, so I threaded it into the machine and started reading.

Roby snapped his phone off and told me, 'We're getting the phone records tonight, Rick.'

I looked up and nodded. 'You might want to make sure they do the same on the hospital's public phones.'

I SCANNED EVERY STORY for an eight month period, from politics to obituaries. What I found out is the local paper carried more about sports than any other topic, with the obits coming in a distant second. When I had finished our local paper's offering for the year, I fished out the local maps Booker had touched and began scouring them for stray pencil marks.

We wrapped it up shortly after midnight. A dozen more of Booker's prints had emerged. Business annuals, high school and university yearbooks, the local Rotary newsletter and a couple of other service clubs. A few thousand names – but most definitely the interest was local. Joe Roby took everything with him. Third shift was under way. He wanted to get fresh eyes to begin making lists and looking for connections.

BEFORE I WENT HOME, I swung by Missy Worth's place, slipping out of the car a block away, crossing the railroad tracks and coming in through the blackest part of the shadows, stepping as softly as I could through the crackling snow drifts.

Missy Worth's house was pitch-black. There was no garage connected to the property, so the place would not have caught anyone's attention on Max Dunn's search. Of course, Will could have left the car somewhere else, like at the bottom of the river, and then walked back into town that night. I slipped up on the back door with a feeling of excitement and dread. I checked the door; it was locked. But anyone could take this lock and not even damage the door. I went around to the side of the house looking into the windows. The curtains were all drawn tight. I passed the front of the house and then slipped along a dark strip between Missy Worth's house and the back of a vacant commercial building next to it. Finally, I found a curtain that was pulled loose. I put my face to the glass and peeked in. That was when I heard a footstep on a brittle patch of snow a few feet behind me.

'WHAT ARE YOU LOOKING AT, PERVERT?'

'DOO!' I shouted, recognising the voice at once. 'It's Rick Trueblood!'

That stopped him. I could see his form in the pale streetlight almost directly behind him.

'Who?' Cautious. Maybe friendly, but still not certain.

'Rick Trueblood,' I answered. 'With the prosecutor's office. I was looking for Will Booker.'

'Here?' He stepped closer and I saw a bat hanging from his hand.

'Sorry, I sneaked up on the place,' I said, 'but I thought Will Booker might be hiding here with the Merriweather girls.'

Doo laughed suddenly. 'Now wouldn't I just love another chance at that boy? Answer to my prayers, man!'

'You're staying here?' I asked.

'It was that or take the cat out to my place. You ever try to move a tom cat on a Harley?'

'Missed the pleasure.'

'Missy's cat has got a bad attitude, man. Besides, this place is okay.'

'When are you going marry this woman, Doo?'

'I'll tell you what, man. If you put us in the same house, one of us would end up dead inside a week. Hey, you want a beer? I got a couple cases in the house. We could bring in the dawn, if you want!'

'Another time, maybe.'

I was almost to the railroad tracks, when Doo called

out: 'You're all right, man!' I turned and saw the big man with that bat of his hanging off one shoulder. 'You're a good man in my book!'

'Why do you say that?' I asked him. I was curious about what had excited his affection.

'Them two girls are already in the ground, but you're still out looking for them. I admire that.'

Chapter 74

Darkness.

PENNY STANDS OVER TAMARA Merriweather. The bloodied bat lies at her feet. Will has tied Tamara to a chair. Her mouth is sealed with tape. Will stands off to the side, his gun in his hand pointing benignly at the floor as he whispers his bargain.

'Give her to me, Penny. If you do, I'll let your family live. Go on, take the bat. Don't worry, no one will ever know you did it. They'll say I was the one. They won't know... not even Benny or your father will ever know.'

Penny stands in silence, staring into Tamara Merriweather's frightened eyes.

'Your father and Benny are going to die if you don't get them help, Penny. You kill *them* if you refuse me. No choice at all kills two people – kills family – but if you pick up that bat and use it, four people live.

'Tammy here is the one who called out when your

322

dad was going to try to break you free. She's the same one that got your mother shot. Give her to me, Penny. I'll never tell. It will just be our little secret. Show me you love your family. You do that and I'll let you have them back. Protect this one and watch your dad pass on first, then Benny after him. One way or the other, someone is going to die. It rests with you to say if its family or a traitor...'

Chapter 75

Saturday 7:52 a.m., March 27.

I SLIPPED HOME LATE, GOT A SHOWER and thought about sleeping until Monday, but the next morning I was dreaming about my mother pulling my brothers and me into a rundown shack with a cross on the front of it. A fine gentleman in black with a fondness for hell's fire and brimstone was naming all the things I couldn't do.

I shook it off slowly, the nightmare of my Pentecostal youth, and came into the light with the feeling that I hadn't quite stepped into the right reality. I was sober, yet feeling hung over. I had done nothing but think about the case, the salvation of two girls I didn't even know, and yet I was feeling defiled. Impure thoughts about a certain librarian? I didn't think so. I think it was that I was lost in time, coming to the end of my search for Sarah's killer and knowing I was going to fail.

I shook it off slowly, enjoying a long heavy breakfast at the twenty-four restaurant down the street. But that was the end of my leisure. I was walking back to the house when my cell phone rang. It was Garrat. The taxi and bus drivers had been checked out, she said. No one knew Booker's face except from TV. The city alleys had been scoured. The public phones at the hospital and library gave us a few leads. Booker had definitely called the Merriweather residence and the pastor's office at Merriweather's church. They were doing follow up on the other calls, but she didn't hold out much hope for a lucky break. If Booker had spent most of his time in the library looking at maps, he could be anywhere in a three or four county area. We commiserated about that for a while, and I finally asked her what she wanted me to do. I was frankly out of ideas.

'What I want from you is an opinion,' she said.

'Honestly? I think it's over.' I looked at the blue sky, the snow-covered rooftops. I breathed the cold air. I was letting go. Saving myself, because that was all I could do. 'I don't like saying it, but if Max can't find him this morning I don't see what else we can do.'

'You might be right, but I wanted your opinion about something else. Which girl do you think he picks?' I grunted in confusion, and Garrat explained herself. 'Which one do you think holds the bat, Tabit or Tammy?'

'I don't know, Pat,' I said into the receiver, still walking back to my house. 'I hadn't really thought about it. Tell you the truth, I don't want to think about it; it makes me sick even to imagine it.'

'Is either of them anything at all like Missy?'

I laughed. 'Not that I can see. Not on Missy's *best* day!'

'That's what I thought. too. This Tammy... she's... the weaker of the two? Is that your read on it?"

'Her mother says she's the more vulnerable of the two,' I said.

'A little bit like Lisa Chenoweth – the girl Booker used to set up the abduction ten years ago.'

'I guess. Maybe. What's your point?'

'I'm at the office; I've been here for about five hours, actually. I was going through the old case, reading the profiles on our victims, and looking at pictures. Everything about Lisa Chenoweth tells me she was the kind of girl who would have been easy to manipulate. But she wasn't the one Booker went to once he had them. He went right for Missy – a troubled girl long before Will Booker showed up in her life.'

'So you think Tabit is holding the bat? Is that what you're saying?' I recalled what Rachel Merriweather had said about the girl. Not anger but depth. Nothing at all like Missy...

'Hear me out on this,' Garrat answered. 'I think Will *spotted* Missy Worth before the attack ten years ago. I think Lisa Chenoweth was his way into the group. A couple of dope deals, a little romance, and then the promise of some cocaine.'

'Tabit Merriweather is a quiet, thoughtful kid, Pat. Her mother said she doesn't show much emotion at all. Walks with God is how she put it. Not exactly the next Missy Worth.'

'Let's say, for the sake of argument, Will Booker is playing his old game, sweet talking a girl into a blood-bath of fury. Only this time he tosses the devil's wager in for good measure – just to see how Connie Merriweather stacks up against Job. How does Booker do it without someone playing Missy Worth?'

'You're saying he's found another Missy?' I had been there already. Garrat might be right, but I couldn't see how it took us any closer to finding his hideout.

'I think he's local. I don't think he intends to move until he's finished with Merriweather. I think he may even give himself up so he can watch Merriweather afterwards.'

'So he's taken over a house somewhere...'

'Not just any house, Rick. He *knew* where he was going. If I'm right, there's nothing random about anything he's done.'

'The guy saw a lot of people, Pat. He went to the mall, the library, the hospital, and the church. Now if he doesn't have to talk to a kid, if he can just spot someone with a problem, which is apparently how he found Missy, then you can toss in a chance sighting on the streets while he's going between points A and B, maybe catching an address where someone walks into a building, then looking up the name of the person in the city directory. Random or otherwise, I don't think we're any closer than before. There are just too many possibilities.'

'You're overlooking one thing.'

'What's that?'

'The devil went after Job's *flock* before he killed the kids.'

Chapter 76

Saturday 8:42 a.m., March 27.

THEY WERE PRAYING LIKE IT mattered when I found the church deacons and Connie Merriweather in a small conference room.

'Dr Merriweather?' I called. I hadn't waited for the prayer to stop and the preacher looked up angrily. I think he almost told me to wait until they had finished, but then something clicked behind his eyes. The thought that maybe if he just quit *talking* to God, God could get a word in edgewise. I don't know; that's maybe giving the preacher more credit than he deserved, but it was the thought I had at the time. Of course I was riding a high, believing Job's flock was Merriweather's flock.

After that look had passed, Connie Merriweather came up out of his seat the way a drowning a man will go after his rescuer. 'Now look,' I said when I had him alone, 'I just spent half of last night on what turned out to be nothing. I don't want you to get your hopes up, but I need the whole congregation's help on this.'

'You have something?' he whispered.

'Will met everyone in the church last Sunday?' I asked.

'Pretty much. I took him around after both services. But everyone's accounted for. Rolly Tincher had us use our prayer line.'

'We're going to do it again. But a little differently this time.'

'Okay.'

'I want to focus on young people, but I don't want to limit it to that. Anyone and everyone has to be accounted for with an actual sighting. Do you understand me? Not just a phone call.'

'A lot of people have been here.'

'Good. That will cut down our work considerably. How many teenagers and college age kids do you have in the church?'

He blew hard, looked at the ceiling, counting. 'You know about our Outreach?'

'Did Will?'

'I'm sure I told him about it.'

'Did you mention it to Detective Tincher?'

'I don't think I did.'

'Including the Outreach, how many young people are we looking at?'

'Church membership is close to two thousand,

including adolescents who have taken confirmation; not all of them regular, of course. Maybe sixty to eighty college kids have some kind of association, but now the Outreach, we serve three-to-four hundred disadvantaged teenagers with that.'

'You're talking troubled kids?'

'Oh, yeah.'

'That's where I want to focus. Can we get a list? Phone numbers and addresses?'

'I think I can patch something together,' he answered.

I pulled my phone out and walked away for some privacy. Max Dunn answered with his usual growl. 'Sheriff!'

'Rick Trueblood, Max.'

'Garrat told me what you're doing, Rick. I've already got two deputies on their way to the church. If you need more, just holler.'

'I'm going to need some undercover people to check out addresses as we go, Max.'

'Whatever I can do, buddy!'

Chapter 77

Saturday 5:32 p.m., March 27.

WITHIN A COUPLE OF HOURS we had everything organized, our list dwindling rapidly. I had ten phones going, four men and six women.

The women were calling adults in the congregation no one had seen since Wednesday. The cover was to ask if they could bring food down. Following this round of calls, they moved on to those college kids who had not yet made an appearance at the church. Those who answered were asked to come to a prayer service that afternoon. If they showed up, we scratched them off the list. If they made an excuse, we sent a plain clothes deputy around to have a look.

The men called those members with teenagers no one had seen, including the all important three hundred-fifteen disadvantaged kids. They claimed to be guidance counsellors who wanted to know why the kids had not been in school for the past three days. As most of them had been to school, they reacted – usually with some genuine anger. Anger was good, but we asked for verification. Had they seen anyone at school? Once we had a name, we followed up with the eyewitness. The kids who had actually been out of sight for the past couple of days we were forced to handle with a great deal more care, and Max's deputies did a drive by. If that left us in the dark, the deputies checked with the neighbours. If no one had seen the kid outside or at least witnessed someone they knew going in and out of the house or if we just got answering machines, the kids stayed on the list.

IT WASN'T TOO MANY HOURS BEFORE Connie Merriweather and I were looking at three kids from the outreach, two college students we hadn't found, one adult couple that had not joined the church but sometimes came, and one family with two teenagers. No sightings, no contact. Nothing on the drive by or neighbours to get them off the list.

I was ready to read my list to Max Dunn and let his people actually go on the property and take a closer look, but just as I was about to hit the speed dial, one of the deacons came up behind me and snooped the list. 'The Lyons,' he said, 'are out of town. A death in the family.'

'You talked to them?' I asked.

'I checked at the business when I couldn't get through for prayers Thursday morning.'

'Who did you talk to?' I demanded. 'I need a name.'

He thought about it. 'Tony Corrigan. One of Ben's store managers.'

'Did Corrigan *see* the guy or just get a call?'

'He saw him!'

I nodded and scratched the family from the list, then punched up Max on my cell phone. I gave him six names and addresses. Then the deputies and I joined everyone in the sanctuary for a prayer that rocked heaven for over an hour. We weren't quitting until we heard one way or the other. There were nearly a thousand of us by then – standing room only. Connie Merriweather was in the pulpit and there were five extra preachers singing and praying to keep things hot.

Meanwhile, Max's people had done their follow-up work and had the list cut down to one very curious case: a girl in Merriweather's outreach programme named Phyllis Hawthorne. She was not answering her phone. She did not go to the door for a special delivery from UPS. The parents were nowhere to be found, and no one we had contacted had seen her at school since Wednesday. What is more, the deputies had a visual through a crack in her curtain. They could be sure of nothing else, only that she was there and not responding to the doorbell. A sure sign something was wrong.

Now Max was as eager to be a hero as any man, so

he and Rolly Tincher huddled. Call Rick or go in? Rolly said he didn't see why Rick Trueblood needed to approve what the sheriff did. That was all Max needed. I expect the worst of it came from the fact that Kathy James had a tip from someone. She was there with a photographer to video the whole thing from inside an unmarked van: a sheriff's SWAT team led by Joe Roby taking the house, one-two-three, like they always practiced it, and Phyllis Hawthorne looking up from her book at five heavily armoured deputies rushing in to save her. It was the first clue Phyllis had that there might be a problem. The girl, as Connie Merriweather could have told us if we had only asked, was deaf.

I got a call on my cell phone less than five minutes after the entry team hit. The church went silent as I listened to Max cursing me.

When I got off the phone, every face in the sanctuary was looking at me. Their eyes were full of dreams and terror. All I could do was shake my head.

Part VII

Treasures of the Snow

Hast thou entered into the treasures of the snow?

Job 38:22

Chapter 78

Darkness.

THE ROOM STINKS WITH THEIR ODOUR, a cloying filth. Their eyes take him in but they do not speak. They are like animals in their pens before the day of their slaughter.

Will wants to see Ben. There is a rattle, a wheeze. The blood is still caked on his swollen, naked chest. His beard is thickening, like the scent of him. 'Ben?' The eyes open. 'One of the guidance counsellors at school has been calling your answering machine, Ben. He wants to know where Boy and Penny have been. Didn't you talk to the principal at that school?' Ben's eyes can hardly hold their focus even as Will pulls the Bernardelli and points it into his face. 'Did you lie to me, Ben?'

From behind him, Tabit tells Will, 'Leave him alone. They always call when you miss class.'

Will twirls around quickly. 'They had an excuse! The principal knew they were leaving town!'

'They just double-check. They always do.'

'On a Saturday?'

'That's when they can find the parents at home.'

Will is dizzy, close to blacking out. His muscles ache with a fire that will not stop. If he could only rest. But he cannot. Not now. 'I won't be lied to, and I won't be tricked,' he tells her.

'Nobody's lying to you,' Tabit answers.

Will thinks about this. He loses a moment. Finally, he draws a breath and pockets the little pistol. Smiling, the good pastor to his flock, 'Have you said your prayers, Tabit?' She does not answer him this time. 'Benny? Penny? Have *you* prayed?' Boy is as silent as Penny but for a different reason. He is fading like Ben.

'Where's Tammy, Will?' Tabit asks. 'Is she okay?'

'Tammy's okay. Ask Penny if you don't believe me.'

Chapter 79

Dawn.

THE SUN WAS UP, BUT I wasn't ready for it. I blinked my eyes, and it hurt. I moaned and heard a woman answer in the same tone.

I opened my eyes and saw Irene Follet beside me. I looked around. Her bedroom, by the look of it. I looked at her again. She was looking back at me. Her green eyes sleepy, amused. 'You don't remember, do you?'

I started to lie, but then I shook my head.

'I think I want a church wedding,' she said.

'I proposed again?'

'Mmmmm.' She nodded and nuzzled my neck.

'You accepted... again?'

'You were so persistent... and cute. And I love the way you dance; it's so... old school. How could I resist?'

I rolled off the bed, put my feet to the hardwood,

and my back to her. The movement cost me some pain and nausea, and I groaned heavily.

'You don't sound so good, Rick.' She was laughing at me.

'I feel great,' I lied. I looked back at her. 'I just need a couple of minutes under a hot shower. I'll be fine.' I stood and staggered some.

She laughed quietly. 'You're still drunk.'

'It never feels as good in the morning, does it?'

I pointed at two doors, questioning her. Irene gestured toward the one on the right. 'Your toothbrush is the blue one. Help yourself to a razor.'

'Have you got a towel I can use?'

'Yours should be dry.'

'*Mine?*'

'We did things right last night, Rick. Showers and everything.'

'I didn't sign anything, did I?'

She giggled. 'We were too busy to bother with paper-work.'

I was in the shower, starting to bring it back, when I heard a knock at the door. I said to come in, and a moment later Irene peeked around the curtain. She was as naked as I was. 'Got room for a friend?'

'My God!' I said with genuine admiration, 'No wonder I keep proposing...'

Chapter 80

Darkness.

TAMMY HAS STILL NOT returned. Penny goes out and comes back. Never a word about Tammy.'

'Is Tammy okay?' Tabit asks.

'Fine,' Penny tells her. 'She's okay.' They are voices in the dark, nothing more.

'Then why doesn't she come back?'

'He's not hurting her, Tabit. If that's what you're thinking, don't worry. He just doesn't want us all together anymore.'

Penny is lying. Tabit knows that much. She thinks that Will is going to pick her out next. She is afraid of rape, afraid to die. That is what leaving the group means. It is the *shadow of death* – nothing like what she had imagined it would be in the comfort of her sunny prayers.

'You *saw* her?' Tabit asks.

'She's okay!'

Lying. 'Did you talk to her?'

A silence like death. Finally Penny answers, 'He won't let us talk.'

Chapter 81

Sunday 8:46 a.m., March 28.

I LOOKED AT MY WATCH, then at the crowd in the restaurant.

'Got a date?' Irene asked me. A bit nervous or sad. I couldn't read her that well.

'Sorry. I was thinking about those two girls. Figuring out how long it had been.'

'You think they're still alive?'

'They disappeared Wednesday afternoon...'

She calculated the thing. 'Fourth morning...'

'Ninety hours,' I said. 'Give or take. The woman who survived this guy last time says she never saw the sun. Never knew when it was day or night. Went on like that for almost two weeks. Perpetual night.'

'I can't imagine something like that.'

I thought about Missy, how crazy she was after Booker was finished with her, but I couldn't tell Irene about that. Instead I watched a big tray of heaping plates of food passing and told Irene about the phone calls we had made on Saturday. 'I was sure we had him.' *The flock.*

'So what now?'

'The thing is we've gone through everything twice. At this point there's nothing left to try. I mean the sheriff's office will keep the pretences up a few more days, we'll all hope for a break, but yesterday was the last big push. Reasonably, we have to assume he took off. Someone in Kansas or Idaho is going to have to make the rescue.' Or clean up the mess, I thought.

'But you can't let it go? You're still counting the hours.'

'When the time comes that I know it's over, I'll let it go. But this is the hard part. It's not really over and yet there's nothing anyone can do. We just wait... until we know.' I told her about my daughter, and then the rest, my failure to get past it. 'There was a point early on... Sarah was already gone, we'd had the funeral, and I was chasing after every lead that came along; the cops were sympathetic, but they had moved on. I could see it, even if they told me otherwise. Me, I wanted revenge. I thought I had to have it or I'd I die. And then one morning I woke up and I just knew it was over. I wasn't going to find him. I was out in Kansas on another bum lead, and I thought about calling my wife, telling her I had tried... my God I had tried! But it was over, and I was coming home. When I touched the phone... I just couldn't call her. I couldn't tell her I'd failed. So I went out and started looking again.'

'Ever call your wife, Rick?'

'We talked on the phone a few times before the divorce. I was into my cups, and I told her I was never going to give up... or some damn thing about as stupid. Just pure ego. My pain is worse than your pain, that kind of thing. When you're full of rage, you don't think about other people. Even the people you love. You keep that feeling long enough, rage is all you have.'

'You lost your marriage over it?'

I thought of Job and that damn Connie Merriweather. 'Business, money, marriage. Everything went when I lost Sarah. The good news is Nicole found someone, a pretty good guy from what I can see. Got some step-kids she loves, took over the business I had been running and she's doing all right with it.'

'What about you?' Irene asked, her smile tender, gently curious. 'Are you doing all right?'

'I've had a tough week. This thing has brought some memories back I thought I was past.'

'This thing is tearing you up.'

'I don't want these girls to die, but I promise you this, I'm going to get past it no matter how it turns out.'

'Because it's a job and not your life?'

'Because I'll know I gave it everything I have. That's

all anyone can do. I didn't know that when Sarah was murdered.'

'So how do you know when something like this is over?'

I shook my head. 'That one they don't put in the manual.'

Chapter 82

Palm Sunday 10:10 a.m., March 28.

'I'D ASK YOU IN,' IRENE TOLD me as we sat on the street in front of her place, 'but I've got three hours before I have to get to the library. I'd like to do some things.'

'Are you going to write a poem?'

'Maybe a line or two.'

'Can I call you tonight? Sober, this time. I promise.'

She opened the car door. 'We don't have to stay that way, do we?'

I laughed. 'We can do anything you want, darling.'

'That sounds like fun. But get some rest today, Rick. Huh? No work. You hear me? You look tired. You look real tired.'

'If you can believe it,' I answered, 'I was thinking about going out to Merriweather's church this morning.'

'Guilt about what the two of us did last night?' She was teasing me.

'I want to touch base with the folks out there. Let them know... well, that it's not just a job. I want those girls back as much as they do.'

'Kind of like going to the funeral afterwards?'

I looked at the sky, 'I'll be there for that, too.'

THE SIGN SAID THE ASSOCIATE PASTOR would speak about *Going Home... to the place you've never been*. Palm Sunday services at eight-thirty and ten-thirty. Everyone welcome.

The church was half-empty. Merriweather's backup was hammering clichés out like burgers on the line. The words were still about hope, but the eyes everywhere told the truth. We came to surrender. We rose and sat, we sang and prayed and listened. I found myself wondering why the innocents seem always to pay for the sins and follies of their elders.

When the service finished, a line gathered in front of Connie and Rachel Merriweather. They had managed it so they weren't quite standing together but could shake everyone's hand as they left. I stood for a minute or so for the ritual, but I got weak in the knees and felt sick with the thought of actually facing Rachel Merriweather. The preacher I could handle. You can talk to a man who knows it's over, but a woman who still believes in miracles...

It was just too much for me, and I cut for a side door like a thief breaking away with the morning's offering. A fast exit and no goodbyes. Just not fast enough.

'Mr Trueblood!'

I had slipped through the commons without incident and was into the hallway, ready to burst into the sunlight and snow. The voice behind me belonged to Rachel Merriweather. How she had gotten there I could not imagine – a secret passageway, most likely. Caught as I was, I turned to face the woman with all the vitality of a pair of worn out shoes.

'Anything?' she asked.

I dropped my chin to my chest as I lied to her. 'The sheriff's still working on it.' She got small and frail, and she shuddered after I spoke. It should have made me a man; instead, her look brought out the professional liar in me and I worked up all the confidence I could summon. 'They'll find your girls, Mrs Merriweather, you have to believe that.'

'Yesterday, I thought...' Yesterday, we had all thought. 'You had such hope in your eyes,' she said, and suddenly there were huge tears running over her cheeks. Her faith had finally broken, and I realized with a terrible sadness that Rachel Merriweather was only human after all.

A woman came into the hall behind her, studied the scene quietly, then retreated. 'We had a good idea,' I said. 'I thought it might work.'

The woman came out again. I looked at her so Rachel Merriweather would turn and see her too. I meant to use the interruption as an excuse to get away, but when the woman saw that I was aware of her, she came forward nervously, her eyes on me alone. 'You're with the police?'

'The county prosecutor's office. Is there something I can do for you?'

She was a tall blonde woman in her late forties, trim, well-heeled, a bit nervous in the soul. 'It's my daughter,' she said timidly. I raised my eyebrows expectantly, 'She thinks there might be something wrong.'

'Wrong with what?' I asked.

'Benny Lyons calls her every night and it's been… well, it's been several days since she's heard from him.'

Rachel Merriweather spoke with tears still flowing over her beautiful face, 'The Lyons are out of town, Faith. A death in the family.'

'That's the thing. Benny was supposed to have a date with Cynthia last night. He didn't call her to say he wasn't able to make it. I wouldn't say anything, but that's just not like Benny. Even if they had to go out of town suddenly.'

Chapter 83

Darkness.

THE DOOR OPENS AND WILL STANDS before them. He is wearing a dress, high heels, and long dark hair. Tabit feels a curdling of acid deep in her bowels. It is Mrs Lyons's hair he is wearing. She rolls to her side, gagging.

'Penny!' Will whispers, 'Time to come out and play.'

Next to Tabit, Penny hisses angrily, 'No!'

Will steps into the room, lifting his gun until it is pointing at Benny, who is unconscious. 'You're dad's gone, Penny. You killed him with your stubbornness. Are you going to kill Benny now, too?'

A CANDLE BURNS ON THE FLOOR, illuminating the room. The furnace tape screeches as Will pulls out yet another strip. He cuts it. Holding the tape and a rag in front of Penny's face, he tells her to open her mouth. Penny knows better than to resist. He will simply go in and execute her brother as he has promised her several times while binding her into this chair. She opens her mouth and takes the rag, then feels the tape covering her lips. Will wraps it into her hair, then smiles as sweetly as he did when he shot Benny in the knee.

'This won't hurt when they take it off, Penny. The dead feel nothing.'

Penny rocks in the chair, seized with panic, but there is no give to the bindings, no way to fight now. Will studies her eyes, blood seeping out from under the hair line. *Her mother's hair, her mother's blood!* 'You should have given me Tammy when I asked you. She's dead anyway. It's not like I didn't warn you, Penny. I *begged* you! Oh, but you got proud on me. Thought you were stronger than me! Well, we'll see how strong you are now.'

He goes to Benny's bedroom and comes back with a metal folding chair. He goes again for the shotgun. 'No,' he says, seeing the fear in her eyes. 'I'm not going to shoot you. I mean for someone else to do it.'

He sets the gun on the chair and tapes the gun barrel down so it points toward her. Low. At the hips, the womb, she thinks. Now he tapes the chair to the floor with several strips of tape to keep it from scooting. Her chair he has tied off with rope, so it is firmly in place. There is no way to move it or even tip it over.

Will leaves again, then returns with a piece of string. Penny can see what he means to do now. All the same it is terrible to watch him knotting the string about the trigger. When he has finished, he goes to her and whispers in her ear like a lover.

'I don't know when they're going to find you, Penny. Maybe you're dead already from the wait, but if you're not, I want you to watch that door open because that's the last thing you're ever going to see. And when you see it opening, you remember to think how if you'd only given me Tammy, only killed a woman who's already dead... why, you could have lived. You and Benny *and* your dad. It's your own stubbornness that opens that door, Penny. You remember that!'

As Will leaves the room, he takes the string. She watches his hand reach back to loop the string over the doorknob. That is the margin she has. About four inches. If the door pulls opens beyond that distance, the string will pull the trigger.

His fingers wave goodbye, all a good joke, and Penny stares into the bore of her father's shotgun.

A gunshot sounds in the next room. She waits for another, hears nothing more. Benny or Tabit? She doesn't know. Hasn't the courage to guess which one he kills.

Her door opens very slowly. She watches the string tightening, certain she is dead. Then she sees Will's fingers coming round the door again. Waving his fingers at her as a child might do, Will says to her, 'Don't worry about Tabit opening the door by accident, Penny.'

Tabit.

Chapter 84

Palm Sunday 12:10 p.m., March 28.

MY CELL PHONE WAS DEAD. I'd left it on overnight, so I called Max Dunn from the church office. Max sounded a bit irritated when he heard my voice. 'What is it now, Rick?'

'A family at the church we overlooked.'

'Listen... buddy... we fought the good fight. Let's put it to bed, what do you say? I can't keep calling the cavalry out on these wild hunches.'

'Max! We've got people nobody has heard from since Booker took off. They're supposed to be out of town for a death in the family, but the boy had a date with his girlfriend Saturday night and didn't call to let her know he couldn't make it.'

'Rick, I had a gal with a pot of a water boiling thirty-five years ago; she had to get home and turn it off or the house would burn down, but the minute she took care of that, why she was going to give me a call! Guess what, buddy.'

'The girl has been by the house several times,' I responded. 'They live in the same subdivision. There's a Bronco and the boy's Toyota parked in front of the garage, Max. The Bronco belongs to the old man. The thing is he's a fanatic about keeping his vehicle spotless. He *never* leaves it out – and it's been there since Wednesday.'

'It's thin, Rick.'

'Men and their cars, Max...'

'People *do* leave town, you know, and they *do* forget things, especially if they're upset.'

'They forgot something else.'

'I'm listening.'

'Family has a German shepherd named Pete. When they leave town, Pete stays in the backyard and the neighbour takes care of him. Dog's a guard dog, never leaves the property. Guess who's not in the backyard, Max.'

'Well... maybe that *is* once too many for a coincidence.'

'Two kids. Seniors in high school. Twins. Boy and a girl. They were in church last week. Will met the boy and his dad before he shook anyone else's hand. The boy is gold, Max. Star athlete, straight-A student. But the girl... Connie Merriweather tells me she's got a lot of issues, lot of anger – a little bit like Missy Worth back in the old days.'

'Holding a bat, you think?'

'It can't hurt to have a look. The family's name is Lyons; they're down in King's Court on Wolverine Lane.'

'*Ben* Lyons?'

'You know him?'

'I know him real well. Hell of a nice guy, Rick. Big contributor.'

'You know the house?'

'No, but the guy is swimming in money – so I'm guessing it's one of the big houses down there.'

'I'll get what I can from the girlfriend on the layout and bring it to your staging area.'

'The university's got a lodge out that way...'

'I know the place.'

'Thirty minutes unless you can get there sooner!'

Chapter 85

Sunday 12:19 p.m., March 28.

THE MINUTE I WAS OFF THE phone with Max, I sat down with Benny Lyons's girlfriend and got everything I could on the Lyons house. Doors, windows, rooms. She knew the house pretty well, especially the basement. Benny's bedroom was in the basement.

We drew up a sketch of the place quickly, as close to scale as she could get it. After we had finished, I took off at a run, only to be caught by Connie Merriweather as I was leaving the building. 'I'm coming along,' he said.

'That's not possible.'

He took my arm. It wasn't a friendly gesture. 'They're my *kids*!'

'I'll call you the minute we know something. What I want you to do is get upstairs to the sanctuary and start praying. You tell them the last four days have just been for practice! The next hour... we're going to need it all! You and I both know that won't happen if you're not there to lead them.'

'I want to *do* something!'

'My mamma used to tell me the Lord listens to the prayers of a righteous man! Why don't you go work on proving her right?' The preacher's hand fell off my arm, and I thought to say something more, but there was nothing to tell him, no hope that we did not already share, and I went on through the door before he could answer me or even give me God's blessing.

I took a country highway south of the church as far as the interstate, then ran west on it for just under five miles, pushing my car as hard as it would go. The road was cleared, but along each side the snow was piled high. I exited onto State Highway 641 and got into some traffic, but a caravan of emergency vehicles was running silently out of the north. When the traffic pulled over, I followed in behind the flashing lights. After the mall we hit the last two miles pushing it up past a hundred. Just outside King's Court, we found a state trooper waiting to help us across the highway. A second trooper made sure we found the staging area.

I parked the car where a deputy indicated and got with Max Dunn, Joe Roby and Cass McCreary. Off from them about ten paces a dozen officers from the city and sheriff's SWAT teams were strapping on armour and checking their weapons. In the distance, I saw one lone reconnaissance officer in civilian clothes running through a woods still deep in snow. He was headed in the direction of the Lyons house.

As I came up to join Max and the two SWAT commanders, I saw Cass McCreary fixing her hair into a teenage girl's pig tails. She looked a bit odd in a bullet proof vest, but when she finished the effect by slipping on a white sweatshirt with a high school logo on it she looked just like a buxom blonde cheerleader I had known a million years ago.

'We need a dad,' Max told me.

I looked at him in surprise.

'Dispatch can't turn up Rolly,' he explained, 'and DeWitt's in church. Won't answer his phone when he's at the church. Our boy William knows my face, and Roby here is taking both teams in.'

'Whatever you need,' I said and handed over the diagrams of the Lyons house. 'Here's the interior of the house, by the way.'

Max glanced at it, then passed it to Roby, who went over to his entry teams with the sketches. As he was doing this, Cass McCreary explained to me what it was going to take to be her daddy.

When the reconnaissance officer returned, Roby came back to get his report. 'It's quiet,' he said. 'Good cover till we get to the backyard. Then...' He shook his head. '...bad news.'

'How much time in the open?' Joe Roby asked him.

'It's a big yard. Seven-eight seconds at a full sprint. Doesn't sound like much, but if he sees us it's enough time to execute everyone.'

'What about the doors?' Max asked.

'Nothing that's going to slow us down. Back door into the garage is particle board or cheap tin, I couldn't tell which. One punch and we're through. Other way in is a glass patio door.' He raised his eyebrows, discounting its potential to slow them down.

Roby looked up from the diagram. 'We're a little thin, Cass. If you can roll off the front and take the first basement window on the southeast corner that will give us cover on all the windows and two full teams going in. One up and one down.' Cass McCreary nodded and Roby looked at me. 'That leaves you moving up on the front door, Rick. Better than even money Booker pops right out into your arms. If I were you I'd strap a vest on and get a weapon.'

'I'll be okay,' I said.

Roby considered me dubiously, then shrugged. It wasn't *his* body.

Max patted me on the back. 'If he's too much man for you, Rick, just dive for cover. I'm coming in right behind you.'

Roby looked at Max. 'EMTs know to come over the top of us?'

'The ambulances are up the highway,' Max told him. 'They're coming in with me.'

362

Chapter 86

Darkness.

THE CANDLE STILL BURNS steadily. At first the shotgun is all Penny can look at. After a time, she forces herself to examine the room. The window behind her at the top of the room has been sealed shut with plastic and cardboard so no light comes in. From there, she thinks, you could see the shotgun and the string to the door – if it weren't covered. She rocks in the chair, but it's impossible to move it. No matter what direction she pulls a piece of rope resists the pressure.

She looks at the window again. The only hope is that someone comes to it, tears out the plastic and cardboard and looks in before they run to the basement for a rescue. Or somehow that she can get her hands loose…

Penny flexes and tears against the tape and rope binding her, but her strength fails her. She cannot fight it, but if she nags it, a little twist one way, then back…

363

Sliding it up now, then down just a fraction. A little at a time. Steadily. Then maybe a chance. She thinks about erosion, water and sand tearing down mountains – with enough time.

She keeps her eyes on the gun. Her wrists burn as she turns them, fighting the tape. Not too hard! she tells herself, just turn it, pry a little, turn again the other way. She has time. She has until that door is pulled open. All the time in the world...

Chapter 87

Sunday 12:59 p.m., March 28.

IN THE CAR McCreary told me, 'Glad you brought the *dad-mobile*, Rick. This thing's perfect.'

'Hey, this was a nice car fifteen years ago!'

'Fifteen years ago I was still a nice girl. What's your point?'

'I'm just saying...'

Cass pulled her Taurus .45 out from under her nice-girl sweatshirt, jacked a shell into the chamber, checked the safety, then slipped it back into place. 'Are you religious?'

'I am this morning.'

'Pray that son of a bitch is in my window, will you?'

'Hey, leave us something to prosecute! Garrat promised me she's taking this case herself.'

'I'm just going to shoot his nuts off, Rick. Garrat can have his ass.'

THE ROAD IN WAS QUIET, and I said something about how still everything was. 'We got it blocked off at either end,' she answered. 'Dispatch has been calling everyone up and down the road for the last fifteen minutes. Telling people to stay inside.'

'That'll get them on their front steps faster than a fireworks display.'

She shook her head, grinning. 'They're telling folks we had a prison break this morning, and we're out here trying to catch them... you know, in case someone decides to start shooting anyone they don't know.'

'Might work for a few minutes,' I said.

'A few minutes is all we need.'

We came around a curve, and I saw Ben Lyons's Bronco covered in snow – but no Toyota. The street was empty. The house darkened, seemingly deserted.

'Okay,' McCreary told me, 'hit the horn.'

I tapped it lightly, then again, a longer shot, then several more taps.

'You see a curtain...'

'I know. I call your name.'

As I pulled to the curb, McCreary jumped out and trotted prettily up the lane along one of the two tire tracks running through the deep snow. At the front of the house, she cut through the snowdrifts and came to the door. Her hands were free and open. She moved with the kind of bubbly innocence of eighteen. I hit the horn again and lowered my window. 'TELL HER TO GET A MOVE ON!' I shouted. Cass tossed me a quick glance before ringing the doorbell. I watched the windows for movement, then hit the horn several quick taps.

Roby's team would be waiting under cover at this point. Will Booker might be checking. Nothing here but a dad and his little girl come to pick up Penny Lyons. As we could be a potential problem, we hoped Booker would come have a look. If we got him to the front of the house, Roby could cross the backyard on Cass McCreary's signal. With no signal from us, Roby moved when he felt like it.

'I THOUGHT SHE WAS SUPPOSED TO BE WAITING FOR US!' I called.

I hit the horn again, a long blast. Across the street I saw a curtain move, but not at the Lyons house. *Come on, Will!* I thought, *Get curious, boy...*

'ARE THEY EVEN HOME?' I shouted.

Now Cass moved off the step and out into the yard. She looked at the windows, edging toward the end of the house without being too obvious about it. She turned back toward me, 'SHE SAID SHE'D BE HERE!'

'WE CAN'T WAIT ALL DAY, SWEETHEART!' I got out of the car, a grumpy but lovable old dad.

'What do you want me to do... just leave?' Quieter. Not overplaying it.

'Well if they're not here!' I said, 'I'm not going to wait here all afternoon!'

'She said she'd be here!' A nice daddy's girl whine. A few steps more to her left, as if tempted to look in a window...

I started to answer. A speech about responsibility and wasn't it about time she and her friends started thinking about it, but at that moment we heard glass breaking.

Roby at the patio door. Now an explosion of wood. The back door of the garage.

We were in.

Chapter 88

Darkness.

THERE IS A CAR, THE SOUND OF a horn. A man's voice. Penny forces her eyes from the wide bore of her father's shotgun and stares at the plastic covering the window. She leans forward now, feeling the flesh at her wrists tearing. She screams into the gag with pain. She struggles to breathe, her nostrils sucking wildly for air. Her chest hammering. She looks at the gun again. The string. The door. She listens. What is the man saying?

Not police, she thinks miserably. A girl answering him? Next door maybe. The Frosts? But that didn't make sense!

Now glass shattering! Voices upstairs, footsteps. Penny looks back at the window. Nothing. They are coming downstairs. *Through the door. Rescue.*

Her eyes flick to the window, now back to the door

as she loses all control, her underpants warm and wet suddenly. The string. The gun.

Her body surges against the certainty of death, but the tape holds her. The gun remains fixed on her, sitting on its little metal folding chair. They are down the steps. Coming for her on the run. *Seconds left*, she thinks. The time it takes to get to the end of the hall and pull the door open...

Chapter 89

Sunday 1:03 p.m., March 28.

CASS MCCREARY BEGAN RUNNING the moment she heard the glass. She had her Taurus .45 out and made the corner of the house quickly before she slipped and fell in a deep drift. There were two window wells looking into the basement on the south side of the house. A second officer was already leaning down into his. Cass scrambled across the heavy snow.

She broke and cleared the glass with a hard sweep of the Taurus. There was cardboard and plastic on the inside. Careful not to cut herself on the shards still in the window frame, Cass beat the cardboard down with two ferocious back-handed swings. When the cardboard and plastic broke free she snapped the safety off her weapon and leaned into the well to get a look at things, her .45 in the lead.

The room was black, illuminated by a single candle.

McCreary blinked away the brightness in her eyes and tried to focus. She saw the shadow of a girl in a chair and started to transmit to Roby that she had a visual on one of the hostages, but she saw the girl looking first at the window and then at the chair placed in front of her with such panic that Cass stopped. Her eyes adjusting, Cass studied the chair more closely. It was positioned oddly between the girl and the door to the room. Then she saw in the murky light that a shotgun lay across the chair. She heard the voices of cops somewhere close, heard their shouts – the order to check the other rooms. They had found something. Cass saw the girl's eyes full of terror. She pivoted her head between the door and Cass and then back to the door. And Cass McCreary finally understood.

She reached the Taurus down further through the window, just as the door pulled back and the string snapped taut.

Chapter 90

Sunday 1:03 p.m., March 28.

I HELD THE FRONT OF the house only a second or so before Max Dunn and the EMTs came roaring into the suburb. I went in ahead of them, kicking the front door open, and found an officer holding the centre of the room with an assault gun. The air was clean. He wore a headset and spoke into it. 'EMTs are coming!' he said.

His voice was cool with the precision that you see in trial runs, and I came up out of my crouch with a feeling of relief. I moved to the side to make room for the medical people. That was when the shotgun blast roared up from underneath us. Not ours. None of us was packing a shotgun.

The officer held his arms up to stop the EMTs, and I took off for the basement at a run.

As I came out of the turn of the stairwell, I saw a

knot of men breaking loose at the other end of the hall. Joe Roby shouting into headset. He needed the EMTs now!

An officer came out of the darkened utility room. 'In here!' he shouted to the men behind me. I joined the crowd and looked past Roby. I saw three figures on the floor. All of them as still as death. I got out of the way of the EMTs and stepped into the laundry room behind three armoured men. Two officers were cutting the tape and rope that bound a nearly naked girl to a wooden chair. I smelled cordite and saw the shotgun. It was strapped to a metal chair that lay on the floor now, but the string that connected it to the door was still attached.

An officer in front of me, a city police, caught my eye and pointed at the chair, then to the window. 'Cass McCreary shot the damn chair over just as we were coming in. Otherwise...'

There was a hole about the size of walnut punched in the metal back of the chair – the result of McCreary's .45. Across the room, I could see the washing machine had taken the shotgun blast intended for the girl. I looked at her wide, unblinking eyes. Penny Lyons. Alive. She looked, I thought, a bit like a picture of Missy Worth I had in my files, when Missy had been a willowy seventeen-year-old. Behind me there was a call to clear the door, and two EMTs slipped into the room.

In the seconds it had taken for me to understand what the girl had escaped, two of the bodies had been cleared from the utility room. The man remained, a thin blanket covering his chest, for all the good it would do him.

'Clear it!' Roby was shouting. 'Everybody up! Now!'

I moved with the rest toward the stairs, seeing several men taking a look into an opened freezer before they climbed out of Will Booker's hell. I noticed several candles set about. It had been the sole illumination until we had arrived. By the door to the utility room there were five stacks of clothes, all neatly folded, a pair of shoes on top of each, odd testimony to Booker's peculiar madness.

When Roby saw me, he held his hand up, stopping me. 'Max is coming down.'

As he said this, Max Dunn pushed past the last of the officers leaving the basement. Cass McCreary was behind him. Roby looked at the woman. 'You couldn't have cut it any closer, Cass.'

'Is she okay?' McCreary's wrist was wrapped in a blood-dappled piece of surgical gauze.

'She's shaken up and dehydrated, but she's doesn't appear to be hurt otherwise.'

He turned to Max and told him what Booker had done to Penny Lyons and then described McCreary's shot just as the entry team was pulling the door open. While he did this, I stepped over to see what the officers had been looking at in the freezer. I saw the fur of the guard dog Pete first, then stepping closer realised it lay on the naked corpse of Judy Lyons. The dog's head had been crushed; Booker had peeled away the woman's scalp.

'We think it's Judy Lyons,' Roby said as McCreary and Max Dunn came beside me to look into the freezer. 'Got another down here.' He led the way and we followed, looking into the room where Booker had kept them. 'Presumably Mr Lyons,' Roby announced.

Max walked in and nodded grimly. 'It's Ben.' Then he swore.

'Booker shot Tabitha Merriweather,' Roby told him. 'Looks to me like he went for the lung so she could choke to death on her own blood. The wound was fresh and they got her out, but I doubt she'll make it to the hospital. He pointed at a piece of bloodstained carpet. 'The boy was here. He was unconscious, already in shock. Got one leg broken at the knee and stinking to high heaven; Booker shot him in the other knee as well. Wound looked a day or two old.'

'Is he going to make it?'

Roby shook his head. 'The EMTs didn't look real happy. They said something about gangrene.'

'How about Tammy Merriweather?' Max asked.

'Her shoes and clothes appear to be over there in one of these piles.' Roby pointed at the five stacks of clothes.

Max shook his head and swore a bit more mildly. 'Son of a bitch!'

'We better get upstairs,' Roby offered. 'He can't have much of a lead on us.'

Before any of us moved, Max looked into Penny Lyons's would-be-execution chamber. 'Captain McCreary,' he said after a moment of silence, 'if Chief Cottrell doesn't know what kind of officer he's got, you come over to the sheriff's department and name your terms. You hear me?'

'Sheriff,' Cass McCreary answered, 'to tell you the truth... I don't even remember pulling the trigger.'

Chapter 91

Sunday 1:13 p.m., March 28.

I CALLED GARRAT with Roby's cell phone. After that I called Merriweather's church. I told the lady who answered to get the Merriweathers down to Regional South. I said I would meet them at the emergency entrance.

'Are they okay? Are the kids alive?'

'Make sure some good people come with them,' I answered.

'Oh, God...'

I switched off before I had to explain myself. Outside, I found Max and Joe Roby. 'You get hold of the Merriweathers, did you?' Max asked.

'I'm going down to the hospital to meet them,' I said.

'Tell the Merriweathers if they have any questions about what we're doing to find Tammy, I'll be up to the hospital as soon as I can get away from here.'

'What *are* we doing to find her, Max?'

'I tell you what, buddy,' Max told me with a wry grin, 'I only feel like lying about it once, so why don't you just wait for me to spoon it out to the Merriweathers?'

'You've got a lot to do here. How long are you going to be?'

'We've got Rolly on the way. Once he's here, I'll drive up to the hospital. We're going to need a news conference – as soon as we contact the Lyons's next-of-kin.'

'The hospital will have facilities,' I said.

'I know. I just wish we had better news. Looking for two girls and we come up with two dead, two critically wounded and one still missing... what a nightmare!'

'We saved one, Max.'

Max looked at the bare spot where Benny Lyons's Toyota had sat, the two sets of footprints leading to the spot and then to the tire tracks leading out to the road. 'Where is he, Rick? Where is my Sweet William?'

I GOT TO MY CAR and rolled back to the highway in no hurry to get to the hospital. I knew that in a matter of minutes every cop in the bi-state would be alerted to keep an eye-out for Benny Lyons's Toyota. With a long afternoon before us and a cold bright winter day, chances were good we had come to the final hours of the hunt, but that didn't mean Tammy Merriweather

379

was going to get through. She had apparently left the house under her own power, but once in the car Booker might have finished it. One child left dying, the other a question mark to torture Connie Merriweather to the end of his days, just in case he hadn't cursed his God yet.

I had my turn signal on at the hospital entrance and was waiting for the oncoming traffic to clear so I could pull in, when I started thinking about Booker and Merriweather and the friendship that had ignited this whole thing. Booker's test of faith for the preacher – the preacher losing everything but God...

Just like Job. In the middle of it all, I happened to remember Frank Cottrell taking the stolen Gideon from DeWitt and reading it to us with such intense thought-fulness: '... *and I only am escaped alone to tell.*' The way he looked up then and pronounced the name of Missy Worth. I started to laugh at the windbag idiocy of the man, something to break the heaviness of the mood that had overtaken me, but the words themselves caught me like a sucker punch. *Missy Worth.*

Booker's survivor. It was Sunday, a little over an hour past noon. Sunday at noon, they were letting Missy Worth out of lock up.

Chapter 92

Sunday 12:41 p.m., March 28.

THEY LET MISSY OUT AT forty-one minutes past noon, forty-*frigging*-one minutes after she was supposed to be released.

Because they wanted money and she didn't have any. 'Your idea to keep me here! I'm damned if I'm going to pay you for it! I don't have no money, anyway!'

What they needed was a signature.

'I'm not signing nothing!'

Doo was there raising hell when Missy took a breath and had to stop cussing them herself. They finally gave up. They would go after the parents. The minute she was done with the bastards, Doo pulled a beer out of a brown paper sack he'd brought along and handed it to her, right there so the doctors and all of them could see it!

Missy laughed and threw her arms around him, slopping beer on his t-shirt and kissing his face with a wet smack. 'I spend another day in here, I *will* be crazy, Doo! A girl can die without a beer, now that's a fact!'

She had her beer down before they were in the parking lot and was working on a second when he kicked his Harley to life.

'Caesar eat all the dope?'

'Hey, that cat is the one that needs to go in there and dry out!' Doo told her. Missy swore, and Doo shook his head. 'Don't worry, I saved your dope.' Grinning, 'Most of it anyway. Between Caesar and me... you're just lucky you had so much!'

'I've been living on cigarettes, Coca Cola, and horse tranquilizers for a week, Doo! I'm ready for something good and plenty of it!'

Doo nodded agreeably. That could be arranged, he said.

'COME TO MAMMA!' MISSY shouted, the moment she was in the house. She was talking to the dope, but Caesar came tripping out of the bedroom, yowling at her. *Where the hell have you been!* Missy was right back at him, chewing him out about eating her grass. Did he know how much that cost her? He didn't pay any attention to it; he wanted his shotgun and nothing was going to shut him up until he got it.

Doo watched the ritual, the cat hanging upside down, Missy with a lit joint inside her mouth, the white stream of dope blowing over his yellow face. When the cat hit the floor, he seemed to wobble a little then catch his balance. Doo shook his head and went to get a couple of cold beers out of the refrigerator. The phone rang while he was coming back, and he picked it up. 'Missy there?'

'Yeah, who's this?' But then the guy hung up.

'Who was it?' Missy called from the front room.

'Nobody!'

Missy turned up the music and started dancing while the joint burned off slowly between her fingers. She handed it to him and Doo took a hit. The world slipped inside out and then he waited while Missy tucked the joint back into her mouth again and blew him a shotgun. As good as Caesar! He watched Missy bring the joint out of her mouth, dance away, and kick a chair over to clear the floor for some serious ass-shaking. 'You got enough beer for Mamma, Doo?'

Doo grinned, the guy with everything under control. 'We got plenty of beer, Missy!'

She hammered the one she had in her hand, swayed easily, and belched like a fog horn. 'So what does a girl got to blow to get another one?'

Chapter 93

Palm Sunday 1:26 p.m., March 28.

WILL DRIVES BOY'S Toyota to Seventh and Elm and sits across the street staring at the house, thinking about the night Missy begged her life from him so many years ago. On her very soul how she would never tell.

Then listening to her lies in court. He shakes his head at the memory of it. Missy, who would do anything to live. But then forgot to keep her promise...

The blood of her kills still excited him. No disappointment in that one! Not like Penny. How she *hated* them! How it grew in her each time the blood splashed over her face and covered her arms. Her sister no different from the rest at the end. Come right down to it, she wanted Mary more than the rest. Pretty Mary that never did anything wrong and sweet as springtime.

Long he contemplates the wickedness of this woman, the power he knows he still possesses over her. How she breaks apart at the news he is back in town. Will smiles in the mirror and wipes a trickle of blood seeping out from under the scalp of hair.

As Will walks toward the house he sees a man coming to the front door. He stares out at Will through a cracked pane of glass. It is the man who answered the phone. The same who caught him at the library. And ain't God good!

Will does not hesitate but in his joy he nearly falls off his high heels and right into a drift of snow. The big man watches him, but he can't see past the dress and scalp of Mother Lyons. He opens the door and leans out. 'Can I help you, ma'am?' Yes, the very same. *They closed?* Kicking. Hissing his threats. His dirty words.

Will whispers now. He reaches into the purse he carries. 'I think I'm at the right place.' He hesitates for effect. Wobbles a bit.

'What are you looking for, lady?'

Behind him Missy shouts, 'Who is it, Doo?'

Will pulls his Bernardelli out. 'Here it is,' he answers, smiling. He fires the gun into the giant's face. The giant falls back with a screaming curse and hits the closet door behind him. Now he swears with his filthy mouth. He grabs his bloodied jaw. He is neither down, nor dead. Will feels a pulse of real fear kick up in him but slips inside the house. He takes aim on the forehead at six inches. Blood hits Will's dress as the gun cracks, and the man sits down on the floor. A moment of wonder, then he falls over dead, the stink of his bowels letting go to prove it. From the back room, 'DOO!' Will steps into the room, looking for Missy but not yet seeing her. 'DOO? WHAT IS IT?'

He sees a mirror in the next room, his own painted features, Mamma Lyons's long dark hair. And wouldn't he have made a beautiful girl?

'DOO, ANSWER ME!' Missy stomps out of the bedroom cursing her dead friend and stops when she sees Will. She is naked to the waist. She has a marijuana cigarette in one hand, a beer in the other. They drop at once as she calls the name of the Lord's son with her wicked tongue.

Whispering, Will steps toward her, 'You didn't think I forgot your promise to me, did you, Missy?'

Chapter 94

Palm Sunday 1:27 p.m., March 28.

I TRIED MY PHONE ONE more time as I came up Seventh Street from the south end at about seventy to eighty miles an hour. The phone was stone dead. I tossed it aside. If a cop saw me, he'd follow, maybe even call in for help.

I pressed the horn and hammered the brakes when I pushed through the red lights. Not a cop in sight. All of them south or headed that way. I crossed Crawford, Poplar, and Ohio. At Cherry I was five blocks out and had a straight shot through. The roads had been cleared of snow, but I had to watch for ice patches. Two more intersections to cross. I saw the needle hit a hundred. I kept the horn pressed while I shot past the U, heads turning on a quiet Sunday morning.

Coming up to Elm maybe fifteen seconds later, I got it down to fifty pretty fast and hit the tracks still braking and skidding. The moment I was over them, I cut right and blew into the snowy lane that ran right into Missy Worth's backyard.

I slid well past the house and then slammed the transmission to park. I jumped out of the car without shutting the engine off or closing the door. I lunged through a couple of heavy drifts and came up to the back door at run. Without breaking stride, I kicked the door to splinters and stepped into Missy Worth's kitchen.

Will Booker was in the room just past the kitchen. He was wearing a dress and Judy Lyons's scalp, his face covered in a pale mist of blood. There was a big Harley Davidson motorcycle between us. Missy Worth was on her knees in front of him, naked to the waist and weeping for mercy. Booker had a little gun pointed at her head, and he was talking. Just talking away.

He looked up at me when the door burst open, but he didn't even blink. All he did was move in tight against the woman, slipping his little pistol into the hollow of her ear.

'I'll kill her!' he hissed.

Missy wept louder. Booker, in his dress and stolen hair and high heels, studied my eyes to see how I was going to handle this. I opened my hands for him to see I had no weapon.

'HE KILLED DOO, RICK!'

'I want you to put your gun on the floor, Mr Law!

You don't do it quick it's the same as killing her,' he told me. 'You want that on your soul?'

What I wanted was for him to point his gun at me. I figured Missy could just about break him in half if she had a chance.

'Put it down now,' he said, 'or it's all over for Missy.'

'PLEASE, RICK! HE'LL KILL ME!'

'We've got ten cops outside,' I told him. 'More coming.'

He smiled, a crooked, dirty grin. 'They find Penny, did they?'

Missy sobbed, 'Rick, *please*! Give him your gun. I don't want to die!'

'I'm not armed,' I said, opening my sports jacket for him to see. 'I can't give you what I don't have.'

I listened for sirens but there was nothing. We were alone. I saw Doo's legs at the front door.

Will pulled the gun away from Missy's ear. 'That bat behind you, Mr Law,' he said, pointing with his weapon. 'Don't pick it up. Just kick it over this way.'

I did as he said. I was maybe ten feet away from them. It was too far to have a chance, but Missy only needed to reach up and grab Booker's wrist. Not that she noticed how easy it was. She was snuffling back tears, murmuring prayers to Will. I'd have given anything to see the snarling bad-ass who ran the Dog Daze. *That* Missy Worth would have taken the bastard out at his knees. Then she would have stomped on him for good measure. This girl, I didn't even know. Maybe it was the Missy who dug her own grave. She was so docile Booker didn't even bother looking at her.

'Pick the bat up, Missy.'

'Will...' Missy's voice was like that of an abused child. The pleading came without conviction or any real hope of mercy.

'Take the bat, Missy!'

Still on her knees, she dropped down on her hands and took the bat. She was whimpering so much I thought she was acting. She had her bat now – her weapon of choice! She could sweep it back at his knees and finish things. I was ready, too, if she did it. I knew how fast she was and the only thing I worried about was saving Booker from getting his head crushed in.

I kept looking at him, damn near ready to smile I was so happy, and he kept looking at me, totally unaware of his vulnerability.

And Missy? She just kept sobbing.

'On your knees,' he told me. To get me down he pointed his gun at the back of Missy's head. I looked at Missy directly now; she was still on her knees, holding the bat.

'I don't want to hurt her,' Booker whispered, 'but you are forcing me...'

'RICK... *PLEASE*!'

I got to my knees, and Missy's suffering eased.

'Stand up, Missy.'

Booker lowered his gun, and I saw him catch a glimpse of himself in the big mirror behind me – liking what he saw. If Missy took one step back, she could swat him with that bat. Hardly more than a flip of the wrist! But she didn't see her chance. She was crying too hard to see anything.

'Kill him, Missy,' Booker whispered.

'Will, please!'

'Kill him now!' he hissed.

I saw her face screw up, her head wagging in refusal.

'Him or you, Missy!' Will raised the gun and pointed it at her.

Missy came round the Harley, cocking the bat behind her waist as she cried, 'I'M SORRY, RICK!'

Chapter 95

Sunday 1:34 p.m., March 28.

I HAD THOUGHT SHE MIGHT turn back, reaching over that Harley when Will Booker least expected it and cracking his pretty skull open. Instead, she hammered me.

I went down flat, the breath in me gone. She had laid into me just behind my arm, catching a rib and muscle. I heard Will hissing his approval and saw his feet give a little dance in his high heel shoes. I scrambled back, working toward the corner of the room, and the next blow I took was a light back-handed brush across the face that blacked me out and left me looking to catch my focus again.

That gave Missy the chance to cock the bat behind her for a full swing, and when I saw her face, all the sorrow and fear had drained out of her. Nothing but rage was left in those mean eyes.

I thought to anticipate the swing, duck under it if I could, but as it came, a gunshot sounded, and she whirled about with a wild yelp, collapsing beside me with a curse.

I looked at Will Booker, but his bloodied face was as astonished as my own. The next shot knocked him to the floor.

I looked toward the front of the house and saw Max Dunn standing in the middle of Missy Worth's living room. His big Colt .45 smoking.

MAX PUT THE TIP OF HIS gun under Will's chin and whispered as sweetly as a lover might: 'Now we play ol' Nat's game by *my* rules, William.'

Booker's eyes darted toward me to see if I would stop it. He will find more sympathy in hell.

'Tammy Merriweather...' Max whispered. 'Tell me where she is or prepare to die!'

'Car.'

I went outside, my breath coming with difficulty. The pain in my rib cage was sharp. I was pretty sure Missy had broken some bones, but I made it to the street and crossed to a brown Toyota. I found the keys in the ignition and went to the back of the car. Pulling the lid up, I saw the bound and gagged form of Tammy Merriweather. She was pale, filthy, and nearly naked. As quiet as death.

'Sweet Jesus,' I whispered, thinking it was over, that

both of Merriweather's daughters had been sacrificed for the folly of their father. Then I saw her eyelids fluttered open. She had a pair of smoky blues that were as pretty as any I had ever seen.

'You're safe,' I said.

Part VIII

The Daughters of Job

And in all the land were no women found so fair as the daughters of Job...

Job 42: 15

Chapter 96

Wednesday 11:20 p.m., December 6.

'A SIMPLE TRIAL,' LEN Griswold said in a conversational tone as he addressed the jury some nine months later. 'No question about what transpired. All of it is just as the prosecution has so eloquently described it to you.'

Here the great lawyer gave Pat Garrat and Steve Massey a congenial smile for the jury to witness. 'No long debates about forensics or pathology.' He hesitated, then tipped his head as he confided to his twelve new-best-friends, 'Not from *our* table, at least.' An affable chuckle from all. 'No. None of the trappings of a murder trial you have all been led to expect from the newspapers. No alibi, no time frames to fit things into, no question of opportunity or motive of the kind any of us can understand. No third man with one arm or any wild lawyerly inventions to distract you! No surprises at all, I'm afraid.' He took a moment to gather them into his hand and focus their attention. 'We are here to try a man for his life, and we have only one question to ask, one simple answer to find. Was William Booker in possession of the knowledge of right and wrong? WAS HE *SANE* WHEN HE COMMITTED THESE HORRENDOUS CRIMES?'

Griswold stepped toward the jury. He was a tall man with silver hair that he kept long. He had dazzling turquoise eyes, broad shoulders and the confidence of a man unused to losing – ever. He wore a white buckskin jacket, pants to match, and cowboy boots that folks could see had been in a stirrup. He had a voice as gentle and reproving as God's own must be.

'Now,' he said, 'I mean to *astonish* you!' He waited, his eyes taking in each juror, slowly and solemnly, just the hint of a wry smile breaking over at the very end of his silence. 'Yes... I'm going to be absolutely honest!'

Another long pause to let the laughter die down. He wanted people to know that he was serious. Life and death serious.

'I don't know the answer to the question! I don't know if Will was sane. Neither does Ms Garrat. My expert witnesses, with their combined psychiatric experience totalling over one hundred years, don't know the answer. The prosecution's psychiatrists don't know it either.' A moment for assumptions to be made, questions to form. 'And you, friends, even you don't know and won't know... can never know the answer! Oh, you'll make the call. I'm quite confident of that. But what you decide, the verdict you deliver, will be a judgement. Nothing more.

'I can see it in your faces already. You don't want to believe me! When this is finished, when all the facts and opinions are expressed, you want to *know* that you've made the right decision!'

He pointed at Will Booker, who was reading his Bible and had not looked up since the judge had appeared and he had been obliged to stand.

'But in this country we don't put to death people who don't understand what they've done. Is this an act? Maybe it is. Maybe Will here is purely as evil as the prosecution contends, maybe his reading of scripture and his ceaseless prayers for the victims are just an act for his gullible-but-kindly lawyer, a piece of show for the good people of the jury who will decide his fate. Folks, I asked Will to put his Bible away during our proceedings here. I said to him, 'Will, no one is going to believe you can read King James all day long! There are preachers I know who can't read that version of the Good Book for longer than ten minutes at a stretch!' And he said to me, "Go in there without my God, Mr Griswold? I can't do that." *Can't*, friends.' Griswold held his hands out to either side and lifted his eyebrows. They could believe Will or not.

'Maybe you have powers to see into the human heart

which I don't possess,' he said at last. 'Maybe you *can* feel certain this is all just an act. Take your justice and know you've done the right thing. God bless you, if you can! But friends... if it's not an act... well, I won't kid you. You've got some hard work ahead of you.'

Chapter 97

Friday 1:10 p.m., December 8.

WHEN GRISWOLD WALKED back to the defence table, he patted Will on the shoulder. Will looked up, smiled, and then resumed his reading.

For the rest of the day and continuing through Thursday and Friday morning, Steve Massey and Pat Garrat presented the bleak outlines of Booker's crimes using a series of witnesses, everyone from police officers and detectives to the coroner. Crimes were detailed, photographs of bodies viewed, weapons displayed, the sheer volume of human loss tallied. And even then the greater part of it entered the record by stipulation, uncontested fact. Throughout the ordeal and this part is harrowing for any jury, Len Griswold was true to his word, posing only the occasional question on cross – always with the aim of showing Will Booker as being something other than a rational being.

By the lunch break Friday, our physical case was outlined. We brought our psychological expert to the stand. Had Will Booker understood the difference between right and wrong? Certainly. The proof of it was in every action he took. These were outlined in review with thoughtful assessment of every choice Booker had exhibited. On his cross Griswold asked the psychiatrist if he had ever spoken to Will Booker. The expert answered that he had, that he met with Booker several times. On Griswold's follow up, the psychiatrist admitted that Will Booker had refused to look up from his Bible to answer any of his questions.

'Thank you!' Griswold answered. 'I have no further questions.'

AT THAT POINT WE WERE ready to introduce the survivors of Will Booker's mayhem.

I met Missy Worth at the prosecutor's office shortly after one. She was wearing a cheap quilted coat against the cold. The shoes had road miles, the pearls at her earlobes were the dime store variety, but she was trying. For Missy Worth, she was all dressed up. A pretty decent makeup job, a charcoal sweater and black pants, a touch of perfume, even some minor successes with weight loss. She smiled at me timidly, almost embarrassed it seemed to be out of her jeans. 'How do I look, sweet cheeks?'

Credible, I thought. 'Beautiful,' I said.

We went through a couple things I wanted her to

keep in mind, then I told her what was going to happen. How she would be called, where she would wait, the whole process, down to her hand on the Good Book. '...and don't give the judge the finger, no matter how mad he makes you!'

This was our running joke, and she gave me a grin. 'I won't let him see it if I do,' she answered.

I think by the time we were out the door and walking across the plaza I was more nervous than Missy. Then we saw Clint Doolittle. Missy's step hitched. She swore solemnly.

Doo was wearing his standard t-shirt and denim but had tossed on a thin leather vest to keep off the frost. Everyone else wore coats. With his bare arms swinging and one hand full of the Bible, he was standing on the courthouse steps. People were returning to the trial after their lunch break, and Doo was shouting like a prophet, 'REPENT, SINNERS!' He held the Bible high in the air, repeating his cry several times. Then he launched into a series of abominations that most of us partake in as a matter of course.

'Did you know about this?' Missy asked me.

'He's stayed away until now.' I looked at the collected media waiting for us. 'I expect he couldn't resist the cameras.'

'He doesn't care about the cameras. He's here for me.'

'That's one view of it,' I offered.

'Tell Garrat she ought to bring his doctors up on criminal charges.'

'She's already considering it,' I answered.

Will Booker's shot to Doo's forehead at point-blank range had failed to penetrate. Twelve hours after taking it, Doolittle woke up with the mother of all headaches and a flock of Merriweather's devotees praying him back to this side. He was so touched by the gesture and so moved by the miracle of being alive that he took up a new calling then and there, but no one knew it until five surgeries later when his jaw was finally working again and he could hit the streets: a born-again-preacher-on-a-Harley, and no soul safe.

He liked to rant against liquor and dope and sex-outside-the-sacred-union-of-marriage. He loved nothing so much as to hit the campuses all over the Midwest, chastising the fornicat-ors, the blaspheme-ors, the drink-ors, the adulter-ors and the whoremong-ors. Lump on his forehead and all, Doo was a preacher who lived for confrontation. He had told me himself that recently some frats down in Attica decided it might be fun to hassle an ex-bad-ass-biker-turned-preacher because his Christian beliefs wouldn't let him take a swing. He told me in all seriousness it was a mistake that came of their not reading the Good Book cover-to-cover. Doo preached his Jesus like a man on fire, but he kept the bookmark on Joshua at the walls of Jericho. The good news, he told me, was that two of the five who went to the hospital ended up 'coming on over to the Lord's side.'

As we got closer, Doo continued to avoid looking at us. I began to hope we were going to be spared a direct assault. In retrospect I admit my optimism was reckless. The moment Missy Worth passed in front of him and the cameras lit up on her, Doo pointed at her and shouted at the top of his lungs, 'THERE SHE GOES, FOLKS! THE WHORE OF BABYLON!'

'Keep walking,' I whispered, taking Missy's elbow and hanging on.

'I'm going to kill him,' she whispered back.

'Wait till *later*,' I said. 'I'll help.'

'JEZEBEL! FORNICATOR! BLASPHEM-OR!'

The shouts followed us all the way into the courthouse. The blessing of it was that Missy Worth didn't even notice the TV cameras.

Chapter 98

Friday 2:17 p.m., December 8.

STEVE MASSEY TOOK Missy Worth's opening testimony, walking her through her perjury ten years ago. He was brutal, completely lacking in sympathy and careful to leave nothing for Griswold to pick at.

When he had finished, Garrat took Missy the rest of the way. The murders of her friends. Forced to do it? No, it was just talk, she said. He beat you? No, he never touched me. Threats? He didn't make any direct threats. 'He just wanted... he said he wanted to let us go free... but Lisa was a problem...'

I had heard it all before, like lines spoken at a play rehearsal, but it was different in the courtroom. The flat inflections, the exhaustion that her face always assumed as she told of her own role no longer seemed empty of emotion. Before the jury she really *was* a victim. That fact read in every juror's face.

'So it was a bargain?'

'Yes.'

'First Lisa, then Kathy, then your own sister?'

'Yes.'

'Each a separate deal with new promises given and every one of them taken as gospel?'

'Yes.'

'Didn't you understand that he was lying to you?' Garrat asked her.

Missy did not look at Will Booker, nor did the accused bring his eyes from his Bible, except once or twice, it seemed, when he tracked Garrat as she moved about the courtroom.

'No.'

'You *believed* him?'

The line we had struggled with came like a piece of spontaneity: 'I *wanted* to believe him.'

'State is finished with this witness,' Garrat announced.

GRISWOLD STOOD FOR the cross examination. We had prepared Missy Worth for a full discussion of her immunity, a brutal exposure of her past. Lots of questions about psychiatric facilities she had visited, and of course her perjury ten years ago. Not once had we thought Griswold might coddle this witness.

'You dug four graves in all, Missy?'

'Yes.'

'You knew the last was yours?'

'Yes.'

'And you lay down in it?'

'Yes.'

Griswold hesitated. 'Did you ask for your life?'

'Yes.'

'And what did Will say?'

'He wanted to trust me but he couldn't.' Her eyes had tears suddenly, but her chin didn't drop.

'And you promised him that he could trust you; you would not tell anyone who had taken you?'

'I wanted to live!' Defensive, some fight in her for the first time.

'I would have made the same promise, Missy. Any of us would have.' He nodded at the jury, including them. They too would kill for the sake of their own lives. 'I just want you to clarify for me, if you will, what took place at that point.'

'I said I wouldn't tell. I swore it on my soul.' She looked defiantly at Will Booker now. Everyone did.

Will Booker simply turned the page of his battered King James.

'A terrible night for you?' Griswold asked.

Missy looked at Griswold as if he had caused it. 'You have no idea.'

'You remember it vividly?'

'Yes!' This was shouted with all the fury I had seen in the woman when she had broken two of my ribs.

'Now let me see if I have this straight. You promised several times not to identify him. He kept saying he wanted to trust you, but he couldn't?'

'That's right.'

'You asked for your life one last time?'

'Yes.'

'And he said …?'

'He said, "You know, I think I believe you, Missy. Just so you believe me…" and then he shot me!' Loud, angry, and as bitter as yesterday. She was off script but still telling the truth.

'He said *I believe you* and then he shot you? That's what you're telling us?'

'Three times! He shot me three times!'

A lesser lawyer would have blurted out the obvious: that it hardly made sense for Will to say he believed her promises and then to shoot her in the same breath. A protest would have naturally followed with some heat, and the judge would have told the jurors to disregard the comment. That was the one thing, of course, they could not have done. I saw Garrat tightening up, ready to leap, but Griswold simply turned and looked at his client. It was a confused look, the kind a parent offers a wayward child, full of questions and not a clue as to why he would behave so… *irrationally*. Now the lawyer looked at the jury, his eyebrows lifting. Could anyone make sense of it?

And then finally, still mystified, 'No further questions.'

Chapter 99

Tuesday 9:15 a.m., December 13.

WHEN TAMMY MERRIWEATHER WALKED into the courtroom Monday morning, she was beautiful. The cherubic innocence of March was gone. So too the long silky blonde hair that had made her look more girl than woman. She was tall and thin now. Her eyes, the colour of blue smoke when photographed, as she often was in the weeks before her testimony, suggested a woman of fabulous mystery, dark secrets and unearthly spirituality. Whenever I was close to her and we had a chance to talk, I saw something else: not mystery so much as a certain terror lagging a step or so behind her. But today, I knew she meant to get a little more distance from it. Her testimony was solid, her courage and honesty exactly the tone the prosecution wanted. In her version of events, Will had plotted murder with ruthless cunning, used her affection for the sake of his plan.

410

She recited in detail the arguments Will had made to Penny Lyons, so Penny might be persuaded to swing the bat she held. When Massey finished his questions, Griswold stood. 'No questions,' he announced.

Penny Lyons came forward next. Penny confessed to an attempt on her father's life, actually pulling the trigger on a gun that was out of bullets. She then provided painfully explicit portraits of her struggle against Will's insistence that she kill first her father and, when that failed, Tammy Merriweather. The temptations Will always held out to her echoed what Missy Worth had described of her ordeal. The effect was to suggest anything but a man incapable of understanding what he was doing. Penny finished her testimony with a description of her being strapped to a chair with a shotgun pointed at her. Will Booker, at that point, seemed anything but irrational. More importantly, his fore-knowledge of what was likely to happen to the girl illustrated, as nothing else had done, that Will knew exactly what he intended and for what reason he acted. When Garrat had finished with her questions Griswold again announced he had no questions.

Garrat, in a fine mood, took us all to Malone's cafe across the street. She was not going to declare victory just yet, that would be tempting fate, but everyone knew Griswold's insanity plea had lost all credibility. The jury didn't have a hard choice to make. The jury was looking at a scheming and cruel murderer who perfectly satis-

411

fied the legal definition of sanity. Booker knew exactly what terror he meant to inflict and that it was wrong to do these things. His arguments to both Penny and Missy Worth proved it beyond a shadow of doubt.

All that remained was to present the jury with a stirring portrait of the ruin he had caused – in preparation for the sentencing phase of the trial. That began after lunch with Benny Lyons. Benny, who had not yet been fitted with two artificial legs, entered the courtroom in a wheelchair. He described his experiences with Will Booker with special emphasis placed on his cunning and those arguments he had offered to Penny when Booker threatened both Benny and his father, if Penny refused him. Finally, Garrat asked Benny about the amputation of his legs. I could see that Benny fought down his tears as he explained all that he had lost in the months following the operation. The world had become for him an entirely different place because of Will Booker.

Out of curiosity I focused on the jury as the handsome boy bravely tallied his losses for their sake. Their objectivity failing, their eyes burned whenever they shot glances at the devil reading Holy Scripture.

CONNIE MERRIWEATHER WAS eager to assist the prosecution, but he was vulnerable on several counts, and Garrat had been careful to present his testimony only after Tammy and the two Lyons kids had testified.

She had meant to show that Merriweather was not the fool most people assumed him to be, but simply another victim of Will Booker's extraordinary ability to manipulate and persuade – hardly the talent of a man who did not understand the difference between right and wrong. She worked the man for more than an hour to illustrate the full nature and extent of Booker's elaborate and quite conscious seduction, paying special attention to Will's reasoning about Biblical stories. Finally, she brought up the issue of faith to finish the testimony. We expected trouble from Griswold on this, but Garrat had decided a series of objections from the defence would have a telling effect on this jury. Griswold needed to look nervous. Repeated objections, though perfectly justified would do that. She had no intention of discrediting Booker's sham piety; this was simply to make Griswold look nervous.

'In your professional opinion,' Garrat asked, 'would you say Will is a religious man, Dr Merriweather?'

I watched Griswold for a reaction, but the expected objection didn't come. 'A student of the Bible, I'd say.'

'A believer, then?'

'Not in my opinion, no.'

'Never was?'

'No.'

'Is not now religious – in your opinion?'

'Not at all,' Merriweather answered. Both he and Garrat looked almost unnerved by Griswold's silence.

In fact, Griswold was paying close attention to everything but did not seem to mind this line of questioning in the least.

Garrat pointed at Will Booker, who was reading as usual. 'That's an act, in your professional opinion?'

The judge leaned forward, staring darkly at Len Griswold, 'Counsellor?'

Griswold stood and smiled pleasantly. He hadn't a problem in the world. 'Your Honour, we are as anxious to hear Dr Merriweather's *professional* opinion as the prosecution appears to be.'

'The defence is prepared to stipulate that Dr Merriweather is an expert witness?'

'In matters of the Christian faith we are, Your Honour. He is therefore fit to judge in these matters, much as a psychiatrist can offer judgement about the mental state of someone.'

Judge Wilson blinked in a bit of contrived confusion. 'The prosecution may proceed.'

Garrat asked the court reporter to read back the last few exchanges, just to score her points a second time, and then prompted Merriweather by pointing at Will Booker and asking him again, 'Is that an act, Dr Merriweather?'

'No,' the preacher responded.

Garrat seemed thunderstruck, 'Do I understand you to say that we are *not* witnessing an act?'

Merriweather took centre stage. 'Not at all. That's a

man reading a book. Will loves to read the Bible. But that is neither faith nor belief. And if you brought a thousand ministers up here, not one of them would tell you that such activity is the same as walking with the Lord.'

'Did Will Booker ever speak to you about voices? Did he ever say God told him to do something – at any time since you've known him?'

'Will never spoke to me about voices. And when he spoke to me about God's desires for his life, it was always in the context of scripture, which he knows very well.'

'Have you spoken to the accused since his arrest?'

'I went to the jail yesterday to see Will.'

'What did the two of you talk about?'

'We talked about what Will did to my family and my friends.'

'The murders?'

'Yes.'

'Did Will blame God for what he had done?'

'No.'

'Did he mention voices commanding him to act?'

'Never.'

'Blame it on scripture – something he read?'

'Leading, your Honour...' Griswold was not letting the prosecution slip Job into its case either by inference or direct reference. Garrat had lost that piece of the case before the trial began.

'Sustained.'

'Dr Merriweather, did William Booker tell you why he kidnapped your two girls and committed multiple acts of murder?'

'He said his own lust drove him to it.'

Garrat turned to Griswold. 'Your witness.'

Chapter 100

Tuesday 2:47 p.m., December 13.

GRISWOLD CAME AT CONNIE Merriweather gingerly. They were former allies, now on opposite sides of an important issue. But they were not enemies, and that was the first matter of discussion. 'Not even a matter of forgiveness,' Merriweather offered with a kindly smile. 'You still believe in Will; I can't.'

'Fair enough. Now I want to ask you about Will's faith, Dr Merriweather...'

'Will has no faith.'

'You brought this man to the Lord!'

'Not to my Lord.'

'Let's try this a different way then. For what reason did Will want to see you at the jail?'

'He said he wanted us to pray together, the way we used to.'

'And did you pray with him?'

'No.'

'You refused?'

'I did.'

'For what reason?'

'Will doesn't believe.'

'Dr Merriweather, did you tell Will you *hated* him?'

'I did.'

'Then why did you go see him?'

'I wanted to face him before I testified.'

'No other reason?'

'As you well know, Will had been asking to see me since his arrest.'

'Any other reason, Dr Merriweather?'

Merriweather had a moment of discomfort, then answered brightly, 'The prosecutor suggested that it could be useful.'

'Ahhhh.' Griswold turned toward the prosecution's table. 'Ms Garrat told you it would be *useful*?'

'Yes, sir.' Merriweather had his feet under him again. He looked honoured to have the opportunity to help such a wonderful woman.

'And why did Will want to meet with you?'

Garrat stood. 'Asked and answered, Your Honour.'

Griswold turned slightly and smiled at Garrat benignly, his eyes twinkling. 'Yes, I believe it was. My mistake. Now, Dr Merriweather, did Will happen to ask your forgiveness at the jail yesterday?'

'He did.'

'Did you give it?'

'No.'

'And what did Will say to you when you refused him?'

'He said he would keep asking.'

'How many times would he keep asking?'

'He had his scriptures mixed up –'

'How many times?'

'Seventy-times-seven.'

'That's a lot, isn't it? Let's see…' Griswold pretended some arithmetic with his fingers.

'It's how often…' Merriweather stopped himself when he saw Garrat's eyes.

Griswold knew where he was looking, but pretended otherwise. 'It's how often… what?'

'It's how often Our Lord tells us we must forgive.'

'Can you find it in your heart to forgive Will, Dr Merriweather? Perhaps at some future time?'

'I can never forgive him what he's done.'

'You are commanded by your Lord to forgive your enemies, are you not?'

'Not this!'

'Do you recall telling me one time that Will was truly the most genuine believer you had ever encountered?'

'Yes.'

'At that time you were convinced Will was not only a follower of our Lord, yours *and* my Lord, but *a giant in his faith*? Isn't that how you phrased it to me?'

419

'Yes.'

'And now you hold the opposite view. That he is not a believer and never was?'

'That is correct.'

'I'm curious. What was it that made you say to me Will was a genuine believer?'

'My own vanity, sir.'

'I see. And are you quite certain that what you now say about his faith is not just your own *hatred*?'

'Objection! Calling for a conclusion!'

'The prosecution has questioned this witness as an expert – asking for his conclusions repeatedly – and the defence raised no objections to Dr Merriweather's judgement with respect to religion, Your Honour...'

'Overruled. Witness will answer the question to the best of his ability.'

'No,' Merriweather said. 'I'm not at all sure. I simply believe that actions speak louder than words.'

'I see. *Actions*?'

'Yes, sir.'

'Dr Merriweather, am I to understand you are no longer preaching?'

'I have no church at the moment.'

'Selling cars, I believe... to keep body and soul together?'

'Yes, sir. That's right.'

'And your marital status?'

'Objection!'

Griswold was ready. 'A vow to his Lord, your honour: *actions* speaking louder than words – according to his own testimony. I only mean to understand his statements, Your Honour.'

'Overruled. The witness will answer the question.'

'We're... our divorce is pending.'

'Have you lost your faith, Dr Merriweather?'

'Objection! The witness is not on trial.'

Judge Wilson leaned forward slightly, glaring at Garrat, 'He *is* on this issue, Counsellor. Witness is instructed to answer the question to the best of his ability.'

'My faith is not what it was. But I still love the Lord.'

'The Lord who instructs you to forgive your enemies... or some other Lord, Dr Merriweather?'

'Objection!'

'We'll sustain that one. Jury will please ignore the last question.'

'I have no further questions of this witness.'

Chapter 101

Tuesday 3:48 p.m., December 13.

GARRAT STOOD TO CALL her last witness of the day. 'State calls Tabitha Merriweather, Your Honour.'

Tabit Merriweather had still not recovered from her gunshot wound. She was in and out of a wheelchair, and came into court that afternoon seated. Her eyes were haunted with fear, like some mad darling who had been locked in an attic most of her life. Her beauty was gone. At sixteen she looked middle-aged. Her face was pasty white, swollen oddly from medications. Her shoulders seemed almost hunched and crooked, her body, like her face, unnaturally bloated. The dead we can too easily forget. Not this one.

Tabit would fix any damage Griswold might have scored with Connie Merriweather, and we had anticipated some damage when the preacher testified. She was the explanation for why a Christian minister was unable to forgive, the reason a good and kind man had become bitter with rage, and, of course, the state's best argument for execution: a visual essay in the continuing suffering and pain William Booker's cruelty had caused.

Garrat went through the experience with Tabit fairly quickly, much of it the same we had heard the others describe. The girl's voice was tiny, uncertain, but all the more moving for its tentativeness. When Garrat asked the girl to describe Will's attempt on her life, her eyes grew wet and distant, but the voice hardly wavered. 'He just walked in and shot me.'

'He said nothing?'

'No. He just did it.'

A minute or two about Tabit's therapy, the nightmares that kept her from sleep, the counselling that could not take the girl from darkness, and then Garrat turned the witness over to Griswold.

Garrat was too good to look pleased, but I knew she was. Tabit had annihilated the defence. Nothing about the girl's condition might move a jury to sympathise with Will Booker – no matter the story Griswold told when he put on the defence. This crime called for blood!

Griswold, knowing he could gain nothing by prolonging Tabit's presence, stood up slowly, as if distracted by something he was reading. He had no questions, he said.

'The witness is excused,' Judge Wilson announced, and made a show of looking at his watch.

Tabit Merriweather looked frightened and confused, but her voice was loud enough to stop the court. 'I want to say something!'

Tabit had been like a shadow as we had prepared for trial. She had something to contribute, but there was nothing we had drilled into her, nothing we had thought to worry about. The truth was her testimony was chiefly about her physical ruin, the imprint of horror that anyone could see in her once lovely face. The sound of footsteps could start her shivering. Laughter might cause her to cover her face in dread. We had always given her room, coddled her more than the others. It had seemed to all of us that we must, that she would break if we weren't careful. And suddenly she was telling the court she had something to say.

I recalled she had asked me once early in the preparation for trial if she would be able to say what she wanted. I had answered, '*You bet, honey!*' The issue had never come up again, and no one had bothered to ask her what she might actually want to say. But suddenly it was a question the prosecution cared deeply about. Garrat stood quickly, 'Your Honour, the state has asked all it cares to know from this witness. If the defence has no questions I hardly –'

Griswold rose. 'Actually the defence would like to ask *one* question. With the court's permission, of course.'

Judge Wilson looked at both attorneys, then at the

forlorn child who wanted to speak but could be swatted to silence with the crack of his gavel.

'Objection, Counsellor?' the judge asked Garrat.

Garrat did not care to fight too hard. What did she have to hide, after all? This jury had made up its mind. You had only to look at them to see their rage: what sort of man would leave a beautiful young girl like this?

'No objection, Your Honour.'

'Proceed with your question, Mr Griswold.'

Griswold gave the girl an encouraging smile. 'What is it you would like to say, Tabitha?'

'Objection!' Garrat answered. 'Improper cross, Your Honour.'

'Your Honour...' Griswold lifted his hands, a soft pleading for judicial discretion. What did it matter? Let the child speak if that was what she wanted!

Judge Wilson considered the thing, then nodded. 'I want to hear this,' he said finally.

Tabit look terrified, and Griswold had to calm her with that honeyed voice of his. 'It's okay, Tabitha. Tell us what you want to say.'

'I don't want Will to die.'

Len Griswold nodded. When it was clear Tabit had nothing more to say on the matter, he asked, 'Why is that?'

For better or worse, Garrat resisted another objection. Tabit's eyes flitted nervously toward Garrat. 'Because I think... I think we should try to be better than that. Miss Garrat has her reasons for wanting to take Will's life, the same as Will had reasons when he asked Penny to kill her father and Tammy, but they're just reasons… just words. Put it all together and it still isn't worth a human life.'

Griswold gave the jury a thoughtful look, then told the judge he had no further questions.

Chapter 102

Tuesday 4:25 p.m., December 13.

I FOLLOWED GARRAT across the plaza at a comfortable distance a few minutes after Tabit Merriweather had made her plea for mercy. Court was finished for the day, but Garrat had called an impromptu meeting. She hadn't said it but her face read clearly enough. Damage assessment.

Irene Follet was at my side, amused. Her job at the library was going to be there whether or not Will Booker was executed, and I felt just a touch of irritation that she wasn't as committed to the death of Will Booker as the rest of us.

'The kid made a point, huh?'

'Not a popular one,' I answered. I was thinking about how many times we would have to hear the echoes of Tabit's speech before the trial ended. And every time

427

the jury would remember our most tragic witness begging for the life of her tormentor.

'You want to know something?' Irene asked.

'Would it hurt your feelings if I said no?'

'The jury ate it up, Rick.'

I found myself nodding. 'The kid made *us* look like killers.'

Irene took my arm affectionately, '*And you're better than that*, aren't you?'

'I think I'm going to be sick.'

Irene nodded in the direction of Garrat and Massey, who were doing their best to look calm and relaxed. 'She won't give it a second thought, will she?'

'What's that?'

'Give Tabitha Merriweather what she asked for?'

I laughed.

'It's a shame,' Irene said.

I looked at her in surprise. 'You think we should let this guy live?'

Irene kissed me on the cheek. 'You're such a man sometimes.'

I stood stock still trying to comprehend what she was saying. 'What does that mean?'

'I'll see you in the Shamrock when you're done here.'

'Are you going to tell me what you're talking about?'

She took both my hands and looked at me affectionately. 'It's hard for men to understand that not everything is about winning and losing.'

IN GARRAT'S OFFICE Massey was shouting angrily, 'The kid is a teenager, Pat! *And* she's a preacher's kid! What's she supposed to say? *Burn him!*'

Garrat grimaced. 'Merriweather did.'

'The kid's weak. Hate to say it, but she is. Physically *and* emotionally. The jury will discount it. My bet is the media slept right through the thing. I'm betting Merriweather is the story in tomorrow morning's paper. That's the damage we ought to be worried about!'

'I'm not worried about the media. It's Griswold who won't let the jury forget this.'

'Griswold is out of ammunition. The guy is going to start tossing rocks pretty soon.'

Garrat looked at me. 'What do you think?'

'What are your options?'

'Prosecution rests... or we bring Clint Doolittle in.'

'I thought you ruled him out.'

Garrat smiled. 'A little of Clint Doolittle's brand of Christianity in the witness stand doesn't sound half-bad about now.'

'Pat, they're going to convict,' I said.

'That isn't the issue, Einstein,' Massey answered. 'Griswold can't find enough doctors in the world to convince this jury to let this guy go to a hospital. He knows it, we know it, and the judge knows it.'

'The problem is,' Garrat interjected, 'the jury likes Griswold. They are going to want to toss him a bone, and Tabit Merriweather just gave them the excuse. When it comes to the penalty phase I don't want them giving him life without parole. I want this monster executed.'

'What do you really get with Doolittle.'

'A reminder that Will Booker scalped one of his victims, and I don't rest my case with the last witness comparing me to Will Booker!'

'She didn't do that.'

'It felt like it.'

'During the sentencing phase,' Massey offered, 'you can discredit the girl by going through the psychological counselling she's had. The emotional distress Will has caused her. Nothing overt, just a little seed of doubt as to her judgement and stability.'

'What happens if you give it away?' I asked. 'Offer Griswold life without parole... and we all go home?'

Garrat laughed at me. 'Then it's welcome to the private sector!'

Massey shook his head. 'Great idea, Rick. World class, buddy. Do you want to know what the media will do to her? They'll say Pat Garrat lost her nerve in the middle of the biggest case of her career. They'll ask what the seven dead people would have wanted.'

Garrat shook her head. 'Not to mention the rest of the survivors. These people *suffered*, Rick! Tabit

Merriweather is not alone in this. Benny Lyons lost both legs!'

'I'm just saying it's something to think about.'

Garrat held her hand up, shutting Steve Massey off before he could insult me again. 'You're serious? You think this is a viable option?'

'Well, it's the one move no one expects.'

'Give us five minutes alone,' Garrat said.

Chapter 103

Tuesday 5:06 p.m., December 13.

WHEN THE DOOR SLAMMED shut, Garrat stood up and walked to the window. The winter's twilight seemed to fascinate her. 'Steve's right about one thing,' she said after a time. 'If I so much as blink there are people who are going to say I lost my nerve.'

'But you're thinking about it anyway?'

'Tabitha Merriweather, in her own quiet way, just turned me into another Will Booker. I'm holding out a bat for the jurors to grab. I'm telling them all they have to do is take a swing and everything will be fine.'

'The difference is you're not lying to them.'

Her eyes cut to me, her expression inscrutable. 'Are you sure about that?' I left her question unanswered. She turned back to look at the city. 'There were some important people at the farm this weekend,' she said. 'They basically told me that if I take Len Griswold to the mat on this, I can be governor in two years.' She didn't look at me, and I realised the promise frightened her. 'They weren't talking about a conviction. That's a foregone conclusion. They were talking about getting the death penalty.'

'Is that a bad thing?' I asked.

'It didn't seem to be at the time.'

'But today?'

'Today it feels like a bargain with the devil.'

'You're not Will Booker telling the jury they have to swing the bat,' I said. 'You're Missy Worth. You're the one *holding* the bat.'

Garrat finally turned away from the window. She offered a sardonic smile. 'I can't say I've ever been called worse.'

'I'm serious! All you have to do is swing that bat and you can have your heart's desire!'

'You could say that about any big case for a prosecutor.'

'You're missing my point, Pat. The minute you fall for that lie and swing, you don't *get* anything. You take a life. If it's the reason you become governor and you don't absolutely believe it was the right choice, you'll sleep with Will Booker's ghost.'

'It's my job to go after people like Booker.'

'How many killers like Will Booker do you know?'

She had no answer for this, but after a long pause she asked, 'What do you figure the old man would do?'

'The Governor?' I smiled fondly, almost seeing her father in the youth we had both shared once upon a time. 'I think most people would tell you he'd fight it out to the bitter end. He *was* a fighter, same as you are, but I'm not sure he'd fight this one – not at this point anyway. You see your daddy was the smartest politician this state ever produced. In a situation like this, I think he'd realise the opportunity Tabit Merriweather just handed him.'

'You call this is an opportunity?'

'A crisis of conscience is always an opportunity.'

'I guess I'm missing something.'

'Up until an hour ago, you had to explain yourself to fewer than a hundred thousand voters. Tabit Merriweather just gave you a chance to go national.'

She laughed, but there was no humour in it. 'Do you know what they'll do to me on national TV, Rick? I'm on record as being *for* capital punishment. Especially for this guy! If they put a camera on me the first thing they are going to ask me is if I lost my nerve.'

'I know what they'll *try* to do. That doesn't mean they get to have their way. Especially not if Lynn Griswold is sitting next to you.' Garrat's head tipped with interest. I'd just given her something she hadn't quite grasped. 'Between the two of you, you make Tabit Merriweather the story.'

Suddenly she was shaking her head. 'If I lose to Griswold at this point, I can work on a comeback in ten or fifteen years. If I give him the case now and I don't sell it on national TV, my political career is over.'

'If you don't sell it, I expect you're right; then again, if you can't sell Tabit Merriweather you probably don't have much a political career to lose. Your old man could have turned Tabit into political hay!'

'You really think I should call Griswold and make an offer?'

'I think you should drop the bat, the way Penny Lyons finally did. After that, I'm pretty sure things will work out.'

'You make it sound easy, Rick.'

'There's nothing easy about it. If you don't believe *me*, go ask Missy Worth.'

Chapter 104

Winter Twilight.

A SNOW STARTED TO fall as I drove from the parking lot. Fat flakes slopping in front of my headlights.

Garrat had called Griswold, wanted to buy him dinner, talk over some options. I wasn't sure what would come of it or even if I really believed we should spare Booker's life. But I felt contentment, and that was something that I hadn't experienced for a long, long time. Like maybe I had let go of the bat, too.

It was a beautiful snow, and I found myself watching the flakes and just smiling. By the time I reached the Shamrock the streets were covered. The quiet that comes with a fresh snow seemed to have settled over the whole town. I parked in front of Irene's apartment house and walked back to the tavern, my footprints filling up almost as quickly as I made them.

When I got to the front of the building, Irene was standing before the door waiting for me. She had left her coat inside and was shivering. I thought maybe she had a snowball for me, like a kid, but all I got was a smile when I took her into my arms.

'What are you doing out here?' I asked.

'Waiting for you,' she answered, her teeth chattering a little.

'Any particular reason?'

She cocked a shoulder prettily, 'I saw you drive by. Thought I'd come out and catch a quick dance before all the other girls make their play.'

'I thought you would want some insider information on the prosecutor's plans.'

'I wouldn't turn it down.'

I slipped my winter coat off and draped it over her shoulders, then took her hand for a slow dance. 'You're a wise woman,' I said, '*and* a great dancer.'

'She's listening to the kid?'

I put my cheek against hers. 'Making the offer to Griswold tonight.'

We danced to music only the two of us heard, and then after a time Irene whispered, 'You know, Rick, the last time we did this you ended up in jail.'

'A crime of passion,' I told her.

Some people came toward us, stomping their feet and brushing the snow off their coats. They were laughing

437

at us. Didn't we know we were dancing in the middle of a blizzard?

We ignored them, turning a neat two-step in the bright silence of the snow and smiling our way into a kiss.

Acknowledgements

First, to my wife Martha: love and gratitude for her continuing support of my passion. Thanks as well to Bud Palmberg and Shirley Underwood for reading and commenting on an early version of this manuscript. For his efforts in support of my writing enduring gratitude to my agent Jeffrey Simmons. Much appreciation as well to Ed Handyside and the team at Myrmidon.

Shortlisted for the CWA Ian Fleming Steel Dagger
for Best Thriller 2011

Cold Rain

**"I turned thirty-seven that summer, older than Dante
when he toured Hell, but only by a couple of years..."**

Life couldn't be better for David Albo, an associate professor
of English at a small mid-western university. He lives in an
idyllic, out-of-town, plantation-style mansion with a beautiful
and intelligent wife and an adoring teenage stepdaughter. As
he returns to the university after a long and relaxing sabbat-
ical, there's a full professorship in the offing- and, what's more,
he's managed to stay off the booze for two whole years.

But, once term begins, things deteriorate rapidly. The damning
evidence that he has sexually harassed his students is just
the beginning as Dave finds himself sucked into a vortex of
conspiracy, betrayal, jealousy and murder. Unless he can
discover quickly who is out to destroy him, all that he is
and loves is about to be stripped away.

**'...an absolute gem of a surprise. This is good, solid
writing piled with suspense and tension!'**

It's a Crime! (or a mystery...)

OUT NOW ISBN: 978-1-905802-34-0 Price: £7.99
E BOOK ISBN: 978-1-905802-59-3